SANGUINE MOON

THE VANESSA KENSLEY SERIES

STEPHANIE MARKS

RED DAGGER

For Erin.

ACKNOWLEDGMENTS

To my editor, Teri, thank you for all of your hard work. I couldn't have done this without you. Again.

"If the apocalypse comes, beep me."

— BUFFY SUMMERS, BUFFY THE VAMPIRE
SLAYER

CHAPTER 1

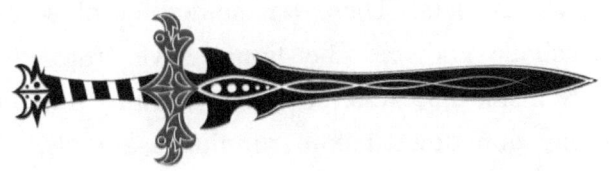

E either this guy was a friggin' track star when he was alive or I'm out of shape from indulging all of those chocolate chip cookie ice-cream sandwich cravings I've been having lately. The crisp air burned my lungs as my feet hammered down the rain-soaked grass. The rich, mineral scent of damp earth and green foliage assaulted my nose as I sprinted across the park grass, steadily closing the distance between the quarry and myself. Slipping on the grass, I skidded to a halt as he lunged over a cement park table without missing a beat. *Oh! To hell with this!*

The smooth, rosewood butt of my gun felt comforting and familiar in my hand as I raised my sig sauer and aimed for my target. Exhaling, I planted my feet and pulled the trigger in two quick successions. I winced at the sound of gunshots echoing through the park. That's what I deserved for not using a silencer, but it was too late to worry about it now, so taking aim again, I fired off two more shots.

The vampire stumbled and fell on one knee as the bullets struck his body. I really didn't care that the shots weren't fatal. There was something oh-so satisfying about knowing the liquid silver that spread quickly inside him was, no doubt, burning like hell. I held my gun down before running again, using his injuries as an opportunity to catch up. *Please, God, don't make me give up the ice-cream cookie sandwiches!*

"Well, that was fun," I said while exhaling heavily and trying to catch my breath. I pointed my gun at his head and added, "but why don't we just cut the shit, yeah? Where the hell is Merrick?"

A sneer flashed across his face and he spat on my boot. The thick glob stuck to the tip of my steel-toed combats in a solid clump. Bad move on his part; you just don't disrespect the shoes.

"Merrick? Sorry, never heard of him," he groaned.

"Right! Of course, you haven't," I nodded while keeping my gun pointed on him as I scanned the park. Swiftly grabbing my knife from my thigh, I plunged it into his shoulder right where it connected to his neck.

He screamed in pain as the silver-edged blade burned into him. Tendrils of smoke rose from his wound and the telltale odour of roasting flesh started to fill the air.

"Let's try that once again, shall we? Where... the hell... is Merrick?"

"I don't know," he hissed as he tried to pull away, but I kept a firm grip on the knife handle. "You think we all get together with him for tea parties and shit? He lit outta here, and I don't know where to."

I pulled the knife from his neck and backhanded him across the face with my gun, sending him sprawling into the wet grass.

"Well, then I guess I have no further use for you."

The soft sound of a snapping branch drew my attention and I scanned the trees behind us again, but the leaves were too dense to see anyone there.

"Oof!" The air came whooshing out of me as the vampire planted his foot in my stomach, taking advantage of my distraction long enough to knock me off balance.

I pointed the gun at him, but he kicked it out of my hand and continued to come at me, his tightly clenched fists swinging for my face.

I jumped back from the first swing and ducked under the second before coming up inside his arms and burying my fist in his stomach. The moment he doubled over, I brought my elbow down hard onto his back, sending him onto his knees before bringing my knee up into his face and knocking him over backwards.

"If you see Merrick, give him a message for me? Tell him to burn in hell!" I whipped out my stake and plunged it deeply into the vampire's heart.

Slowly standing up, I realized I was panting as the vampire briefly hardened before dissolving into ash.

"Never mind; I'll tell him myself!"

The rain started again and I wiped the fat raindrops out of my eyes and ran my hand over my head. Strands of hair came loose from my ponytail and were plastered on my face. I tilted my head back and let the rain wash my face clean of the sweat and frustration, just as it washed away the ashen body at my feet as if it never existed. But it had existed. And before it was ash, it was a vampire; and before becoming a vampire, he was a man. Maybe even a good man. But I couldn't dwell on that. It wasn't his life that mattered to me, only his afterlife, and his choices after his heart stopped beating while he continued to walk the earth. They were very bad choices.

I sniffed and frowned, then sniffed again. Lowering my face, I listened closely as the faint scent of marijuana reached my nostrils. *Shit. Someone is definitely watching me.* I walked over to where my gun lay as casually as possible, then meandered over to the trees where I heard the branch snapping earlier.

The bushes shook violently before a young man exploded from them, blind panic filling his eyes as they met mine. He hastily took off across the grass towards the parking lot. *Seriously? More running?*

I ran after him and tackled him from behind, dragging him to the ground.

"Get off me!" he yelled. "Help! Help!" He bucked

wildly while clawing at the grass and desperately tried to extricate himself from my grasp.

I grabbed his belt and pulled myself up his body before flipping him over and covering his mouth with my hands. He swung at me and connected with my face, his punch catching me right below the eye.

"Ow! Fuck!" I removed one of my hands from his mouth and grabbed his wrist while keeping the other hand firmly on his face.

"Shut up, just shut up!" I snapped at him. "Everything will be okay, I swear, but you really need to stop yelling, seriously."

I couldn't help but feel sorry for him as the hot air inside him came out in bursts on the side of my hand and his eyes darted frantically back and forth. If I were he, the sight of what just happened here probably would have scared me witless too. But I couldn't just let him go. I had to make sure he forgot what he saw here tonight; and I couldn't do that until I got him to stop freaking out.

"Look, I want to let you up, okay? And I want to take my hand off your mouth, but I can't do either of those things until I'm sure that you won't scream your head off, or try to run, or do anything stupid like that, okay?"

He nodded his head really fast as his chest continued to rapidly rise up and down.

"I'm having a bit of a tough time believing you, so why don't you just take a few deep breaths for me, okay? Nice and easy, slowly in and out." I watched him carefully as he breathed deeply through his nose a few times and his heaving chest started to slow down.

"Okay, all right, there we go. Nice and easy. Now I'm going to take my hand away from your mouth. You just keep your eyes on me, okay? Just keep looking at me. Are you ready?"

He nodded slowly this time, and I smiled. What a complete shit show the night turned out to be! Another dead-end and a terrified witness. All I wanted now was to get out of the stupid rain and into my nice, warm bathtub. Was a cozy night at home really so much to ask for?

I kept a firm grip on his wrist (in case he got it into his head to try and take another swing at me) before slowly removing my hand from his mouth. When he didn't start yelling, I allowed myself to relax a little. Maybe everything would be okay after all.

"Hi," I said, but he didn't reply. Oh, well, silence was infinitely better than screaming. "I'm sure you're very scared and have lots of questions, but I promise you everything is going to be much better in a moment."

I let the energy flow over me as I opened myself up to the hunger and leaned in towards him, all the while keeping his gaze riveted on mine. One little kiss and I could easily put this mess of a night behind me.

"Hey! What's going on over there?" A homeless man was walking towards us, pushing a grocery cart heaped high with his treasured possessions.

The man beneath me shoved me off him with an unexpected burst of energy, the connection between us hopelessly lost by the vagrant's unwelcome arrival.

"Damn it!" I swore as I started to run after him.

He fled through the parking lot and across the busy street, dodging the traffic, and I followed after him through the four-car lanes. Hearing a double blast of a horn, I managed to jump back just in time to avoid being hit by an SUV. When the vehicle passed, I made the final dash to the other side of the street, but I couldn't see the witness anywhere.

"Shit!" I yelled as I looked up and down the street, trying to find him amongst the few people still hanging around. "Shit!" Elizabeth would have my ass when she found out about this.

I fished my cell phone out of my pocket and punched in William's phone number, continuing to silently curse myself as I waited for him to pick up.

"Hello, love, get anything useful?" His English accent washed over me and I couldn't help smiling at the sound of it. Cocky, arrogant and a serious pain in my ass, but none of that prevented me from wanting to jump him the moment he got within ten feet. I was amazed that I managed to keep my hunger under control at all when he was around.

"We've got a problem," I closed my eyes and pinched the bridge of my nose. I could already feel the start of a tension headache coming on.

"What happened?" All humour vanished from his

voice. A muffled sound came from his end of the line, followed by a thump and a sickening crunch.

"William? What the hell is going on over there?"

"Nothing to worry about, love, it's all under control. Hold on a moment, will you?" I leaned against the wall of the instant cash loan business and watched the cars speeding by, their windshield wipers swishing frantically back and forth as the rainfall increased .

I could hear lots of puffing and cursing over the line as William ostensibly dealt with his own problems. Looked like everyone was having an interesting night.

"Sorry about that, pet; you were saying?"

"Everything all right over there?"

"Oh, yeah, he was just young and stupid."

"And now dust?"

"Very much so. Now stop stalling and tell me what's wrong."

"Someone got away from me. A human someone. A, umm... human witness someone," I held my breath and anxiously waited for the news to sink in.

"Vanessa, love," William said sweetly, "a witness to what, exactly?"

"He saw me dust my lead. I caught him hiding in the bushes and was about to glamour the memory away when we were suddenly interrupted and he used that moment to bolt. I lost him in traffic."

William was silent and I started to grow impatient. It wasn't like I didn't know how badly I screwed up, I really didn't need for him to emphasize the point with a dramatically-timed silence. This wasn't a goddamn spy movie after all.

"Will you please say something?" I snapped testily.

"Have fun telling Elizabeth," he laughed.

"You're a real asshole, you know that? I think I'll tell her from the safety of my own home."

"Aren't you coming over tonight?" His laughter was tempered by unmasked disappointment.

"No, I think I'm just going home and calling it a night. If Elizabeth doesn't have me killed, I'll call you tomorrow, all right?

"Sweet dreams, love," he whispered.

"Watch your back," I answered before hanging up the phone.

CHAPTER 2

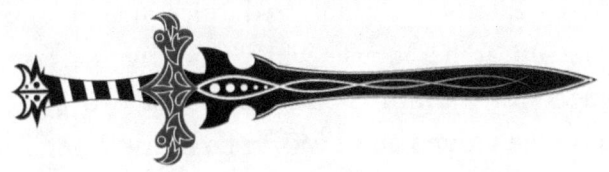

Seriously, more rain? What the hell, Silverlake? I turned the heater up in my Mustang and snuggled deeper into the thermal seats while trying to keep my eyes on the road. I let my mind wander as I listened to the rhythmic swish of the windshield wipers, parting the curtain of rain that hammered against the glass. It wasn't easy, but I tried to appreciate these last few minutes of peace before getting chewed out again.

It's not like I wasn't expecting Elizabeth's unhappy reaction to getting the news from the night before. Preventing any witnesses from escaping is pretty much Task Force Rule Number 1. Not having any witnesses in the first place? Even better. And now that I was living completely on the Silverlake Coven dime, the less I pissed off the Coven leader, the better; but calling us all in tonight seemed a little over the top. It was simply one teensy, weensy human witness. Couldn't we all just be debriefed over a conference call or something? Why drag everyone out to the middle of nowhere in the midst of a damn typhoon?

I pulled into the circular driveway that graced the front of Elizabeth's giant, red brick manor and sat staring up at her house while enjoying the last few moments of warmth. There was about two inches of rain on the ground and I was in no hurry to get soaked to the skin.

William's electric blue Mercedes sat in the driveway behind a rusty, beat-up, bright orange pick-up truck.

That heap must be Thatcher's. Rolling my eyes, I turned off the ignition. Groaning at the sizable distance from my car to the large double doors of the mansion, I threw my car door open and made a mad dash up the front steps, crashing through the heavy wooden doors, and slamming them shut behind me.

"Vanessa!" Anastasia called as she waved to me from the top of the staircase in the entry hall. She swayed elegantly down the stairs, and I tried to squash a spike of envy at her striking good looks. Her white-blonde hair fell in a heavy, bone-straight curtain down her back. I couldn't help wishing my hair were a more interesting color than chestnut brown. And really, who even needs cheekbones that sharply defined? Eastern Europeans had all the good genes.

She looked me over from head-to-toe and tried to cover a giggle. "You've started your own lake."

I looked down at the puddle beneath me and rolled

my eyes. "Great, something new to add to the list of reasons why I won't make it out of here alive tonight."

"Don't worry," she said, looping her pale, slender arm through mine. "I'm sure tonight will be nothing more than us trying to come up with the best way to find this missing witness of yours."

"Oh, so you heard all the gory details, huh?"

She waved a delicate hand dismissively as we headed toward the main library. "More or less. It was bound to happen sooner or later. Honestly, seeing how reckless the Renegades were this summer, I wouldn't be surprised to find more witnesses running around out there that we don't even know about. How do you think vampire lore first got started?" She wrapped both of her arms around mine and squeezed it comfortingly as we entered the library. "Don't worry, it will be fine."

"Well, there she is," Thatcher drawled as he leaned against Elizabeth's wide, oak desk and slowly clapped when I entered the room. "Nice work there last night, darlin'."

"Bite me, Thatcher."

"Don't mind if I do," he said with a grin before flashing his fangs at me.

Sighing with disgust, I ignored him and eyed up the chairs in the room. They suddenly all looked incredibly... expensive, and I was still dripping small lakes in my wake. *Maybe I'll just stand instead.*

"Well, now that you're all here, maybe we can begin, hmm? Let's discuss how best to deal with this little mess." Elizabeth tapped her perfectly manicured, seashell-pink nails against the top of her desk and stared us down.

Thatcher cleared his throat and gazed at the plush carpet beneath his feet. He might have been a little, loudmouth redneck of a vamp, but if anyone could put him in his place and shut him up, it was Elizabeth. That was one of my favorite things about her.

"William?" Elizabeth called him over and nodded towards the slim, silver laptop on her desk.

William looked at me and mouthed, "Sorry," before opening the laptop and spinning it so the screen faced us.

"This little gem was up on the internet today," Elizabeth said, pointing to the screen. "Would anyone like to take a guess and tell me what, exactly, we're looking at?"

I stood rooted in my spot, staring at the picture in front of us. There I was on the screen, frozen in action as the vampire and I went at it in the park. *Were those fangs? Could you actually see his fangs?*

No way, the picture was too gray and blurry from the rain for that kind of detail; I was just freaking out. And my back was to the camera. It's not like anyone could actually identify me. The vampire's face was much more in focus though. Not that it really mattered, since no one would ever see that face around town again. It's not like people could track him down and question him, or ask, "Hey, who was that hot chick giving you the serious smackdown in the picture?" Right? Of course, right.

"Looks like you're famous, chicky," Thatcher snickered.

"Really? I don't know, looks like the vampire is much more famous to me," I said lightly as my eyes darted to Elizabeth. "So, where was this picture found... exactly?"

"It was put up by a charming fellow who calls himself The Informant." Elizabeth hit a key on the computer and the picture minimized to show The Informant's blog site.

"Oh, you have got to be shitting me!" I looked up at the ceiling and flopped into the closest chair, no longer worrying that I was still soaking wet. She could send me a bill for the dry cleaning. "This guy again? Really? Are you telling me the witness that got away from me last night was the bloody Informant? Of all the people in the city, it had to be that fear-mongering, hack journalist? Oh, this is so not my day!"

"And what a headline, 'The True Monsters of Silverlake?' How... poetic," she said, raising her delicately arched eyebrow.

"It makes us sound like we should all be lurking under Loch Ness," I snorted. "The guy is a complete idiot. I still can't believe that anyone listens to a word he says. He sounds like every other whack-job conspiracy loon on the net."

"That may be so, but we know it's true and the

Renegades certainly will as well if their eyes ever land on this article."

"And they may not like what they see," Anastasia added. "One of their own exposed like that? It doesn't matter if the article is believable or not, there's no way they're going to allow him to continue broadcasting the existence of vampires in Silverlake City."

"The chance of being outed would put a serious crimp in their plans, and that's for sure. It's a whole hell of a lot harder to launch a sneak attack of oppression on a population when they see you coming," I agreed. "Oh, man," My head dropped down in disappointment. "When we find this guy, we're going to have to do more than just glamour him, aren't we? Do we operate some kind of vampire witness protection program that I don't know about?"

"We will figure out what to do with him later. For now, our main priority is finding him before the Renegades do. Just find him!"

"How hard could it be to pin down the location of the IP address where the blogs were being posted from?" I asked. "Let's get one of the techie vamps on it. Once they get the address, I can swing by and pick this guy up. Nice and easy. I mean, when you think about it, he just made finding him that much easier for us than if he were some random guy. Right? Right?" I looked around the room, still clinging to the small glimmer of a bright side to the situation, but they all just shook their heads at me.

"Let's just get him before anyone else does, shall we? Now go, I have plenty of other things to do." Elizabeth dismissed us and we all headed for the door. "Not you, Vanessa. One moment please."

Damn. So close. "Yes?" I turned back to her and smiled. William squeezed my shoulder gently as he left the room, closing the door behind him. *Traitor*.

"That was a good idea you had about tracking the IP address. Technology isn't where my expertise lies. You just saved us a lot of time."

"Thank you, but let's be honest, this whole mess is my fault in the first place. I wouldn't have to save us time if he had never gotten away from me."

"Vanessa, I have no doubt that you understand just how important secrecy is to our continued survival. Vampire, succubi, we all live more peaceful lives when we don't have to constantly look over our shoulders for the torch and pitchfork-wielding mobs. Having dodged a few of those in my day, let me tell you that I will do whatever it takes to keep this life we have strived so hard to create for ourselves intact here."

"I know that, Elizabeth, and I don't know how many ways I can tell you I'm sorry—" I started, but she held up her hand to silence me.

"You misunderstand me, child. I know that you're sorry. What happened was unfortunate, but it's not as if it's the first time it ever happened. We will find this so-called Informant and we will silence him. If possible, we will find a way to protect him from those who

17

would like to silence him in a more permanent manner. But I want to make sure that I am very clear here. If it comes down to the life of this human versus the exposure of our kinds, I will always choose to protect my people. Things are precarious enough right now. We still don't know where Merrick has fled to, and even though the gruesome displays of bodies that plagued us over the summer has stopped, it is highly unlikely they have abandoned their plans."

"There is no way Merrick would give up. He's still out there, somewhere, building his army. Crazy like that doesn't just give up."

"Exactly; things are too tenuous in our world for us to allow this human to focus his mortal eyes on us. Find him and bring him to me by any means necessary. Do you understand?"

"I don't want to hurt him, Elizabeth. I'm not going to hurt him."

"I understand your reluctance to hurt him; I do. He has done nothing wrong. And believe me when I say that I don't want him hurt either. But make no mistake, you will be faced with some tough choices in the days ahead and if things go awry, he may turn out to be only the first of many."

I gritted my teeth and jerked my head in a nod. What else was there to say?

William was waiting for me when I left the house. The moment I got outside, I felt the pressing weight of Elizabeth's words finally lifting off my chest. It all seemed a little less real out in the night with the damp smell of the forest and the grounds surrounding her home enveloping me. The rain lessened to no more than a soft drizzle when we were inside and it cooled the angry flush in my cheeks.

William pulled me into his arms and rested his chin on the top of my head.

"How was it, love?" he asked.

"She's willing to kill him." The words sounded strange coming out of my mouth. "She didn't say it in so many words, but that's what she meant. If it gets too messy, she's willing to kill him, just like the Renegades would."

William didn't say anything, but just held me tightly in silence.

"You knew that though, didn't you?" I looked away in disappointment. Sometimes, it was so easy to forget what he was, what they all were. Vampires. Killers. Just because the Silverlake Coven did not kill the people they fed from it didn't mean they wouldn't hesitate to kill if they felt it necessary. And no matter how much it pained me, I could see how the continued secrecy and protection of their existence could easily outweigh a single human life.

"I'm not surprised, no. Elizabeth will do whatever she feels is best for the Coven and its survival."

"And you agree with her." I stiffened and started to pull away, I already knew the answer and my heart felt heavy again, but he tightened his grip on me.

"I'm hoping that it won't come to that," he replied as he kissed the top of my head and then released me. "Come home with me. I missed you last night."

"I don't know." I averted my gaze and focused on a spot over his shoulder, unable to look him in the eye.

"Don't be mad, pet, please?" He placed his hands on my hips and pulled me into him again. "We won't talk about it, I promise. No Task Force, no Coven politics, nothing. Just you, me, and a nice, long bubble bath. What do you say?"

He bit my earlobe and I could feel my resolve slipping away. I hadn't fed in a while and it really sounded nice to spend some time with him.

"All right, fine, I'll come over. But there had better be wine."

"There will be wine, buckets of wine," he laughed.

"Ugh, tonight sucks," I pouted.

"Well, let's go make it better then," he said before giving me a smacking kiss on the lips and sauntering off towards his car.

I couldn't suppress my grin as I watched him walk away. What better way to brighten up my day than by spending rubber ducky time with the sexiest vampire I knew? Hey, a girl's gotta eat.

CHAPTER 3

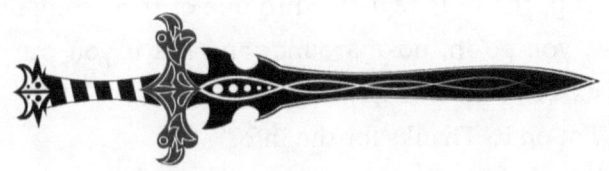

"Your phone's ringing," William called from his kitchen where he was pouring me a glass of wine, "It's Mouse."

"Great, toss it here." Standing up from the couch in the living room to catch my phone as William threw it half the length of his penthouse apartment, I deftly plucked it out of the air when it came straight toward me. Sure, maybe we were asking for a touchscreen phone disaster, but there was something to be said about vampire aim.

"Hey, Mouse, what have you got for me?"

"So I tracked the IP address on the blog. It wasn't too difficult, of course, pretty basic security."

"Basic for me? Or basic for a techno geek like you?"

"Basic for me; you would have cried."

"Hmm... I want to argue with you, but you're probably right. So where is this guy?"

"You're never going to believe this, girl, but it looks the he works for our very own daily news."

"Oh you have got to be shitting me. That guy works for the *Silverlake Daily*?"

"Yup, the IP is registered to one of their computers. I say, you go in, poke around, and see if you can find out exactly who this guy is."

"I'm on it. Thanks for the info."

"Go get him."

I hung up the phone and tucked it back into my pocket.

"Sorry, babe, looks like food has to wait. Mouse managed to get me a lead on this guy."

"Do you want me to come with you?"

"No, this shouldn't be too crazy. Why don't you go out and I'll call you as soon as I get his name?" I walked into the kitchen and leaned over the wide expanse of granite counter. "Kiss for good luck?"

William reached over the counter and grabbed me by the back of my neck, entangling his hand in my hair and crushing his mouth against mine. I opened my mouth wider to allow him entrance as he deepened the kiss. My hunger increased and I gave into the urge to feed off him, pulling his energy inside me and floating on the rush.

I broke off our kiss before I took too much and gave him a quick peck on the lips.

"Yup," I winked at him, "that should do it."

After parking across the street, I scanned the dark windows of the *Silverlake Daily News* office building. Breaking and entering really wasn't my thing. I had absolutely no idea how I could get past any alarm systems they might have. *Why do I only think about these things when it's too late to do anything about them? How the hell am I going to get inside here?*

I reached into my glove compartment and pulled out the silencer. Not the most suave way for getting things done, but I fell asleep in Lock-Picking 101 so it looked like I'd just have to shoot the lock off.

I screwed the silencer onto the barrel of one of my guns and slid it back into my side holster before zipping my leather jacket up over my top to conceal my weapon.

Luckily, the street was deserted. It seemed like the rain kept everyone inside tonight. About time someone up there finally gave me a break. I darted across the street with my head down, heading directly for the newspaper's front doors. If someone did happen to pass by me, the less suspicious I looked, the better. Who would think twice about a reporter coming in late to beat a deadline?

I gave the door handle a swift tug and had to take a hasty step back when the door swung open. I was nearly smacked in the face. It certainly looked like someone was really putting in a little overtime tonight.

I stepped inside quickly and shut the door quietly behind me. Passing through the reception area, I ducked down low beneath the door behind the reception desk. Through the window in the door I could see the main reporting area, and all the reporters' desks that were laid out in rows of cubicles.

The room was dark and it didn't look like anyone was inside at their desk or working. I couldn't make out so much as the tiniest beam of light from a desk lamp. So why was the front door unlocked? Pulling out my SIG Sauer, I reached up and opened the door to the offices as quietly as I could, while crouching down low before I snuck into the room.

I could hear the soft murmuring of two people talking as I made my way down the rows. Shit, the last thing I needed was two more witnesses, but I didn't have the option of abandoning this lead. I turned the gun around in my hand so the butt was facing outwards. If I snuck up on them quickly and quietly enough, I could probably knock one out and glamour the other before they even realized what happened.

As I got closer to the voices, I began to perceive the low moans accompanied by a rhythmic thumping. *Oh, you have got to be kidding me! Well, no wonder there were no lights on in here.*

I ignored the sexual energy flowing off the couple as I reached the last desk before theirs. Adjusting the grip on my gun, I stepped out and prepared to knock out the person nearest to me when the woman threw her head back. Her wild, red hair gave me pause.

The woman opened her eyes and screamed as she saw me standing there with my gun held high before toppling off her equally astonished partner.

"Vanessa!" she screamed.

"Karen? What the fuck?" I yelled as her partner tried to scramble off his chair.

"You!" he exclaimed while anxiously trying to haul his pants up and cover his privates at the same time.

"The goddamn Informant?" I accused her as I pointed the butt of my gun at him.

"Why the hell do you have a gun?" she yelled.

"Why the hell do you have no pants?" I pointed my hand at her lower half.

Flushing so brightly I could see it despite the dimly lit room, she quickly pulled her skirt back down over her hips.

"Karen, run," the Informant said to her. "Just run. She's here for me."

"Why would she be here for you?" Karen asked him. "Why are you here for him? How did you even find out about us?"

I held up my hands in surrender. "Hey, I had no idea until just now. Is this why you're constantly dodging our questions about your secret boyfriend?"

Karen's face suddenly went very pale. "Vanessa?"

"No seriously, Karen, I know you like his blog and everything, but really?"

STEPHANIE MARKS

"Vanessa—"

"Okay, sorry, that's not really supportive. Obviously, you knew we would completely take the piss if we ever found out who you were dating, but come *on*."

"Vanessa," she whispered, "why do you have a gun?"

I looked at my hand just as the Informant tried to leap out of his chair. Ignoring Karen's question, I grabbed the Informant and shoved him back into it before aiming the gun at him.

"Please don't do that again."

Karen slapped a hand over her mouth and her eyes opened wide. "Vanessa, I know you don't like him and you don't think he's good enough for me, but this is ridiculous."

"What?" I looked back at her, confused for a moment before it clicked. "Oh, sweetie, no! I'm sorry, this is so not about who you choose to date. Your boyfriend and I actually need to have a little chat, but we can't have it here. We have to go. Now."

"I'm not going anywhere with you. I saw you. You killed him. She's a killer, Karen."

"Umm..." she trailed off, looking back and forth between us.

"Yeah? See? That's why I'm here, because you keep running your mouth off about what you think you saw." I poked him in the forehead. "Crack bit of journalism you did there. Unfortunately, it also got you noticed. Hopefully, only by us, but that's pretty unlikely. So now I get to spend my evening saving you from yourself," I snapped at him. "Seriously, Karen, your boyfriend just isn't making the best first impression here, ya know?"

"Colin, I don't understand. What did you do? Nessa?" Karen's eyes started to tear up and I swore in frustration.

"Awww, Kare, come here," I crooned. I pulled her into a tight hug while keeping my eyes firmly on Colin. "It's okay, Karen, but Colin wrote an article on a subject that he shouldn't have, and now some very bad people may be out to hurt him."

Karen started crying in earnest now and squeezed me tighter. "But what does that have to do with you?" she choked out.

"I—"

"She's here to shut me up permanently," Colin interrupted. "She thinks she can keep the truth hidden. But the people deserve to know. They deserve to know what's going on, and what's really out there. Well, you can't shut me up! I have freedom of speech, I have—"

The front door of the newspaper building crashed open, cutting him off, and I dragged them both down to the floor.

"Yes," I hissed at him, "you have freedom of speech, but right now, it looks like you also have the freedom to die."

"Oh, God! Oh, God! Oh, God!" Karen's voice started to rise higher in pitch. I slapped my hand over her mouth and stared into her eyes, shaking my head slowly.

Lowering my voice to barely above a whisper, I placed the gun back into its holster. "Believe me when I say that whoever is out there *is* there to kill you. And they don't give a shit about your freedom of speech, got it?"

The door to the offices opened and I heard footsteps on the linoleum floor.

"Come out, come out, wherever you are," a rough voice sang. "I know you're here. I can smell you."

"And I can hear your hearts beating," a second voice joined the first. "Sounds like they're ready to jump right out of your chests. Maybe I'll save them the trouble and just tear them out instead. And then eat them."

Tears were streaming down Karen's cheeks and my heart clenched. *Not again!* I refused to lose another of my best friends to these bastards.

Brushing back one of the wild, curling tendrils of her bright, orange-red hair, I kissed her on the forehead before glaring at Colin. I drew my hand sharply across my lips, indicating that he stay quiet.

"Oh, I think they want to play hide-and-seek," the first voice laughed.

Jumping out from my spot behind the desk, I pulled the stakes out of their holders.

"Looks like you found me," I said.

The vampires ran at me and I stepped forward to meet them, opening up my growing hunger. I wouldn't allow them to get anywhere near Karen.

The energy rose until it began to consume me, and the edges of my vision blurred to red as I focused on their attack. I had to get Karen and Colin to safety as soon as possible, which meant I didn't have time to play with my food.

When the first vampire reached me, I didn't hesitate. Sidestepping his attack, I brought the stake up and drove it into his chest. I didn't bother to make sure if it finished him off, I simply moved on to the second vamp. His steps faltered and I heard a loud thump behind me: a body hitting the floor.

"Wish I had more time to have some fun with you," I told him as I continued forward, "but there's somewhere else I have to be."

The vampire's fangs descended and he lashed out at my face, aiming straight for my eyes, and hoping to blind me. I spun out of his reach and grabbed the keyboard off the desk behind me, which I smashed into the side of his head, sending him off balance.

Coming up behind him, I shoved him forward against the desk partition and planted the stake into his back.

The vampire crumpled into ash, his remains joining those of the other vampire on the cheap, scarred floor.

The hunger in me howled, clawing at me for more, urging me to go out and satisfy my craving, but I restrained it. I had a job to do and I couldn't let my hunger consume me. The power was coming to me more readily now, but I still needed more practice in controlling it.

I dusted off my hands and slid the stakes back into their sheaths. It probably wasn't likely that anymore vampires were on their way, but there was no point in hanging around there any longer than we had to.

I walked back to Karen and Colin's hiding spot and found them crammed together, huddling beneath the desk. My heart went out to them. Karen never should have gotten mixed up in any of this. And Colin? Well, okay, I was still pretty annoyed at him for putting us all in this situation in the first place; but it was not like he actually *asked* for any of it either.

I sighed and held my hand out to them. "It's all clear. And if you were wondering, this is pretty much the point where I say, '*Come with me if you want to live,*' so why don't we all get out of here before we really push our luck?"

Nodding, they scrambled out from beneath the desk, and Karen brusquely wiped the tears from her eyes with the back of her hand.

"What... what were they?" Karen asked as they hustled after me, trying to keep up with me as we ran from the room.

"Monsters, Karen," Colin hissed. "There are monsters in Silverlake. Didn't you see their teeth? They looked like they were..." he trailed off and shook his head, unable to voice the truth.

Karen grabbed my hand as we stepped out onto the street. She tugged me around to face her.

"Monsters?" she asked in a small voice.

I wanted to comfort her, but we just didn't have enough time. I knew I would have to explain everything to them eventually, but standing in the newspaper office with vamp dust under our feet just wasn't the best place to do that.

"My car's over there." I pointed across the street and ignored the confusion clouding her face.

Fishing my car key out of my bra, I hit the *unlock* button on the remote before pulling my cell phone from my pants pocket. William picked up on the first ring.

"Vanessa, how are things going?"

"Made a couple of new friends, but I found him."

"Great, now we can get him before the Renegades do."

"No, I mean *I found him*, found him." I opened the driver side door and leaned the seat forward, urging them to hurry up and get in the back. "We're on our way to my place now."

"I'll meet you there," he replied quickly and hung up.

I slid into the driver's seat and closed my eyes for a moment. I'd fulfilled my mission and found the Informant, now I could only hope that the Coven voted to let him live through the night. I would be so annoyed if

I had just gone through all of that for him to end up dead anyway. Besides, Karen would never forgive me.

CHAPTER 4

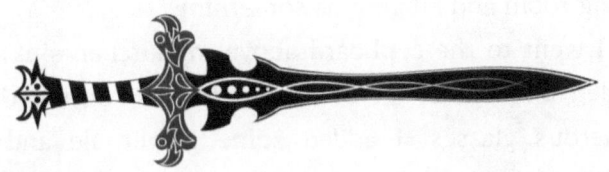

I unlocked the door to my apartment and let them inside. While there was no doubt that I loved having my own personal space again, sometimes I still missed waking up to William every day. Sure, I was forced into cohabitation with him by the police for my own safety. That's just what happens when you pick up a mentally unstable vampire stalker who's hell-bent on convincing you to become his succubus queen. But pushing all that aside, looking back on it now, I really loved spending that time with William.

However, there was no way I could move in with him permanently. That was just pushing our relationship forward too quickly. Going from zero to living together in two shakes of a dead body just didn't seem like the most solid foundation for a long-lasting relationship, you know?

"Make yourselves at home. Can I get you guys anything?"

"Got anything to drink?" Colin choked.

"Yeah. Karen, why don't you guys head into the living room and I'll grab us something."

I went to the cupboard above my kitchen sink and pulled down a bottle of Crown Royal. Pouring three generous glasses, I added some ginger ale and ice before placing them on a tray and taking it out to the living room.

Karen was curled up on my cream leather couch, tucked tightly against Colin's side, but both of them jumped up quickly when I came over.

"It's okay," I tried to reassure them as I handed them their drinks, "you guys are safe here." I took a sip of my own drink and sat in the matching recliner next to the couch, pulling it around so I could face them better.

Looking around the room nervously, Colin sat down again, taking Karen's hand and pulling her back on the couch with him.

No matter what I thought about his journalistic skills, or more accurately, his complete *lack* of them, it was touching to see him looking out for her. It seemed like he really did care. It was too bad that Karen believed we wouldn't accept him. Sophia and I would have come around eventually... probably.

"I'm sure you guys have a lot of questions and I'll try to answer them to the best of my ability so go ahead."

"Who were... what were those men?" Karen asked.

"Colin was right in a way, they were monsters. But if you want to get right down to it, they were more than that. They were vampires."

"But vampires aren't real!" Karen protested.

"You're right. There's no way they can be real," I told her. "They're myth and magic and made-up stories to scare little kids into eating their greens. But they're also here, now. And it doesn't matter if you believe in them or not, they'll kill you just the same."

"There are vampires living in Silverlake?" she mumbled weakly.

"There are vampires living in Silverlake. More now than ever before. Although not all of them are bad." I had to think about that for a moment. I suppose when it came to feeding off people and then wiping their minds of the memory, a person's sense of "good and bad" were more or less subjective. It's not like I was all on board with it when it happened to me.

"So what?" Colin scoffed. "They aren't all going to try to kill us?"

"No, no! Of course not. I mean, that's why I came to find you tonight. You never should have seen what happened yesterday. You were a witness and letting you get away was a huge screw-up."

"You killed him!" Colin shouted. "I saw you kill him, and you were going to kill me too! I could see it in your eyes!"

"I was never going to kill you, you idiot." I found myself rapidly losing my patience with this guy. "I was just going to help you forget what you saw. And if you had only let me do that, maybe you wouldn't be in the position you're currently in tonight. Especially, if you had kept your mouth shut instead of rambling on all over the internet about monsters hiding under the bed."

I shoved my chair back and got up to pace back and forth in front of the couch before taking a healthy swallow of the whisky.

"And by the way, can I just ask? What kind of an idiot sees someone *kill* someone else, and thinks that person is then going to kill *him*, and reacts by putting a picture of the whole thing out there for the entire world to see? Are you sure you weren't hoping to get taken? Because that sounds like some serious death wish shit to me." I crossed my arms over my chest and cocked an eyebrow at him, waiting for him to explain himself.

"Look, I hadn't planned on saying anything." He hastily put his drink down on the coffee table. "I was just so freaked out by what I saw. I drank, okay? I went home and I drank and I tried to forget about it and pretend that it wasn't real. But it just wouldn't go away. I saw it over and over again. The way you just stabbed that stake right into him." Colin looked me straight in the eye for a moment before his gaze darted away. "You kissed him. You kissed him and he turned to dust. Just, dust. Forget about them, what the hell are *you*?" he asked me accusingly.

"Umm, that's a little more complicated." I took another sip of my drink and let my eyes wander around the room.

"Vanessa? Are you a monster too?" Karen shrunk further away from me, sinking into the plush cushions of the couch and I could feel my heart beginning to break.

That was why I never shared my secrets with any of my friends. Even though I loved them like the sisters I never had growing up, I was always afraid of seeing that look in their eyes. That cutting expression of confusion and fear. The same look that Karen was giving me right at that moment.

"I'm not a monster. I'm just... a bit different. And vampires aren't monsters either, not really. I mean not in the sense of their biology, you know? They're more monsters by deed..." I trailed off after seeing the blank looks on their faces. "This really isn't helping very much, is it?"

"No, Vanessa." Karen frowned at me. "It's really not."

There was a knock on the front door and they both went very still.

"It's okay, I'm expecting company."

Taking a stake in one hand, I walked quietly towards the front door and checked the peephole to see William on the other side. Relaxing, I undid the deadbolts on the door and opened it wide for him.

"Nice to see you're taking more precautions with

your safety, love," he teased, wrapping me in his arms and kissing me.

"Yes; well, I realized something during my forced vacation this summer. That whole, handy entry by invitation rule doesn't work on a glamoured human that gets sent here to take me out. I feel much safer with the locks and deadbolts."

He nodded, thinking it over, "You have a point. Now, why don't we take this guy to Elizabeth so that we can get it over with?"

"Yeah, about that." I walked him to the living room where he saw both Colin and Karen. "I kind of ended up bringing along one more person than I intended."

"So you've just started collecting witnesses now, have you?" His voice was tight with annoyance.

"Look, she was there, I couldn't just *leave* her."

"That's exactly what you should have done."

"She's my best friend!"

"Excuse me?" He stared at me as if I had just grown two heads.

"She's my best friend, who also happens to be dating the Informant. I mean *Colin*. So I brought her with us. There was no way I could leave her behind. Especially not after what happened to Colleen."

I turned my back on him and stormed over to the bathroom, slamming the door shut behind me. I needed a moment alone to collect myself. My stomach felt as though it was about to tear itself apart. The loss of Colleen was still too fresh for me to be able to speak about and stay calm. *Damn him for making me bring it up!*

I splashed some cool water on my face and took a long look at myself in the mirror. Dark circles had formed under my eyes and my cheeks were tight and drawn. Beneath my flush of anger, my skin looked ashen and pale. I could almost pass for a vampire, myself, these days. When did life become so damn complicated? And so messy?

A light knock on the door pulled me out of my dire thoughts and I towelled off my face and cleaned up my ponytail before opening the door.

I was greeted by Karen's tear-streaked countenance. She opened her mouth before closing it again and stepping into the bathroom, wrapping her arms around me, and embracing me in a tight hug.

"I miss her too," she said, rubbing my back.

I felt so guilty. I couldn't tell either Karen or Sophia what happened to Colleen. When she never came home, her mother filed a missing persons complaint on her, firmly believing that her daughter had become a victim of the serial killer that was running loose in the summer.

And she was right. Colleen was a victim, being turned against her will into a vampire plaything for Merrick. They dangled her life like a carrot in front of me and snatched it away in a swift blink. There was nothing I could do to stop it.

But how could I tell that to her mother? Or our

friends? I had to keep the truth of our world a secret. Now, they believed Colleen was just another missing person in a growing pile of people that seemed to be slipping through the cracks of our city.

I allowed myself a moment to cry and the hot tears rolled down my cheeks, nearly drowning me with their incessant presence. I wept for the bright spark and light that Colleen once was, and raged at the abomination she had become.

"We have to go now," I sniffed.

"I trust you," Karen hiccuped. "I'm scared out of my mind right now, but I still trust you."

I clenched the back of her shirt and squeezed my eyes shut to stop the flow of tears. "It will be okay," I promised.

Karen nodded and continued to hold onto me, a familiar life raft in a turbulent ocean. "Just don't leave me, okay?"

"Never." I grabbed her by the shoulders and stared into her eyes, willing my words to be truth. "I'll protect you, Karen. I swear to you that I'll protect you both. I won't let you out of my sight, I swear to God."

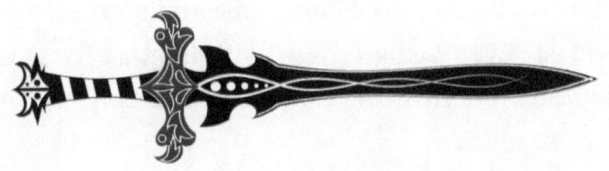

CHAPTER 5

Elizabeth's large, circular driveway looked like the finalist round of a "Show-and-Shine," with exotic candy-colored cars crammed into every available space. Judging by the look of things, everyone had come out to catch a glimpse of the person that could have single-handedly undone centuries of careful deception.

I glared at William over the hood of my Mustang as he stepped out of his car, looking completely bored with the whole situation.

"Made a few calls, did you?" I asked him as I waved my hand at the packed driveway.

"I called Elizabeth and the team. I had nothing to do with the rest of this."

"Right," I drawled as I let Karen and Colin out of the back seat of my car.

"Wow," Karen sighed as she looked up at the huge face of the manor. It brought back memories of the first time I ended up here, when William literally snatched me off the street and brought me here against my will. Of course, that was only after first trying to eat me for breakfast. Even being furious with him, as I was then, it couldn't diminish the awe I felt at seeing this place for the first time.

"I know." I smiled at her. "It's just as amazing inside. Come on."

I took Karen by the hand and left the guys to follow us up the stairs, but hesitated for a moment. I kept my hand on the doorknob briefly before pushing the door open.

I was instantly hit with a blast of excited chatter as I stepped into the entrance hall. Vampires, deep in conversation, stood around in groups, or hovered on the staircase, vying for a better position. It all stopped the moment the four of us passed through the front doors.

It's always awkward when you walk into a room with the sneaking suspicion that everyone was just talking about you. It's an even worse feeling when you know for a fact that they were talking not only about you, but also about whether or not someone would live or die that night, thanks to your epic mess-up.

"Do you know where Elizabeth is waiting for us?" I asked William as I angled myself in front of Karen. I was trying to obscure her from their view.

"Yes, she—"

"Thank you for finding him so quickly, Vanessa." Elizabeth appeared at the top of the grand staircase, dressed from head-to-toe in a black pants suit. Her hair was pulled back from her face in an elegant chignon, and large diamond studs sparkled in her ears as she moved. She looked more like the CEO of major company than the leader of a one of the largest vampire covens.

"Mouse did most of the work in helping me find him really," I told her. That was true. That he happened to be in the first place I looked was pure luck. Obviously, slightly tainted luck, seeing as how he wasn't alone and all.

"So modest," she said, smiling at me indulgently.

"So what's next?" I shifted my weight from one foot to the other as I tried to ignore the stares of the vampires in the hall. Some of the looks they were sending our way were downright hostile, and I didn't want to be there for much longer. It would give them too great a chance to deal with the situation as they saw fit.

"Since so many of us have shown up here tonight, it seems more appropriate to hold this meeting in the ballroom. It is large enough to accommodate all of us."

She made her way down the stairs and off to the right, heading from the libraries and offices where we usually held our Task Force meetings. Everyone obediently filed out of the room after her. The silence was heavy and eerie, as if we were attending someone's funeral, or following the hearse.

The ballroom was beautiful. Even though I had yet to hear of a single event happening there in the few months that I had been part of the Coven, there still wasn't a single speck of dust in the room. Three giant chandeliers dominated the ceiling, which swirled with intricate, deeply cut molding.

An entire wall of the room was comprised of floor-to-ceiling windows, overlooking the vast landscaping behind the house. As I made my way across the marble floor, I could hear the ghost notes of an orchestra playing a haunting waltz. I imagined all the Coven gathering here to dance from dusk until dawn.

Maybe they would once again when things were a little more peaceful and we had some time for celebrations.

Elizabeth took up her position in front of the giant windows and turned to face us as we gathered around her.

"Bring him forward," she commanded, her voice resonating across the expanse of the vast room.

I took Colin by the upper arm and he stared at me, his face the shade of sun-bleached bones as I walked him to the front of the crowd.

"What is your name?" she asked him as he stood there, swaying, in front of her. I stood behind him, prepared to catch him if he ended up fainting.

"Colin." His voice didn't carry as well as hers did,

but for all his nerves, he still managed to keep it steady and looked her directly in the eyes. I had to respect him for that.

"Well, Colin, I am Elizabeth, leader of the Silverlake Coven. Do you know why you are being presented to us today?"

Colin turned around and looked at me with wild eyes. He seemed to be seeking direction before answering her. "I saw something that I shouldn't have, and now some people want to kill me."

Elizabeth nodded gravely and looked him over. "You tried to expose something that you know nothing about, while clinging to your ignorant insistence about freedom of speech. Speech without thought or consideration is a sure recipe for disaster as you have, no doubt, learned tonight."

Colin nodded his head frantically. "I know that now. I know. I will never say another word about it. I swear to God. I hadn't planned on saying anything in the first place; it was all a huge mistake."

Elizabeth held up her hand and smiled at him sadly as she shook her head. "I'm sorry, Colin, but what's done is done and you cannot take it back. If we had been the only ones who saw it, that would have been feasible, but as it happens, we were not the only ones, were we? There are others of our kind, vicious and unreasonable, and sadly, they have also become very aware that you have knowledge of us."

"But I won't say anything," he protested.

"I'm sorry, Colin, but we can't just let you go back to your normal life now. You will need to stay here for the night where you will be safe. I need some time to think of the best way for us to protect you."

"But you're not..." He paused and swallowed audibly. "You're not going to kill me, right?"

"No, you have my word on that; I will not kill you."

"Thank you, thank you so much." Colin started to shake as he took a step back from her.

"Vanessa, take him upstairs to the guest rooms and see that he's comfortable and well guarded. We still have more to discuss."

I nodded, feeling relieved that it all went so well.

"William, watch Karen for me. Don't let her out of your sight; I'll be right back."

I walked through the crowd ahead of Colin, parting the way for him, when there was a rush of movement behind me and someone stumbled into my back.

"What the...?" I turned in time to catch Colin before he fell to the ground, his eyes staring blankly into nothingness and his head twisted almost all the way around. "No!" I screamed as I fell to the floor, cradling his body in my lap. "Who did this? Which one of you fucking did this?!" I screamed at them, scanning the crowd, desperately trying to detect a guilty face, or satisfaction, anything. "One of you saw who did this, I know you did. Which one of you was it?"

I stood up and grabbed the vampire nearest to me,

shaking her in rage. "Who was it?" Taking the next vampire in hand, I stared into his eyes and shook him too. "Who was it?"

In my own blind fury, I could barely make out the sound of Karen's weeping as she shouldered herself through the crowd and fell to her knees beside Colin's body. Her sobs sounded far away as my anger started to overtake me.

The edges of my vision began to haze and turn red as my eyes landed on Elizabeth amidst the crowd. I lunged forward, making my way towards her.

"You!" I shouted, pointing at her. "This is all your fault!"

I burst through the throng and started to rush her when an iron band wrapped itself around me, holding me back, and restraining me across my chest.

"Vanessa, don't! Calm down, you have to calm down."

"Let me go!" I struggled against William, now desperate to get free. "This is her fault! She promised him! She promised him that he would be safe. This is on her head!"

My anger turned to frustration and my frustration to tears as I struggled with impotent rage, unable to touch her. She stood just beyond my reach, looking at me like an indulgent mother watching her child having an unwarranted temper tantrum.

"They broke your law, your word," I shouted at her.

"Don't you care? Why don't you care? Why don't you care!"

"I care." She looked beyond me and snapped her fingers.

There was murmuring and shuffling of feet as two vampires marched a third forward, which they escorted between them. The third vampire looked smug and even winked at me as he passed.

My breath caught in my throat when I realized he was Colin's killer. So quietly, so quickly, they found and brought forward Colin's executioner and I didn't even see it happen. Why didn't anyone say anything? Why did they let me think he could get away with it?

"You broke Coven law," Elizabeth said to him.

"I did what you were too weak to do. You know as well as I that there was no other way. They would find him and kill him anyway, and in your foolish attempt to protect him, you would have brought war even closer to our door. How many of our kind would you have allowed to die in order to save this one, loud-mouthed human? What I did was necessary for our families to continue to exist."

"You broke the law," Elizabeth repeated. Then moving so fast, I almost missed it happening, she snapped the vampire's neck. His head was also twisted almost completely around, the same way Colin's was, before she tore it right off his shoulders. The head and the body both turned to ash, and the dust cloud rolled over her feet before hitting the ground and coating her once spotless pants up to the knees.

I stood there, frozen, staring at Elizabeth. I raised my hand to grasp William's arm around me and squeezed it tightly. The anger that I felt only a moment before was quickly replaced with relief and gratitude, and his presence now seemed more like that of a protector than a captor. Thank God I hadn't reached her! In my idiocy, I probably would have lost my head as well.

Elizabeth looked at me unblinking before walking from the room. The rest of the Coven followed after her. The situation was firmly behind them now. The threat to their security had been quickly dispatched, and Coven justice was dispensed all at once. There was nothing more for them here.

With the hall now empty of all in attendance but Karen, William and myself, the sound of Karen's sobbing echoed in the ballroom. The acoustics amplified every heart-wrenching tear.

I pulled against William and this time, he let me go. Free of his grasp, I staggered over to Karen and fell to my knees beside her to stare down at Colin's lifeless body. I failed to protect them. Again.

I rested my hand on her shoulder and she tore herself away from my touch. Staring at me with unmasked loathing, she raised her hand and slapped me across the face.

I closed my eyes and inhaled deeply as the burn spread across my cheeks. Saying nothing, I turned back to Colin with my head bowed as she pulled his body into her arms and began to sob again.

I sat there by her side in silence, watching her pour all of her fears and sorrow onto the spotless ballroom floor until I could take no more.

"We have to go," I whispered.

"No, no! I'm not leaving him here."

"You have to, Karen. I have to get you out of here, right now."

"No, I'm not leaving him in this place. I'm not leaving him here alone."

I grabbed her and jerked her roughly to face me. When she tried to pull away, I held her face in both my hands and forced her to look me in the eyes.

"We are leaving. Now." I stood up and grasped her arm, hauling her to her feet. I didn't want to leave Colin's body there either, but that was out of my hands now. All I could do now was get her out of there as soon as possible.

I jerked her sharply and she stumbled as she skirted around his body. With one last, disgusted look at William, I started running towards the front door of the mansion.

We made it to the driveway without incident and I shoved Karen into the car before diving into the driver's seat and gunning the engine. I peeled down the long, private driveway as quickly as I could, anxious to put as much distance between the Coven and me as possible.

As I traveled the half hour back into Silverlake City, I couldn't banish the sight of Colin's dead body from my mind, nor the blank expression on William's face when I ran from the room.

CHAPTER 6

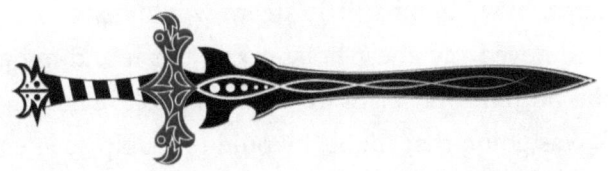

I kept my arm firmly around Karen, supporting her weight as I walked her through my apartment to the spare bedroom. Her eyes were barely open and she trudged heavily across the cold boards of my hardwood floor. It was as if she were completely weighed down by the events of the night, the reality dawning on her like great slabs of rock dropping onto her shoulders, and then being commanded to bear them across the scorching Sahara Desert.

I didn't turn the lights on in the spare bedroom as I lay her down on the bed. After helping her stretch out, I very gently removed her shoes and tucked her under the covers.

I left her there in the dark, alone with her sorrow and regret, giving her some much-needed privacy. But I couldn't sleep, I was too amped up to rest my head anytime soon, and the frustrated energy coursed through me. I wanted to rage, and hunt, and feed.

The night was still young and there was bound to be a Renegade or two hunting somewhere in the city. Perhaps, blowing off a little steam would help.

I removed my chest holster and put it and my guns in the bottom drawer of my bedside table. The way my luck was going that night, I would probably have ended up getting stopped by the cops and being booked for walking around with not one, but two! concealed carries. It was better to just stick with my long knife and a single stake. Besides, I was definitely in the mood to get up close and personal.

I checked in on Karen before I left, poking my head in the spare room to see the steady rise and fall of her chest. She would ache tomorrow, and more than likely, feel as if her whole world had been torn apart before her eyes; but at least for the next few hours, she might get a small semblance of peace and sleep.

I locked the door of the apartment behind me and rode the elevator down to the lobby from the twentieth floor. I couldn't imagine having another apartment close to the ground. That was one thing I learned the hard way this summer after being dragged into this supernatural world. Even though the vampires couldn't enter my home without permission, it certainly didn't stop them from throwing a grenade through my kitchen window. The harder it was for them to find creative ways to blow me up, the better I felt about the whole thing.

The air outside was cool, now that the scorching summer had turned into a lingering fall; and despite being November, we were yet to see even a hint of snow. Hopefully, the season would stretch out for as long as possible. I just wasn't ready yet to face the icy, harsh bite of winter as the frozen winds rolled off the lake, gripping the city in its relentless grasp. Patrolling in that weather really sucked.

The streets were almost deserted as I strolled along under the street lamps. I looked up at the sky and the faint stars winking through the clouds. The light from the pale sliver of moon was outshone by the artificial illumination coming from the buildings and stores around me.

Now that I was living in a more central location of the city, I had better hunting opportunities, not to mention, how much I liked the constant hum of life. It was a permanent connection to the other lives that scurried through the streets every day.

A tripping shuffle came from behind me, pulling my attention back to my surroundings. I kept walking so as not to alert them. I didn't want them to know I noticed their presence, and my ears strained as I listened for more sounds.

Stretching my arms above my head, I turned to face the street, looking both ways, as if checking for oncoming traffic before darting across the road to the other side at a casual jog. I used the opportunity to glance back, but I didn't see anyone else on the sidewalk behind me.

I continued my walk down the street, remaining very alert. Even though I couldn't see anyone around, I couldn't shake the feeling that I was being followed.

I pretended to trip slightly, rolling my ankle and hissing loudly. I dropped down to check my ankle and kept my head low, allowing my hair to fall forward and curtain my face.

A low, rough growl came from behind me and I whipped around to introduce myself to my new friend, but froze in fear at the sight of a giant canine approaching me. It was huge, standing a good four feet at the shoulders. Its sharp teeth snapped at me as it slowly made its way closer.

I scrambled backwards in an ungraceful crab walk before eventually finding my feet. Grabbing my dagger, I held it out in front of me, the blade trembling slightly in my grip.

I really wished then that I had taken my chances with the guns; if I stuck my knife in the beast, it would probably do no more than make it very, very angry. Oh, well, maybe it would eat me faster.

Do wolves play with their food? The image of it batting me around like a shredded, blood-covered rag doll came to my mind and I brought my other hand up to grip the knife as well, while continuing to take slow, deliberate steps backwards.

The wolf suddenly lunged towards me, snapping its huge jaws ferociously when two arms wrapped around me from behind. I was instantly hauled off my feet and dragged into the alley.

I kicked out, screaming, and any attempt to devise a strategy flew out the window as old memories of my former kidnapping this year flooded my mind. The terror of being chained for days in a dark basement, only to die again overcame me, and I kicked out even harder as I struggled against my attacker.

The giant wolf followed us into the alley and blocked the entrance and any chance for escape. Even if I were to break free, the monster would have been on me in seconds.

"Well, now, you sure don't fight like a vampire," a lilting drawl laughed in my ear, "but you've sure got their stink all over you now, don't you?"

"Let me go!" I snapped as I continued to struggle.

"Sure," his arms dropped away from me quickly as he shoved me roughly with both hands on my back, and sent me sprawling onto the pavement of the alley in the direct line of the wolf.

I lay on my stomach and pushed myself onto my elbows, my eyes frozen on the giant paws now padding towards me.

"What do you want?" I asked, trying to stay calm and keep my voice steady. *Animals can smell fear*, I remembered. I just needed to stay calm. If they wanted to kill me, I would have probably already been dead.

"We just came to have a little chat about how you vampires are getting mighty sloppy around here these days. Having your picture taken and the like. It's not just bad business for you lot, you know. Your kind are so damn arrogant. You forget that you aren't the only ones trying to preserve your lives of privacy."

"What do you mean?" I eyed the wolf warily before turning around to see the man that grabbed me; but he was already on top of me, and turning me to face him.

I inhaled sharply as his brown eyes turned a bright amber and his teeth started to elongate in his mouth. Not just his fangs, like a vampire, but *all* of his teeth.

"Don't play with me." The command came out almost like a guttural bark. "You think we don't know about the picture? The article? We have just as much invested as you do. And we *will* be included in the decision on how the matter is ultimately dealt with."

"It's too late." I shook my head. "It's too late, he's already dead... What *are* you?" The question flew out of my mouth before I could hold it back.

Shaking, I turned from him to look over my shoulder at the giant wolf behind me, and then back to the glowing, yellow eyes that were boring into mine.

"Oh, no! Oh, no, no, no, you have *got* to be shitting me! A werewolf? Are you a mother fucking *werewolf*? There are *werewolves* now?" I could feel my grip on reality and my composure slipping. This night was definitely becoming way too much.

"You don't know my kind?" He leaned in closer to

me and inhaled my scent deeply. "Hmm, you smell of vampire and something else." He looked at me curiously before letting me go and standing up again.

I followed him, and dusted the dirt and dust off the front of me before tossing my hair over my shoulder and holding up my hands.

"Okay, wait a minute. I just need one minute, okay?" I asked him as I looked back at the wolf again. It tilted its head to the side and sat back on its haunches. "Oh, God," I groaned.

"Okay, so you," I said, pointing at him, "and you?" I turned around and pointed at the wolf behind me. "You're both honest to God, real life, howl-at-the-moon werewolves?" I took a deep breath and nodded. "Okay, okay. Obviously, this is totally plausible because hey, there are vampires, right? And there's me. And I'm not a vampire, by the way, so... yeah. Werewolves."

I put both my hands on my face and closed my eyes for a moment, trying to block everything out in order to grab just a few seconds of sanity in a night that was quite rapidly spiraling down the drain.

"And you're here because of the picture on the Informant's... on Colin's, website? Well, you're too late for that one. He was killed tonight. One of the vampires got to him first and just... killed him."

"Well, that's one problem solved then," he said over my shoulder to the wolf behind me.

"Hey!" I shouted, storming towards him and shoving him. "That was my best friend's boyfriend. So watch

59

your damn mouth! He wasn't just an annoyance, or a problem. He was a goddamn human being who didn't deserve having his life stolen from him. He didn't know what the hell he was getting into; and he sure didn't ask for it. Nobody *asks* for this. Or to be dragged into this life. So show some damn respect for the dead!"

I stood before him, my chest heaving as I tried to catch my breath from my outburst. All these damn paranormals cared about was their precious secret; never mind how much blood they had to spill, or who had to be sacrificed in order for them to keep their identities unknown.

"I'm sorry, I should have shown a little more tact. I'm sorry for your friend's loss, and your own, judging by the looks of it."

"It wasn't my loss, it was just my mistake. I never should have trusted his safety with them, not when it came down to their precious secret and the life of one insignificant human. I keep forgetting what killers they are. Every last one of them. It doesn't matter if they sit around in their fancy houses playing nice. Deep down, they'll kill just as mercilessly as the Renegades if they decide it serves their purpose."

"Yeah, well," he said with a shrug as he tucked his hands into the front pockets of his faded jeans. He rocked back on the heels of his scuffed workman boots and looked up at the sky. "Vampires have always been a bunch of arrogant sons of bitches."

"And you?" I looked at him skeptically. "Look at you!

Hauling me off the street and trapping me in an alley. Do you really expect me to think that you wouldn't have killed him just as quickly? Because I don't believe that for a second."

I took a step towards him and looked him up and down. Now that the panic was gone, I had a moment to really study him. His thick, chestnut hair was long enough to run my fingers through, and he was overdue for a trim. But that and the rough, new growth of his beard made him look solid, even real. Sometimes, the refined beauty of the vampire coven, and the uncontrollable madness of the Renegades made me feel like I was looking at them all through funhouse mirrors, distorted and not quite real. They almost had a dreamlike quality to them. But this man, this wolf, was earthy and real and strangely solid. Maybe that was because he was still alive, whereas the vampires were already very much dead. But it didn't matter.

"You want to guard your secrets just as badly as they do. So don't look at me and pretend like you wouldn't have snapped his neck just as swiftly if you thought it would suit your purpose."

"So you've got us all figured out then, have you? You think you know the score?"

"Yeah, I think I do."

He nodded and looked around the alley before letting out a tired sigh. "Well, it looks like our business here is done for the night. Really no point in hanging around these dirty alleys like a bunch of rabid raccoons.

Why don't the three of us go and have a drink so we can get better acquainted?"

I could feel the familiar tug of hunger low in my belly as I contemplated his offer for all of a half second before dismissing it. "No, thanks, I'm finished here. And with you." I turned to walk away.

"Oh, come on now, you can't tell me you aren't the least bit curious. Like you said before, we're real life weres. You didn't even know we existed, and now you've met two of us." He paused and looked over at the wolf. "Sort of. And I sure as hell am interested to find out what you are, exactly. So what do you say? How about a quick drink to further the werewolf, vampire, mystery woman relations?" He smiled innocently and cocked his head to the side. "I promise we're house trained."

A burst of laughter escaped and surprised me, the sound seemed so foreign.

"Sure, why not?" I shrugged. "In the name of furthering cross species relations."

"Why don't we just give my brother here a little privacy for a moment so that he can change?" He held out an arm in front of him, indicating that I should walk out of the alley first and they would follow behind me.

"So how long were you trailing me?" I asked as I leaned against the wall of the building on the street and looked straight ahead.

"Just a couple of blocks. We were trying to pick up

the scent of any vampires out tonight when we came across you."

"You were just walking around, hoping to stumble across a vampire tonight?" I snorted. "Doesn't seem very efficient."

"Yeah, well, it's not as if we could just stroll into the Coven manor uninvited. What do you think Elizabeth would do if we both brazenly showed up at her door without any invitation or notice?"

I shrugged and looked away. "How should I know? I didn't even know you existed before a few minutes ago. No one bothered to tell me there was anything else out there. No one seemed to think that was very important information apparently."

My annoyance was beginning to blossom into life again and I tried to squash down the niggling sense of betrayal that I felt towards William at that moment. How much time did he have to tell me there were more out there, so much more to this supernatural world? And yet, not once did he even hint at anything else. Vampires really were bloody, self-centered egotists.

I turned at the sound of movement coming from the entrance of the alley and saw a young man emerging. He was tall like the first man with the same chestnut hair and bright, brown eyes, but not as fully filled out. The muscles on his long, wiry body were lean with youth and the last vestiges of puberty.

"This is my little brother, Michael." He tousled his brother's hair and Michael shoved his hand off, his eyes darting toward me in embarrassment. "And I'm Kane." He held out his hand to me and I shook it.

"Vanessa," I told them.

"Well, Vanessa, where would you like to go for that drink?"

I looked over at Michael. "Are you even old enough to drink?" I asked him.

"I'm twenty-two," he sneered.

"Well, then," I said with a grin, "I know just the place."

CHAPTER 7

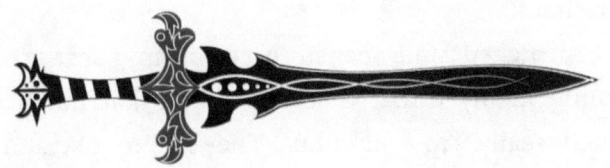

I settled into the booth at the Roxy and took a long drink of my beer. Not being the weekend, the bar wasn't as fully packed with people, or as loud as it normally was.

"I haven't been here for a long time," Kane remarked, grinning over his beer.

"I love this place, it's so relaxed." Since it was the middle of the week, the Roxy was running more like a pub than the hottest weekend dance club. That meant we didn't have to scream above the music to be heard or understood. I relaxed in my seat and took a moment to watch the handful of people out on the dance floor, grooving to the eighties rock blasting over the speakers.

"So what are you?" Michael asked so abruptly that my sip of beer went down the wrong way. I pounded on my chest and coughed before glaring at him.

Kane smacked Michael in the back of the head and

looked at me apologetically. "Sorry, he's young, and apparently, hasn't learned any manners at all. But I'd be lying if I didn't say I was just as curious. I've never heard of anyone that wasn't a vampire being so thick with them."

I shrugged and leaned back in my seat as the burning in my throat eased up. "Not that much of a stretch, really. I'm a succubus. They like to joke and call me 'vampire lite.'"

"Well, now, you're about as rare as a five-leafed clover then, aren't you? The Pack likes to keep to itself for the most part, and I can't think of a single one of us that actually met a real life succubus before. I was told your kind were a myth."

"*I'm* the myth?" He couldn't be serious. "You're joking, right?"

"Okay, you have a point. To the humans, we're all make-believe. But in our world, most people don't believe succubi are real. You're pretty much the folklore of our folklore."

"Yeah, and you know, I don't think I'm ever going to get used to that," I told him, taking another long swallow from my bottle.

"How do we know you're really a succubus?" Michael asked skeptically.

I looked at him and leaned forward slowly, a sly smile playing across my lips. "Would you like me to prove it to you?" I asked in a sultry voice.

A dusky blush crept up his neck and across his cheeks as he looked away, shaking his head.

"Good," I said with a laugh, sitting back against the booth cushions. "It's probably better that you just take my word for it anyway." I raised my beer bottle to him in a silent salute.

"So?" Kane changed the topic as he chuckled at his brother's discomfort. "How'd a nice succubus like you get mixed up in a coven like that?"

"One night, one of them tried to eat me. Luckily for me, I didn't taste right."

"So one of them tried to eat you, and now you're all just best friends, or what?" Michael sneered.

"Yeah, Michael, something like that. Apart from the fact that I'm pretty pissed off with them about what happened tonight, they're pretty much my family now. I didn't know there was anyone else out there even remotely like me until they came along. Of course, now I'm learning that there are more people out there like me than I ever thought possible."

"And you still trust them?" Michael pressed. "Even after they kept you in the dark about the rest of us?"

"Yeah, okay, see, so who *are* the rest of you? Because when you say it like that, I'm starting to get the sneaking suspicion that you're talking about more than just a few weres."

"Oh, yeah, there are loads—"

"I think," Kane cut him off, "that maybe we should take this a little more slowly. Why don't we order another round first? You've been through a lot tonight and we'd hate to overload you all at once."

"What?! You think I can't take it? I'm not afraid to know what's out there. What I hate is walking around thinking I've got all the facts and the next thing I know, a dog the size of a small horse is looking at me like I'm his dinner."

"Wolf," Michael corrected.

"Whatever." I rolled my eyes at him.

"I'm not trying to say that you can't take care of yourself, or you can't handle it," Kane said softly. "But this, *this* is a big deal, and once you know about everything else that's out there, you can't un-know it."

"Is it really as bad as all that then?"

"No, not bad, it is what it is. But you didn't seem so thrilled to belong to the small corner of the world you've already discovered. Are you sure you want to take all the rest on?"

I sat there thinking it over. He was right, at the moment, I had my hands more than full with the problems between the Coven and the Renegades. Did I really want to start borrowing trouble?

"What if someone else attacks me though? What if they come around wanting info on the person who wrote the article and I'm not prepared?"

"It shouldn't be a problem. You said that it's been... dealt with, by the Coven. So my brother and I can put the word out for you that it won't be a problem any longer; and everyone can breathe a little bit easier."

"I'm not sure. I really feel like this is something that I should know about. I can't just hide under the covers and pretend it's not out there just because I'm having a bad day."

"Tell you what, why don't we call it a night? You look like you could use a good, long sleep. If you're feeling up for it tomorrow night, why don't you meet us back here around nine o'clock and we'll tell you all about it?"

I nodded and finished off my beer. "All right. Let me get some sleep, and tomorrow I'll deal with this fresh. But if you're not here, I'm going to be seriously choked."

"Don't worry, we aren't going anywhere. It was nice to meet you, Vanessa."

"Nice to meet you too." I smiled at Michael. "Both of you. And thanks for not eating me, Mike."

I slid out of the booth and patted Michael on the shoulder before walking away.

I was standing at the stove, frying up breakfast, when Karen padded in, shuffling her feet and rubbing the sleep from her eyes. Her normally wild shock of curly, red hair was standing on end, and I wondered if she accidentally stuck her finger in an electrical socket at some point last night while I was out.

I wanted to say something to her, something

enlightening and comforting and heart-soothing all at the same time, but my mind drew a blank, so I decided to play it safe.

"Are you hungry?" I gestured towards the pan of bacon I had sizzling. "I can make you a breakfast sandwich on a bagel."

She shook her head and got a glass down from the cupboard before moving to the fridge and pulling out one of my ever present cartons of apple juice. Between the two of us, it was surprising a worldwide apple shortage hadn't been declared.

I watched her fill the glass to the brim and polish off the entire thing before filling it up a second time. She looked at me with puffy, red eyes, evidence of all the hours of intense crying the night before. Then she lowered her head and shuffled back to the guest bedroom, closing the door silently behind her.

I finished making breakfast and fixed her a sandwich anyway. Even though she felt unable to eat now, after hours of crying, she would eventually be starving. That always seemed to be the way it went after a good, hard cry. After pouring out everything you have, you can finally start over again and suddenly, you become desperate to fill up all the cracks and hollow canyons inside you that you allowed to run dry.

I knocked gently before entering and tiptoed inside so as to not disturb her. She lay curled up on top of the blankets in fetal position with her head hidden beneath one of the many pillows piled high on the bed.

I sat outside at the small, wrought-iron table on my balcony with my feet up on the other chair of the simple three-piece set. Shoving aside my half-eaten sandwich in disgust, I let my head fall back, enjoying what little warmth the early morning offered.

There was no point in pretending like it was just another morning; that wouldn't get me through this. What I needed were answers, and as soon as the sun went down, I knew exactly which lying vamp I was going to drag them out of.

(something) ... several ... (illegible) ... with ... term.
Eleven (billion) ... ted up the ... total end of the
could ... they (illegible) act on the ... made ... behind
... (illegible) ... ded off back towards
... (illegible) ... to ... carry ... ing on and.

There was no point in returning how to another
... (illegible) nothing had even there ... and through this.
Vaguely ... (illegible) ... or (illegible) ... and was as that
... (illegible) ... I have ... up with (illegible) ... down for
... (illegible) ... on.

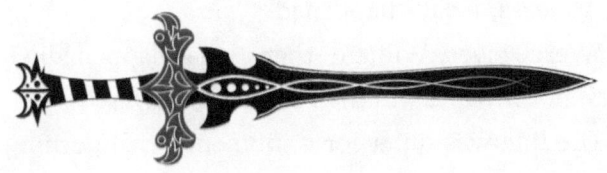

CHAPTER 8

"Vanessa, I'm glad you called."

I ignored the traitorous need that was tugging in my gut at the sound of his voice, remembering this was the same man that had been lying to me for months now.

"You know what, William? I don't care if you're glad or not. I have questions and I bet you have the answers; that's all this is about."

"I didn't know he was going to die, Vanessa, and not like that, if it had to happen at all, I promise you. I didn't expect anyone there to go against Coven law like that, especially in Elizabeth's presence. We were all just as stunned as you were."

"That's not what I'm calling to talk to you about," I ground out between clenched teeth as my grip tightened on the phone. I had to resist the strong urge to throw it across the room.

"Then what answers do you think I have for you, love?"

"Don't call me that! Don't you dare call me that!" I snapped.

"Vanessa, what's happened?"

"Werewolves, William, that's what happened! Giant, hairy, not mythical, in the flesh werewolves."

The line was quiet for a moment, with nothing but the sound of his stereo playing in the background.

"Are you hurt?" he asked, finally breaking the silence.

"Should I be hurt? Are werewolves something that can hurt me? Because I was under the impression they were make-believe. Not something I have to watch my back for when I'm out at night. And it sure as shit seemed like something I should have known about last night."

"Are you finished?"

"Nope, pretty sure I'm not. In fact, I'm thinking I'm just getting started because I want to know why, in all this time, no one thought that maybe I should know about the big ass werewolves that just wander around Silverlake City."

"Vanessa, I didn't tell you because I thought you had enough going on already. It wasn't some huge secret. There was no conspiracy to keep you in the dark about the other supernaturals. But they just aren't our main priority right now. We have much bigger problems within our own clan; and a few shaggy mutts were the farthest things from anyone's mind, including my own."

"Clans? There are clans now? What the hell is a clan?"

William sighed and I could almost see him pinching the bridge of his nose in frustration. "Each supernatural type is referred to as a clan. The werewolf clan is broken down into packs, the vampire clan is broken down into covens, etcetera."

"And the succubi clan?" My curiosity was getting the better of me.

"I actually don't know. Succubi are so rare that most of us have never even met one, let alone, heard of a large group of them in one place."

"Oh," I said quietly. I nudged aside the sting of disappointment, and wondered if I would ever get to meet another succubus.

"So you met a werewolf last night..." he prompted.

"Actually, I met two, and after we cleared up a few things, they seemed to be pretty all right guys."

"What did they want?"

"What do you think? They wanted to find out about Colin. They weren't overly impressed with my little photo shoot."

"And what did you tell them?"

"Well, the truth obviously. It's not too difficult for some of us. I told them Colin is dead and just like the vampires, they seemed perfectly satisfied with that."

"You know how important the continued secrecy of

our kind is. The world isn't prepared to hear the truth about our existence yet."

"Especially if they learned there was more than just the occasional vampire out there sucking them dry, right? I get it. Extreme secrecy required. But that doesn't mean I, in any way, condone the killing of innocent humans to preserve that."

"Well, then? What would you like to have seen happen last night? I know you're angry with the way it turned out, but I don't see you offering up any other solutions."

"Are you happy that Colin is dead?" I gasped.

"No, I'm not happy about it. But I understand why it was for the greater good."

"I can't have this conversation with you right now. I just can't."

"Vanessa—"

"No, just stop. Look, I'm going out to meet these guys tonight and I'm hoping they can give me some real answers. You can keep your secrets and preserve your greater good."

"You're crazy if you think that I'm going to let you meet those dogs alone."

"Do you even hear yourself right now? I don't need a damn chaperone; and anyway, you're not invited."

"Vanessa, don't be stupid. In their wolf forms, two against one, you wouldn't stand a chance."

"They aren't going to attack me, William."

"You know that for certain? You've known them for all of one night and you're sure they won't harm you?"

"You tried to eat me for breakfast the first time we met, and yet somehow, I still ended up sleeping with *you*, didn't I?"

"You've got to let that go, love, I said I was sorry."

"Did you? Because I don't actually remember you apologizing for it."

"Stop trying to change the subject, I'm coming with you tonight. They may have news for me to pass onto Elizabeth anyway, so it would be good for me to be there for more reasons than just to make sure that you don't get fleas."

"Oh, my God," I gasped. "You're a racist. You're racist against werewolves."

"No, I'm not."

"Yes, you are. Talking about me getting fleas. Calling them mutts. You're a walking, talking, racist against werewolves, vampire cliche. Oh, my God, I'm so embarrassed for you. Seriously, William, if you're coming with me tonight, you had better check up on what millennium this is first. Racism just isn't cool anymore."

"I'm not racist. They *are* dogs. Dogs get fleas."

"Uh-huh, tell that to the Confederate flag."

I walked into the Roxy at exactly nine PM and tried to ignore the brooding shadow hovering so closely behind me. More than once, I thought he would step on my heels. I still didn't like the idea of William acting as my undead babysitter, but if he could use this time to deal with Coven business, then it really wasn't my call to stand in his way or mess it up.

"They're over there." I pointed to Kane and Michael who were watching the door for us from across the room. William didn't say anything, but followed me as I waved to them and joined them in the booth. William and I slid in across from the wolves.

"Glad that you could make it." Kane smiled at me, but his eyes went hard as they slid over to William. "I see you brought a friend."

"He kind of brought himself," I said with a defeated sigh.

"Vampires are always sticking their fangs in places where they aren't invited," Michael sneered.

"How about we try to keep this friendly?" I smiled at Michael and William before rolling my eyes at Kane. "All I meant was, William wanted to talk to you about Coven and Pack business, or something like that, and this seemed like a good opportunity, so he came along."

"There are a few questions we wouldn't mind having answered while we're in town." Kane pushed his glass out of the way and stared intensely at William. "Like why the hell vamps have been skulking around Pack territory?"

William's eyes narrowed sharply. "What do you mean? We have no need or reason to go out there."

"That's exactly what I've been saying, and yet, we've been picking up your scents at the edges of our land lately."

"The members of the Silverlake Coven know better than to go anywhere near your land. Whoever's been out there isn't one of ours."

"Is that so?" Kane rubbed the stubble on his chin.

"You don't believe this mosquito, do you?" Michael looked at his brother, getting disgusted. "He's lying. Why would he tell us anything about their plans?"

"Plans?" I looked at him, confused. "I really don't think the Coven has any kind of plans against the werewolves. I mean, we kind of have our own problems right now."

"Vanessa," William warned, putting a hand on top of mine.

"What, William? If vampires are out on their land, and they aren't supposed to be, then it sounds like our problems concern them too."

"We don't know that for sure. It could have just been a nomad."

"Is there something you would like to fill me and my brother in on?" Kane asked William.

"No," said William.

"But they should know."

"It doesn't concern them. It's Coven business."

"Well, whatever this Coven business is seems to be spreading a little out of your control there, William.

Because there have definitely been vampires in our area and more than that—"

"Kane, no," Michael interrupted, "that's Pack business."

"Oh, for crying out loud!" I slammed my hand down on the table and glared at the three of them. "I have had it up to here with this. By the sound of things, we're all in trouble here, so why don't we just cut the crap and get it all out on the table, okay?"

Michael sulked and slid down in his seat with his arms crossed over his chest. I interpreted his body language as telling me that was the closest I could get to an agreement from him. William and Kane sat in silence, glaring at each other, but didn't contradict me.

"Good. Now, the Silverlake Coven has been having a serious problem with a few of its vampires. And it's looking like it's not just a few random malcontents like we first suspected. There is an entire breakaway faction of the Coven running around out there, stirring up a shit storm. You know all those murders this summer that we all believed were the work of a serial killer? It was just a huge cover-up scheme conceived by the Renegades to hide their murders. They were killing the humans they were feeding from."

"Holy shit," burst out Michael, and I nodded in agreement.

"Holy shit is right, but there's more. They weren't just killing humans, they were turning them as well. We now have a whole new crop of young vampires running around out there, all killing their feeds and getting up to who knows what else. If you've been smelling strange vampires where they shouldn't be, then it's probably a good bet that it's them."

"You know they're out there right now, and you haven't put a stop to it?" Kane gaped at us. "What the hell have you guys been doing all this time?"

"Everything that we can," William said with icy resolve.

"Yeah, it sure looks like it," said Michael.

"It's complicated," I sighed. "This is... it's bigger than any of us thought when we first learned the vampires were the ones doing all the killings."

"And now the killings have just stopped? I haven't heard anything about more bodies being found for over a month now." Kane sipped his drink.

"That's right, and to be honest, I don't know what's scarier." I rubbed my arms as a sudden chill ran down them. "Something is up. They don't need the exposure to cover up their kills anymore, but there's no way they would just stop killing. They seem to feel they're *owed* the death. Like it's a right that they've been denied for too long."

William squeezed my hand reassuringly. "They're planning something, we just haven't been able to figure out what."

Michael looked silently at Kane with worry in his eyes and a silent message passed between the two brothers.

"It's a pretty safe bet then that they're planning something big." Kane lowered his voice and leaned in towards us. "Ours isn't the only pack that smelled vampires on their land, but it's worse than that, much worse. Wolf pups have been taken from some of the other packs."

My eyes widened in shock. "What?" I choked out. "They've kidnapped your children?" Horror and disgust, coated with a thick layer of fear, bolted through me. My eye caught Michael's who was shaking with barely contained rage, but his head jerked in a nod.

"Four have been taken so far that we know of," Kane continued. "All of them were under the age of five. Thankfully, none of them were from our pack. No one under the age of fifteen has been allowed out of the sight of the elders. There are regular patrols in place as well."

"I can't believe this is happening. Why would they take the children?"

"We don't know. But from what you've said, I think they're just another part of a bigger plan. "

"They plan on challenging Elizabeth," William stated with certainty.

"Are they crazy?" I paused. "Scratch that, they're obviously certifiable, but I thought the Silverlake Coven was the largest in the area? A very wide, wide area."

"It is, for now. But if the werewolves' children are being kidnapped from other packs, that means the Renegades have probably spread much further than we estimated. Who knows how many vampires they've turned by now?"

It was starting to sink in. "That would also explain why they haven't bothered to cover up their killings anymore. If they've set up satellite covens in other major cities, then depending on their size, who would notice a few more deaths?"

"Especially if they're killing transients," Kane added.

"Junkies, runaways, and the homeless," I listed, ticking them off on my fingers. "Who would look closely if a few more of them turned up dead?"

"It gets worse." William closed his eyes and sighed.

"Worse? Worse how, exactly?" My whole life seemed to be increasingly getting worse. At this point, what was one more bombshell?

"As you know, the Silverlake Coven was formed because a few of the elders voted to end the killing of humans."

"Right, because they deemed it needless. So?"

"Well, while there are certainly other vampires out there that agree and also don't kill their feeds, there are also a lot that still do."

"Oh, my God," I whispered.

"Exactly."

"What is it?" Kane asked, confused.

"Recruiting season," I explained.

"Wherever they've been setting up their smaller covens, I bet you they've already reached out to the others in the area," said William.

"Would the solitary vampires even want to join a coven?" I asked.

"Do you really think the Renegades are going to take their feelings into consideration?" William asked.

"Vampire civil war," Kane mumbled. "Just what our world needs."

"And it's spreading like a virus, infecting the rest of us!" Michael shot daggers at William.

"We have to get the children back," Kane announced. "We have to find them and bring them home."

"We don't even know where to start looking," I said.

"Then start killing these Renegades until you do," Michael demanded.

"Michael," Kane warned.

"No, he's right," I said. "I'm sorry, Michael, you're right. We have to get these kids back no matter what. William, we have to help them."

"I'll take all of this to Elizabeth. She'll want to know." William agreed.

"So do you guys think you can stop taking cheap shots at each other long enough for us to work together on this?" I asked.

The guys all looked at each other and nodded their consent.

"We will," Kane answered for them.

"Good," I leaned back in my seat. "So how do we get these kids back?"

CHAPTER 9

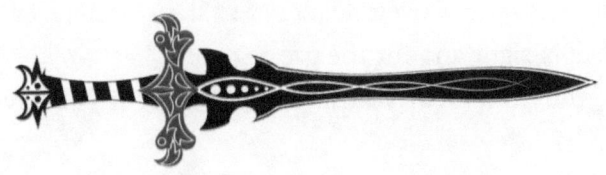

"We are in serious trouble," I said as I sat on William's couch with my feet resting on his coffee table.

"You noticed that, did you?"

"Hey, watch the snark. I know I'm stating the obvious here, but at the moment, the obvious is all I've got."

"Sorry, love, I'm just wound a little tight." He leaned over and kissed me on the top of my head.

"I know, and I guess I can't really blame you. How do you think Elizabeth will take the news?"

"She'll be even more determined to put an end to this quickly, of course."

"But what about the wolves? How do you think she'll feel about us helping them get their kids back? I wish this weren't something I had to ask, but I can't even begin to guess where that woman's priorities will fall on this one. The Coven comes first, right? No matter the cost. What if she considers those kids as nothing more than collateral damage?"

"I can't answer that," he shook his head. "She's an elder and the Coven leader. She'll do whatever she thinks is right and for the greater good."

"And you? Will you follow her even if she says to drop it?"

"No," he said firmly. "No, I won't. I can't ignore this, Vanessa."

"You would go against Elizabeth? You would actually knowingly disobey her for the werewolves?"

"You don't have to sound so surprised," he sneered. "I do know the difference between right and wrong."

"No, it's just—" I started to apologize, but he held up his hand to stop me.

"We fucked up, love. We all know it. We let Merrick get away from us this summer. We don't know who else he's working with, and we don't know where he is. Now, his vampires are kidnapping children and I don't, not even for a second, believe that this isn't just the beginning."

I sighed in relief. Even though it hurt to admit it, I just didn't know where William's loyalty to Elizabeth ended and his own conscience began.

Elizabeth was reclined in a plush armchair in her main sitting room, gently swirling the contents of her wine glass. The deep red liquid clung to the crystal and I sat mesmerized as the light from the fireplace danced across the delicate pattern of the glass.

I had never seen William, or any of the other vampires drink except directly from the source before, but it was highly doubtful that she was savoring a nice merlot. She took a sip from the glass and sighed in satisfaction as William and I sat quietly waiting for her answer.

"These are very serious accusations that you've brought me," she said mildly, taking another sip from her glass. "I find it hard to believe that the wolves would be so careless as to let their pups be taken so easily."

"I don't think it was a matter of carelessness, Elizabeth." My throat was tight as I tried not to let my annoyance seep into my voice. The image of her tearing the head off the vampire that went against her word was still fresh in my mind.

"Well? What would *you* call allowing your enemy to come so close as to take your own child?"

"But they didn't know they had enemies to watch out for. We didn't tell them. I didn't even know they existed."

"Vanessa, dear, sometimes your naïveté amazes me. After this past summer, haven't you yet learned that *everyone* has enemies? It doesn't matter if the weres knew of the Renegades or not, they are werewolves and as such, know just as we do, that there are those out there who would bring them harm. Human, vampire, were, it does not matter. We keep a constant vigilance when it comes to protecting our clans. This is a werewolf matter and it will remain that way."

"But it's not just a werewolf matter. The Renegades are vampires; and if they took those children, then that makes it our problem. Furthermore, as the Silverlake Task Force, it is our *job* to get those kids home. We can't just turn our backs on them."

"We are having a hard enough time controlling the situation as it is, and now you want to distract yourself with this wolf problem as well? No, you have one job and that is to find Merrick and bring him to me so that we can put an end to this entire mess."

"But if Merrick is behind the missing children, or knows who is, then how can we just ignore this lead? It's the biggest news we've had since the killings stopped. Or at least, since they stopped being so public."

"Elizabeth," William cut in, "we are getting nowhere hunting down the Renegades one-by-one. You know that as well as I. If any of them knew where Merrick was, they have not given him up. We need this lead."

"Neither of you even know for certain that the Renegades are behind this," she sniffed.

"No, we don't." I shook my head. "But it's too much of a coincidence to ignore. Who else would have the gall to sneak onto Pack lands and take their children? They are werewolves, for Christ's sake! If you're going to take that kind of a risk, then you'd better have a damn good reason to think it's worth it. No one in their right mind would take a wolf pup on a mere whim."

Elizabeth sighed and set her glass down on the end table next to her. She looked off to the side at the fireplace silently before continuing. "The peace between vampires and werewolves is a new and tentative one. Getting involved in their business is not a step that can be taken lightly. Even if the Renegades aren't behind the kidnappings, the fact remains that they believe vampires are doing it. That means, you will be going in there at the peak of their suspicions. They have no reason to trust us. And now, even more reason than they've had in a long time, to reopen old wounds."

"We will be careful," I promised her, "but we have to try."

She nodded, but continued to stare into the flames, seemingly caught up in whatever memories played out before her there.

"Go. Find whoever did this. Bring back the children if you can," she ultimately relented before falling silent again.

I opened my mouth to reply, but closed it again before rising with William and slipping quietly from the room, leaving her to her private thoughts.

CHAPTER 10

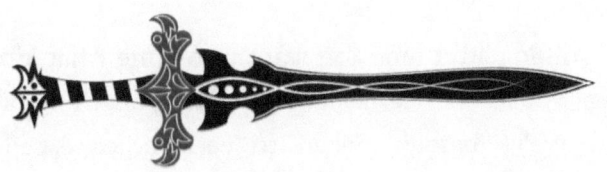

"I want you to stay close to me," William said as he shot a glance in my direction before focusing on the road again.

His jaw was clamped tightly, and I caught a glimpse of the deep grooves etched between his eyebrows before he turned away from me.

He barely spoke two words to me during the whole drive out to the Pack lands, choosing instead to sit and brood. I was determined not to let his mood cloud my own impression of the pack, but none of the vampires on the Task Force seemed overly thrilled about going out there. We would be surrounded and outnumbered, which had them all on edge.

"I'm sure it'll be okay. We're going out there to help them. Besides, I seriously doubt Kane would let anything happen to us."

"Maybe not to you," he mumbled under his breath.

I stiffened, "What was that?"

"Nothing, nothing, just forget it."

"No, what did you mean by that?"

"I just don't like the way he's sniffing after you, that's all."

"Sniffing after me? You want to tell me what kind of drugs you're on? He hasn't been doing anything of the sort. We've barely spoken to each other except to arrange for this meeting to happen."

"Open your eyes, Vanessa, it's written all over his face every time he looks at you."

"Get real, William, you're seeing things that aren't there. I don't know what your problem is, but you really need to get over it."

He opened his mouth to argue with me, but settled for a nasty look instead. The skin of his hands stretched tautly over his knuckles as he squeezed the steering wheel.

I bit my tongue and exhaled deeply through my nose. God save me from sulky vampires.

"Oh, wow," I sighed, "that is amazing." I leaned forward to look out the window, awed by the house suddenly looming in front of us.

William said nothing, but I was sure I heard a soft snort from his direction.

All three cars slowed down and came to stop in front of a beautiful, two-level log house with huge, floor-to-ceiling windows on both levels. The lights were ablaze on the main floor, affording us a clear view of the spacious living room. Inside, we could see a few men and women chatting. The golden light spilled out onto the large, wraparound front porch that boasted a very inviting two-person porch swing. I couldn't help smiling; the home, although large, looked incredibly welcoming. I couldn't wait to get inside. Elizabeth's manor was breathtaking for all its size and grandeur, but this home had something that I didn't realize hers was missing. It had *heart*.

I hopped out of the car and didn't wait for William, but hurried to the bottom step of the front porch where Kane and Michael were already waiting for us.

The vampires hung back for a moment, appearing uneasy as they peered at the gathered werewolves through the window.

"Are you guys coming or what?" I asked, grinning before following Kane and Michael up the steps and into the house.

Once inside, I glanced over my shoulder to see them standing on the other side of the door with varying degrees of annoyance on their faces. William's expression was thunderous as he glared at Kane.

Michael snickered and Kane looked puzzled for a moment before offering them an apologetic smile.

"I'm sorry, please come in," Kane offered. Apparently, the rule about vampires not entering a home without an invitation didn't only apply to humans.

"This is your home?" I took in the high ceiling of the entrance hall and peeked through the large, open archway into the living room. Some of the werewolves were shuffling anxiously. No one seemed overly keen on having this meeting tonight.

"Yes, I built it a few years ago." He looked around his home proudly. "Moving in was a dream come true."

"I don't doubt it, it's absolutely beautiful."

"Thank you." He smiled at me and I felt a light flutter in the pit of my stomach. My eyes flickered over to William and away again when I saw the cool, blank expression on his face.

Noticing my sudden discomfort, Kane glanced at William for a moment before placing a hand lightly on my back and leading me into the living room.

"Why don't we get this meeting started then?" he suggested.

The werewolves cleared the way for us as we entered the room, taking seats, or leaning casually against the walls.

"Let me introduce you to everyone. My brother, Michael, you already know." I waved at Michael and he returned my greeting with a small smile before focusing on the vampires with barely concealed hostility. Kane shot his brother a knowing look before continuing on. "This is Keegan." A scruffy-looking man who seemed to be in his late thirties gave us a curt nod, but didn't speak. "And that is Sheena and her sister, Lena."

Sheena appeared the younger of the two, and the bangs of her ash-blonde hair fell over her face as she looked at us with intense curiosity. Conversely, Lena's hair, although the same color, was pulled back in a tight, serviceable ponytail, and her expression was much more suspicious than curious as she examined us.

"As you all know, dark times have come to the Packs." Kane looked around the room at those gathered there, making eye contact with each one as he spoke. "Pups have been taken from us, stolen off our very lands! And while none of the Silverlake Pack children have been taken, the scent of vampires has been detected in the area. Right now, protecting our remaining pups is our highest priority. They will not be taken like the others."

"Stolen by bloodsuckers," Keegan said, glaring at us.

"Yes," Kane nodded. "They were taken by vampires. Which is why we need them to get our children back so quickly."

"But how do you expect us to trust them?" asked Lena. "For all we know, they could be in on it."

I could hear the members of the Task Force shifting behind me as the wolves murmured amongst themselves.

"Because I trust them," Kane replied, keeping his voice level, "and because our Alpha trusts me and my counsel while he is away."

The rumbling quieted down, but we were still impaled by their hostile glances. I took a deep breath and exhaled slowly before stepping forward beside Kane.

"My name is Vanessa and I'm a member of the Silverlake Coven Task Force. I know that you don't trust us, and while we've never met before, I'm also aware that the animosity between the two clans runs deep. But if we're going to have any chance at all to get those kids back, we will have to work together. We don't have the luxury of nursing old wounds and indulging our prejudices right now, not when there's a much larger problem heading our way."

"Vanessa is right," Kane said. "Now isn't the time to be stubborn. The vampires have a situation that affects us all. And while normally, each clan mostly keeps to themselves, this will likely drag us all down with it."

"Leave it to the vampires to make a mess and leave the rest of us to clean it up," the loud-mouthed wolf spoke up again.

"That's enough, Keegan," Kane snapped.

"No, he's right," I said, cutting off whatever Keegan was about to say next. "This is a vampire mess."

"Vanessa," Thatcher barked behind me.

"Give over, Thatcher, it's the truth and you know it just as much as I do. Vampires slaughtered humans this summer. Vampires kidnapped the werewolf children. Vampires turned on other vampires and tried to kill us. We were betrayed by one of our own team. If this isn't a vampire mess, then you tell me what the hell you prefer to call it. But my point is: absolutely none of that matters now! The Renegades have shown they are fully prepared to make this *everyone's* problem."

"We have to work together to find a solution," said Anastasia who came to stand beside me. "Can you not see that this is exactly what they want? And no less than they would have reason to expect? They rely on our distrust of each other; why would that keep us from stopping them?"

"But why do they want the children?" Lena asked.

"We don't know," Thatcher said. "But it ain't for anything good. All we know is that it's probably in line with this new world order plan of theirs."

"What new world order plan?" Keegan asked. The wolves started quickly talking over each other, the tension in the room heightening with every passing second.

William walked to the closest wall and leaned against it, glaring at the wolves with annoyance. I was starting to get really sick of his elitist attitude.

"Do you want them back, or not?" William asked so quietly that I could barely hear him. The whole room went silent.

"Of course, we want to get them back, vampire," Michael sneered. "They may not be from our Pack, but they are wolf pups. We will help the other packs."

"Well, then, there's only one way we can do that, *dog*."

"What way is that?" Kane asked, putting a hand on

Michael's shoulder, who turned a shade of deep red at William's emphasis of the word "dog."

"We have to set a trap for them," William replied with a shrug.

"What kind of a trap?" My stomach clenched, afraid he was about to suggest the unthinkable.

William pushed himself off the wall and faced Kane, speaking only to him instead of the whole room. "We have to let them take one of your children."

The room exploded at his comment. Every wolf but Kane advanced on us and the vampires dropped into defensive stances and prepared to protect themselves.

Keegan was the first one to attack. Lunging at William, his outstretched hand started to grow and elongate, his fingernails transforming into sharp claws.

I didn't stop to think, but simply threw myself in front of William. Without much time to maneuver, Keegan tried to reach around me, so completely focused on reaching William that his eyes widened in surprise when I collided into his chest.

With no time to waste, I wrapped my arms around his neck and pressed my body against his, taking advantage of his confusion. Lifting my face up, I kissed him, grabbing the back of his head as my hunger flared. I channeled his energy into me. As soon as I felt his body starting to relax, I let go of him and he slid to the floor.

Kneeling down to check his pulse, I was relieved to feel a strong, steady heartbeat in his neck. I was sorry I had to use my power on him, but I couldn't trust that William wouldn't have killed him if Keegan had actually reached him. If that occurred, this whole thing would have fallen apart, and we would have made an enemy of the werewolves as well.

"So," Kane coughed and I looked up to see every pair of eyes in the room on me. While Thatcher seemed almost mildly impressed, the wolves' faces shifted between confusion, interest and bald fear. "That's how you do it then?" he asked.

"Yeah," I said rising to my feet. "That's how I do it. And I really don't feel like having to do it again anytime soon, so why doesn't everyone just calm down so we can get back to coming up with some kind of plan?"

"I already came up with a plan," said William.

"Yes, William, you did. Your plan was that of a crazy person. Maybe we should at least try to come up with something a little less... insane."

"You can't deny that it makes sense, love," he argued.

I held up my hand and shook my head at him. "Are you trying to get us killed here? Is that why you're doing this? You want to get us torn apart in this room?"

"If we are going to win this war, we have to make some hard choices."

"Now you're starting to sound like Elizabeth."

"That's because she was right. We aren't going to get anywhere if we don't start taking chances and doing things that we don't necessarily want to do."

"*Start* taking chances? I've done nothing but take chances since I met you," I snapped.

"And you think we can work together?" Michael sneered, "You guys can't even stop fighting amongst yourselves."

"We aren't fighting, dog, we're hashing out the details," William countered lightly.

"Right," Michael drawled.

"I don't want to do it," Kane said softly.

"Of course you don't," I glared at William.

"But it may be the only way," Kane conceded.

"What!?" I exploded. "You can't be serious."

"We could follow them, find out where they're keeping the others. It could lead us directly to Merrick," William nodded.

"This may not be a complete waste of time," Thatcher agreed.

"That's outrageous," Lena growled, pacing back and forth.

I looked at Michael, sure that he would back me against such insanity, but he just stood there, silently shaking. His face flushed red with anger and his fists clenched so tightly that his knuckles turned white.

"You people are insane," I spat as I shoved my way through them before exiting the room, in desperate need of fresh air.

Shivering in the crisp air with my arms wrapped around my legs and my forehead resting on my knees, I stiffened at the sound of the front door opening and closing behind me, followed by heavy footsteps on the porch.

"You're going to freeze out here." Kane sat down beside me and I absorbed the light warmth that was radiating from him.

"Doesn't seem like that's something you have to worry about."

"Nope. Has to get a lot colder than this."

"How can you do it?" I asked, and he knew I was talking about the plan, not his supernatural ability to keep warm.

"Because we don't have much of a choice."

"There's always a choice. You could say no. You could demand that we find another way."

"To what end? So that we spend the winter running in circles chasing our tails? No. As Beta, I am expected to make these decisions. To take action, no matter how distasteful the choices may be."

"But how can you ask them to make a sacrifice like that? To put the child at risk? And that poor kid will have no say in any of it. What if something goes wrong?"

"I can't think about that."

"How can you *not*? This is the life of a child we're playing with! If we're too slow, or if we're outnumbered, or beaten back and that kid is taken..." I dropped my head onto my knees as the tears started to slide down my face. I didn't want him to see them, or think I was weak. But how could they not see how wrong that was?

Kane put his hand on my back and I could feel the heat seeping through my jacket and warming my skin. I shifted slightly closer to the heat source and we sat there in silence while my tears dried up.

"I don't want to do this."

"Neither do I," he said, squeezing my shoulder and rising before holding his hand out to me. I took it and he pulled me to my feet.

Still holding my hand, he raised his other arm and I held my breath when he gently wiped away the last of my tears from my cheeks. Then, releasing me, he turned without saying anything and headed back inside. I followed him through the open door, now determined to get it over with.

"Have you all decided then?" I looked at each of them in the eye, a stubborn part of me still hoping that someone would demand a different plan, but I knew there was no point in trying to preserve much hope.

"We will follow our Beta," Sheena said softly, her eyes downcast.

"I have decided that William's plan is the one we will use," Kane said gravely, avoiding my eyes. The wolves nodded in agreement, and I felt my last bits of hope crumbling. The final decision was made.

"Who..?" I trailed off, unsure of how to ask, "who could you possibly ask to do that? I mean, who has a child they would be willing to..." I shut my mouth, unable to find the right words.

"I will do it."

"Lena, no!" Sheena grabbed her sister and shook her head in disbelief.

Lena's face was drawn, but her voice was steady. "We can't make a decision like that and then ask someone else to do what we will not. I understand why it must be done, but I cannot, and I will not, ask another of our Pack to do it."

Sheena wrapped her arms around her sister and held her tightly as Lena sat there unmoving, her jaw clenched in stubborn determination.

"Dammit, Lena," Keegan whispered, although he didn't try to talk her out of it.

The vampires stayed silent as the Pack members made their decision. Their faces were completely devoid of life or expression. I couldn't help wondering what they were really thinking.

Michael walked over to the couch and sat on the other side of Lena, taking her hand in both of his.

"We will protect him, Lena, you know that," Kane promised. "We will protect your son to our last, dying breath."

Lena looked up at him and nodded once before getting up and walking out of the house.

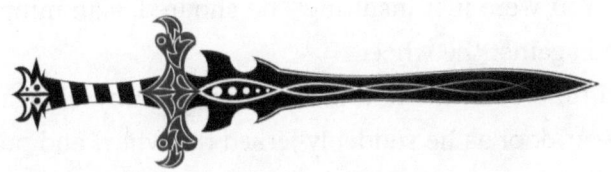

CHAPTER 11

"So are you ever going to speak to me again?" William asked as he looked straight ahead out the windshield. We were driving away from the Pack lands.

"Eventually." *Possibly once hell freezes over, or pigs fly, or I wake up one morning with a burning desire for Thatcher's touch.*

"We had to do something, Vanessa. We were getting nowhere, we would have been talking in circles for hours."

"So is that why you did it then? I know you didn't want to be there in the first place; you made your feelings about the Pack abundantly clear. So did you agree to it just to save yourself the *inconvenience*?"

William sat quietly, the cords of his throat pressing against the skin of his neck from the force of his tightly clenched jaw.

"Is that what you think of me?" he finally asked, his voice barely above a whisper. Even sitting next to him, I could hardly make him out.

"I was just asking—"

"You were just insulting!" he shouted, slamming his hand against the wheel.

I jumped at his outburst and pressed myself against the car door as he suddenly jerked the wheel and pulled over onto the side of the road. Gravel pinged the under-side of the car as it slammed to an abrupt stop.

"Get out!" he commanded.

"What?"

"I said, get the hell out of the car!" he snapped.

He levelled his pit-black eyes on me and I scrambled to undo my seat belt. My hands slipped on the buckle, wet with damp and fear before throwing myself out the passenger side door and onto the cold ground.

A moment later, he was around the car, clamping his icy hands down tightly on my arms and hauling me to my feet before shoving me back against the car. I couldn't catch my breath. I stood frozen in fear as William brought his face, hardened with anger, close to mine. My eyes flickered at the sight of his fangs before returning to the black pits of his eyes. My entire body tensed as he brought up his hand and wrapped it around the back of my neck, fisting my hair. I closed my eyes, unable to face what was coming next.

"Look at me," he demanded.

"No, I can't. I can't see you like that."

He shook me gently and pulled on my hair to tilt my head back. "Look at me!" he demanded, taking his other hand and trailing a finger down the side of my face.

I slowly opened my eyes and only had a moment to notice that his eyes had returned to their familiar shade of green before his mouth covered mine.

Relief turned to confusion and then anger in less than a second. I pulled myself away from him and slapped him across the face.

"What the fuck, William!?" I shouted, pushing him away from me. "What the hell do you think you're doing?"

"What does it look like I'm doing?" he growled before pulling me towards him and kissing me again.

The hunger inside me burst and for a brief moment, I was held captive in the kiss as the energy started to flow into me. Struggling to control myself, I tried to clear my head and pull away again, but he pressed me against the car and deepened the kiss a few moments longer. Eventually, he stepped back to let me go.

"Now," he said calmly, the anger in his voice replaced by concern, "why don't you tell me what the hell is going on with you, love?"

"What's going on with me? That's rich. Where the hell do you get off scaring me like that? I thought you were going to *bite* me, William, or worse."

"Well, maybe you needed a bit of a scare. Shake you out of that bitch mood you've been in for the last few days."

"I haven't been in a bitch mood!" I snapped, causing him to raise his eyebrows at me. "And even if I have been, it doesn't give you the right to vamp out like that on me."

"You were out of line."

"*You* were out of line!"

"All right, so maybe we were both out of line," he hissed in frustration.

"Well... maybe we were," I snapped.

We stood on the side of the road with our arms crossed, refusing to meet each other's eyes.

"Well, then?" he coughed. "Are you going to tell me why I feel like I can't do a single thing right by you these days?"

I opened my mouth to say something scathing, but he held up his hand to stop me. "And I'm not just talking about tonight. Ever since the we found the informant, Colin, you've been upset with me, and I can't seem to do a thing to fix it. You've been hurling barbs at me every chance you get. Now I want to know why."

The urge to fight evaporated from me and I slumped against the car, letting my head fall back. "I've been a horrible bitch to you, haven't I?"

"You've been sweeter."

"It's like I can feel it all slipping away from me. Before I met you, any of you, I thought I was alone. It was strange, *I* was strange, but I was okay. I accepted that. And then you came along and dragged me off and my life turned to nothing but pain and death and betrayal ever since then. It's not your fault, I know it's not your fault. Lachlan and Merrick found me before you did so I would have been dragged under eventually anyway. But you're here and they aren't; and I *trusted* you. I trusted you to keep me safe, but when I was cornered by the werewolves, I knew, I just *knew* if they intended to kill me, I wouldn't make it out alive. I had no idea how to protect myself from them because you never told me they even existed. I could have died because you never bothered to give me all the facts. My friends' lives are being torn apart. And now there's this. A child, William, we're using a child as bait. And did you even see your expression in there? Blank, just... nothing. I know that we have a job to do. But I don't know if I can do *this*."

He stepped forward slowly and wrapped his arms around me, resting his chin on the top of my head and I melted into the comfort.

"We have lived for a very long time, and our world is filled with violence. This is not the first impossible decision that we've had to make and it won't be the last. We didn't make the choice easily, but we have to stay focused on the bigger picture. Right now, that's all there is. We will do this because it's all that we *can* do."

I shivered as the wind picked up and the fog of my breath swirled in the air around us.

"Please, just take me home," I whispered.

"Come home with me, love. You haven't spent the night in ages."

I nodded as I reached for the door handle, "Okay."

As soon as we entered William's apartment, he shoved me against his front door and I gasped as his hand found its way under my shirt before squeezing my breast. I roughly dug my fingers into his hair and pulled his face down, pressing his mouth on mine.

He inhaled my scent as he buried his nose in my hair, at the same time reaching around my back to unhook my bra before tearing my shirt over my head.

"God, I've missed you, he growled. He pulled my bra straps from my shoulders, deftly taking one of the nipples of my newly freed breasts between his teeth.

I groaned and pressed myself harder against him, reveling in the feel of his soft tongue flicking over the hardened nub.

Gasping, I was suddenly being lifted off the floor. I wrapped my arms around his waist as he walked us up the stairs to the second level of his condo and into his large bathroom.

Without setting me down, he reached into the large, glass-encased shower to turn on the water, and moments later, the room was filled with thick, hot steam.

We rushed to undress each other, tearing at each

other's clothing, neither one daring to waste any time until we were blissfully naked at last. He picked me up again and carried me into the shower.

The hot water felt wonderful as it pounded down on my back and shoulders. William lifted me even higher before I slid down onto him.

I gripped his shoulders for support and let my head fall back as he thrust inside me, slowly at first, and then with more speed. The energy built up inside me as he pumped harder and I screamed out and bit down on his shoulder when he pushed me over the edge. Upon my completion, I heard his own shout joining mine a moment later.

I tightened my shaking legs around him as he lowered us carefully to the shower floor. We sat wrapped together and let the hot water wash away the day.

CHAPTER 12

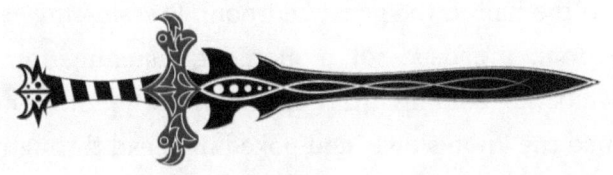

Slipping into my apartment as quietly as I could, I pulled off my boots by the front door to prevent the heavy sound of my footsteps from carrying down the hall. The soft gray light of early morning sneaked its way through the crack in my living room blinds, promising another depressing day of fog and rain.

The sleek, metal handles of my kitchen cupboard felt cool against my palm as I pulled a heavy glass from the shelf and went to the fridge in search of apple juice. I wasn't procrastinating or anything, I just wasn't ready for my early morning dose of heart-wrenching guilt. Not just yet.

Sighing, I finished off the juice and placed the glass in the dishwasher before stripping off my weapons and arranging them on the counter. I let my hand linger on the hilt of my knife, trailing my fingers over the flat side of the blade towards the point before snatching my hand back in a shaking fist. *This is my life now, and maybe the sooner I can stop bitching about it and just accept it, the sooner I can actually start keeping my friends alive.*

I turned my back on the weapons and made my way down the hall to the guest bedroom. Pressing my ear to the door, I paused for a moment, listening for any movements coming from inside. Hearing nothing, I turned the knob slowly and poked my head through the doorway, scanning my eyes around the room and over to the bed. I could barely make out the wild mass of Karen's hair as I welcomed the rhythmic greeting of her deep, steady breathing. A fist tightened around my heart for a moment before releasing it slowly, exacerbating the guilt that constantly ate away at me. I retreated from the room, softly pulling the door firmly, but quietly shut behind me.

As I opened the door to my bedroom, the soft buzz of my phone went off in my pants pocket. Fishing it out, I looked down at the caller ID. *William.*

"Hello," I whispered so as not to wake Karen before I closed my bedroom door.

"Hi. I just wanted to make sure you got home all right."

"What? You didn't think I'd be able to walk the few blocks between your place and mine without getting kidnapped or attacked?"

"Well, you never know. It's a crazy world out there these days. Can never be too safe."

"Tell me about it," I sighed.

"Then again, maybe I'm just calling because I wanted to hear your voice one last time before I went down for the day."

There was a light fluttering in my belly at his words and I couldn't help but smile. "Well, you've heard it. That should hold you over for a while."

"Hmmm, I'm not so sure about that. You snuck out without saying goodbye."

"You were asleep," I laughed.

"Just resting my eyes, pet. You could have woken me up for a goodbye kiss, at the very least."

"But you looked so peaceful, I didn't want to disturb you. Or ruin your beauty sleep."

"I like being disturbed by you." His voice was a low, soft rumble and I flushed with warmth at the sound.

"Well, maybe if you keep being nice to me, I'll disturb you some more. But right now, I'm in desperate need of a shower and some sleep so you'll just have to disturb yourself," I laughed.

He chuckled and the sound lightened my mood. Neither of us had really laughed in a while, and it was comforting to hear him feeling playful.

"Sleep well, love," he whispered.

"Sleep well, William," I whispered back.

I tossed the phone onto the bed before slumping back against the door and sliding down it until I was sitting on the floor. My en suite bathroom seemed miles away instead of just a few feet, and a shower seemed like much more trouble than it was worth. *Shower later, sleep now.*

Stripping off my clothes, I let them fall to the floor and stepped over them before pulling back the covers and sliding naked between the bed sheets. Cocooning myself in the warmth of the heavy blankets, I curled up into a tight ball and fell instantly asleep.

I stepped out of the shower, and the bathroom tiles felt cool beneath my feet amidst the thick clouds of steam in the air. Reaching for one of the thirsty, white bath sheets on the shelf, I wrapped it around my body before turning to face the large mirror and wiping clear a wide streak in order to see myself.

I cringed at the dark circles I saw beneath my eyes and my pale, drawn skin. *So much for my so-called beauty sleep.* Rolling my eyes at my reflection, I went to the bedroom and pulled on a pair of indigo jeans and a deep v-neck sweater before padding barefoot into the living room where I found Karen sitting on the couch, watching TV.

"I thought you were going to sleep all night too," she said in a quiet voice without looking away from the screen. "I checked your room sometime this afternoon, but you were out cold."

"Yeah." I shuffled awkwardly, drawing patterns on

the floor with my big toe. "I didn't get in until this morning. It was a really long night."

She nodded and nibbled on the corner of her thumb as she curled up smaller on the couch, pulling her knees tightly into her chest. "Were you... working?"

"Yes." I nodded as I cleared my throat, looking around the room at anything but her. "Yeah, I was working."

She nodded again before looking up at me, her pale hazel eyes holding me fast. "Did you... did you kill anything?" she choked out.

"No, no! Nothing like that. It was just a meeting. We needed to figure out a plan, so we... had a meeting..." I trailed off, feeling utterly uncomfortable.

Her eyes moved from mine and a small breath of relief escaped me. I suddenly had no idea what I was doing there. Should I go back to my room? Or join her on the couch? Should I just leave the apartment and let her have some space to herself? I couldn't just stand there forever, frozen like an idiot.

"Want to come sit with me and watch this?" she offered, her eyes still glued to the TV.

I nodded and moved slowly towards her. It felt strange, but I worried that any sudden movement might scare her out of this rare moment. It was the first time in days when she wasn't completely inconsolable. Was the worst actually behind her? Or did I just fall into a deadly, eye of the storm-type moment? I didn't want to risk saying or doing anything that might set her off again.

"What are you watching?" I asked as I sat down on the other side of the couch, putting as much distance between us as possible.

"I don't know." She shrugged. "One of those dating shows where a bunch of vapid bimbos try to win the heart of the hot dude with tons of money."

"Anyone pull out anyone else's weave yet?" I smiled.

"Not yet, but give it time." Karen glanced over at me and a small, fleeting smile passed over her face before she looked away again.

The tight, ever-present grip around my heart loosened and fell away as I hastily turned my head from her. I tried to subtly wipe my eyes as they began to water, while grinning with relief.

A few hours later, Karen and I were curled up together under my giant, black, faux fur throw blanket. We were watching trash TV and eating greasy pepperoni, bacon and mushroom pizza, washing it down with a case of beer. We laughed together as we booed the ridiculous, shameless antics of the latest fame-grasping reality TV family.

"Can you believe these people will never have to work another day in their lives after this show runs its course, and the world gets sick of watching them making fools of themselves?" I raised my beer and pointed at the flat screen. "Three years of letting cameras follow them around and they're set for life. Why can't *I* be set for life?"

"Because you aren't a trashy, gold-digging pseudo-celebrity. You are doomed to a life with neither fame nor fortune, Vanessa. I'm sorry, but that's the choice you made." She giggled and hiccupped before taking another swig from her beer can.

"Damn my life choices! No one told me about becoming a reality TV celebrity. It was never an option when I was in school. It was strictly doctor or lawyer."

"Or vampire slayer?"

Nervously, I glanced over at her, but she still had a smile on her face.

"No," I said slowly, "I didn't know that was an option either."

Karen put down her can and picked up my free hand with both of hers. "I don't blame you, you know," she said with a steady voice. "I did, at first. I was so scared and hurt and..." She let out a heavy sigh. "I can't even begin to explain what I was feeling, but I hurt so much and I blamed you because you were the only one I knew how to blame."

"Believe it or not, I've been feeling and doing the same thing a lot lately," I mumbled, thinking of William.

"Doing this, what you do, it isn't easy for you, is it?" She bit her lip and I looked down at our joined hands.

"No, it's not. I still don't really know what I'm doing most of the time, I just kind of go on instinct. But I'm not doing a very good job of it. People keep getting hurt or killed... or worse. And I can't seem to stop any of it from happening." I looked Karen straight in the eye. "I failed you."

A tear ran down her cheek, but she brushed it roughly away and shook her head. "No, you didn't. You tried to protect us. You didn't kill Colin, that *thing* did. And it's not fair of me to keep blaming you for it."

"Thank you. I really... really needed to hear that." I cleared my throat and she reached for me. After putting my can down on the table, we wrapped our arms around each other and squeezed as tightly as we could, trying to find our way out of the confusion and back to forgiveness and trust.

"I want to know," she said.

"What do you want to know?"

"I want to know about you. What you are, and what *they* are. You're my best friend and I want to understand. I don't want you to feel like you have to hide who you are from me anymore, okay?"

"Okay," I sighed as I squeezed her again.

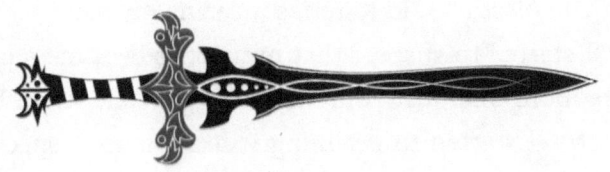

CHAPTER 13

"My mom died from cancer when I was eight years old. She was beautiful. Even when the sickness tore through her and sucked away her strength, I can remember this... this light that shone from inside her. She never seemed scared, not even at the end, and she always had a smile on her face when I went to see her. Looking back now, my dad and I practically lived in Silverlake City General Hospital for those few months. By the time she was gone, I knew all the nurses on her floor by name. They would bring me candy and coloring books to work on while she slept. After she died, my dad just... fell apart. Some days, dad wouldn't even get out of bed, he would just lie there, clutching her nightgown and staring at the ceiling. Or he would drink, a lot. He was never a bad father; he never hit me and I never went hungry. I never went to school in dirty clothes either, but he was always very sad. Once she was gone, it was as if all the beauty and laughter in our house disappeared too. And he never recovered. A few years ago, he died. Wrapped his car around a light post."

"Oh, Nessa," said Karen, squeezing my hand.

"I started to suspect that my mom's bedtime stories were more than just your standard fairy tale when I hit puberty. I started to get hungry at all hours, especially around my time of the month. But the hunger wasn't just for food, it went... deeper. It felt much more painful and started from right down inside the very core of me. It would come over me in waves, burning hot, then cold. Some days, it was all I could do to resist the urge to tear at my flesh, trying to rip it right out of me, that incessant, screaming hunger. It blinded me with need, and often drove me to tears. I would lock myself in my room so my dad couldn't hear me raging. Having to leave the house and go to class during those days was scary too. And dangerous. I was afraid to be around people. Afraid I would hurt them, afraid I would slip and give in to whatever beast was clawing at the cage inside me, desperately trying to emerge.

"I think it was that fear that allowed me to get through those days without hurting anyone. Beyond those cravings in the back of my mind was always the greater fear of what would happen to me if I did end up hurting someone. Would I go to jail? Would people think I was crazy and convince my dad to lock me away? Or maybe they would just think I was a sad girl that simply lost her mother too young. Or consider it nothing more than a sad, desperate cry for attention. So I kept such a tight rein on myself that I kind of... shut down. I tried to stomp it so far down inside me that I could pretend it wasn't there. Eventually, I just couldn't press it down any farther, and my hunger flared up on me so hard and fast one day, I almost killed a boy that I was fooling around with."

"Oh my God!" Karen gasped.

"The moment I saw him lying there, foaming at the mouth, his eyes rolled up in the back of his head and so pale that I could see the veins beneath his skin, every single story that my mother told me about our fore-mothers came rushing back to me. I knew exactly what I was then, and what I'd done.

"When the paramedics came, they found some cocaine on him and assumed he overdosed. I got tested for drugs too, but they had to release me since I had nothing in my system. You know, I never even knew he did coke before that. It ultimately would have saved him from ending up in a coma. I never would have agreed to go out on a date with him if I had known that.

"After that tragic event, I had to learn to accept what I was real fast. I'd already spent too much time in the luxury of denial and it almost cost a guy his life. I just kind of... fed on instinct after that. Sometimes, all I have to do is let the sexual energy in a crowded room flow over me to keep me level, but other times, I get properly hungry and have to take the energy from a more direct route. Either way, I learned to accept what I was a long time ago. It's just that now, I'm learning there's more to me than I originally thought. I'm much faster and stronger than I probably ever would have realized if I hadn't been drawn into this mess last summer. And no matter how horrific things get, I have to admit that I'm glad to know."

I looked at Karen and tried to decipher the unreadable expression on her face. Staring at me, she took a large swallow of her beer, paused, and then returned the can to her lips. She tilted her head backwards and finished it off in a few long gulps before taking a deep breath.

"Does what you are still scare you ever?" she finally asked.

"Sometimes it does. As my powers grow, or because of what I've had to do with them. But I've had so much scarier things to deal with lately that it's really not that bad."

"Well, it's... definitely different. But we've been best friends for a long time now, Nessa. You're a good person, and I love you. It might take me a little while before I can fully wrap my mind around all of this, but I want you to know that you don't scare me, okay? Not one bit."

Karen threw herself on me and wrapped me in another tight squeeze before letting me go and settling back beside me on the couch. "Now as to the vampires," she continued, "they scare the heck out of me. I don't know how you can work with them. Aren't you worried they may try to eat you one day?"

"One of them already tried actually." I threw my head back and laughed.

"Okay..." Karen drawled, side-eyeing me as if I had just become unhinged.

"I'm sorry; but the first time I met William, I was really hungry and he was really hungry; and to be perfectly honest, we both tried to eat each other. Of course, I didn't really see it that way at the time, so I was pretty pissed off at him for trying to take a bite out of my neck. But... he made up for it later." I looked away with a smirk.

"Uh-huh, I bet he did." She nodded, seeing right through me. "So is that how you ended up working with them then?"

"Pretty much. William found me and took me to Elizabeth and everything kind of took off from there. It's a good thing too, seeing how my stalker turned out to be a vampire as well. He was an insanely psychotic one however. God help me if he had managed to get to me before William." I shuddered at the thought and wrapped the blanket more tightly around me.

"So you're saying that these vampires you took me to the other night... They're the good vampires?"

I sat in silence for a moment, thinking it over. "I think that on a vampire scale of good and evil, yes, they are good vampires. On a human scale, however, things become a little more fuzzy and gray. But they don't go around killing people for no reason and that's a serious plus. However, I would say their moral compass is a little more flexible than the average bear."

"So you don't think they would try to find me, or hurt me, or anything, like they did with Colin?"

"No." I shook my head so hard, I almost gave myself whiplash. "There is no way! Colin messed up big time. I'm sorry, sweetie, but he really did. It's not just because of what he saw; it was because he plastered it all over the internet. Anastasia told me vampires expect to be seen every once in a while. It just happens. Hence all the folklore, right? But trying to expose them by yelling it at the top of your lungs is what gets you into trouble."

"So if I just keep my mouth shut and promise to never say anything to anyone. Ever. Eveeer…"

"Then you should be perfectly fine!"

Karen sighed with relief and fell back against the couch to look up at the ceiling. "Well, that's something, I guess. So what happens now?"

"What do you mean?"

"With me. I can't stay here forever, right? I have to get back to my life eventually. My work, my home. I can't just hide here, sleeping all day and watching terrible TV."

"You can stay as long as you want, I'm certainly not going to rush you out of here. But I probably should talk to Elizabeth to see what's what before you head home. I don't want anymore surprises."

She blanched, her eyes going wide, "Do you think there will be more surprises?"

"Nothing specific, but that's what makes it a surprise. I'd rather just make sure instead of taking anything for granted."

"Okay. Are you going over there tonight?"

"Yeah, I might as well head over there right now and get it over with?"

"Be safe?"

"I will."

I stood pacing outside Elizabeth's study. *Well, this is what I get for showing up unannounced. Relegated to the waiting room.*

A moment later, one of the heavy, wooden doors opened and a small man hurried out, his head down and his face buried in the collar of his coat. Curious about what business he may have had with Elizabeth, I stared after him as he raced towards the front door.

"Why don't you come in, Vanessa?" Elizabeth's voice floated out into the hall.

Putting the man out of my mind, I opened the door wider and stepped into the room before pulling it shut again.

"Thank you for taking the time to see me, Elizabeth, I know I should have called ahead."

"No worries, darling. Whatever it is must be very important to bring you out here so hastily."

"I want to talk to you about Karen."

"Who, dear?" she looked puzzled.

"Karen, my friend that I brought here for protection."

"Ahh, yes, of course, the other human."

"I want to know if you had any... plans for her."

"Plans? Whatever for, dear?"

"I don't know, Elizabeth, that's why I came to ask. I want to make sure that she's not in trouble... or anything."

"Should she be?" Elizabeth tapped a perfectly manicured finger against her lips and raised a flawlessly shaped eyebrow at me.

"No, she shouldn't be. But I thought I had better come out here and check," I said slowly.

"Not to worry, Vanessa, I'm sure that you have the situation with your friend firmly in hand. It's not as if she has any foolish intentions of exposing us, or does she?"

I shook my head no.

"Well, then, no one has anything to worry about; and you and your friend can rest easy. I'm sure it must be nice for you to finally have someone from your former life to confide in. Take some joy in that." She rose to her feet and walked with me to the door.

"Besides," she added as she held the study door open for me and I stepped into the hall, "if she ever *does* become a problem, I have every faith that you will handle the situation accordingly." She smiled at me with a warmth that didn't quite reach her eyes before closing the door firmly in my face. I stood there, unmoving, my mind refusing to examine too closely exactly what her final words meant. For now, however, all that mattered was: Karen was safe to go home; and I didn't have to worry about protecting my best friend from the entire Coven.

CHAPTER 14

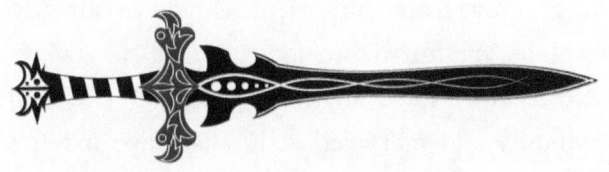

I was lying on my couch three days later with the living room windows open, enjoying the warmth of a rare sunny afternoon when my phone rang with an unassigned number.

"Hello?"

"Vanessa? It's Kane."

"Oh." I sat up and swung my legs off the couch to place my slippered feet on top of the dining room table. "What's up?"

"I have to come into the city a bit later and I was wondering if you wanted to get together with me for a drink? Maybe do some hunting?"

"I uh, I'm surprised you aren't bringing Michael, or one of the other wolves with you if you plan to go hunting." I tapped one of my feet against the table and tried hard not to wonder what he might look like in wolf form.

"Well, to be perfectly honest with you, Michael is starting to drive me a bit crazy out here. Every time I turn around, he's right there, getting ready to butt heads with me about something. I wouldn't mind an evening away from him. Unless you've already got other plans," he hurried to add.

"No, I don't have anything planned." I looked out the window and marveled at how strange it felt to be talking to a supernatural when the sun was still high in the sky.

"Nothing going on with William?" he asked a little too casually.

"Nooo," I drew out, "nothing planned with William." I tried to ignore the light fluttering of guilt I suddenly felt. *I can have a drink and go hunting with whomever the hell I choose.* "Meet me at my apartment later and we can figure it out from there?"

"Sure, where do I go?"

I gave Kane my address and hung up the phone, glancing down at it for a moment before looking out the window again. The soft clouds floated past in the pale blue sky. *I guess daytime is no longer automatically me-time anymore.*

Checking the clock on my phone once again before snatching another glimpse of my outfit for the umpteenth time, I had a feeling that Kane's idea of hunting and mine were just a tiny bit different. I decided to dress for a tumble instead of a seduction. A violent tumble, that is, and I chose tight, black stretch pants and low-heeled, calf-high boots with a tight, low-cut, forest green long-sleeved shirt. I finished braiding my hair into a single, long, plaited ponytail when I heard the knock at my door.

I opened the door and found Kane filling my door-way. His soft, wavy, brown hair curled around his ears and a lock of it fell forward over his eye when he looked down at me. He brushed it away and smiled as I opened the door wider to let him in.

"Hi," I said. The apartment suddenly seemed unfath-omably small with him in it once I closed the door. *Had he always been so tall?*

Sparing a moment to take him in while his back was turned, I could only admire the fit of his faded jeans and the broad expanse of his back and shoulders in his worn leather jacket.

"I like your place," he said, turning to face me as he slipped off his jacket.

"Thanks. Here, let me take that." I held out my hand for the jacket before hanging it in the hall closet. I was trying not to stare at his forearms when he pushed the sleeves of his brown sweater up to his elbows.

"Can I get you a beer?" I brushed past him towards the kitchen before he had a chance to answer, ducking my head and avoiding his eyes when the familiar tug of hunger pulled in my abdomen. It had been days since I last ate, and without a mirror, I had no idea if my eyes would betray me.

"I'd love one, thanks," he said from right behind me.

I jumped, not realizing that he was standing so close to me. Tripping over my own feet, I stumbled into him and he caught me by my upper arm, pulling me upright before I could fall flat on my face.

"You all right there?" he chuckled, setting me straight.

"Yeah, I'm fine, thanks. Just a bit clumsy." I smiled at him.

He looked at me, somewhat puzzled for a moment before taking a step closer to me and asking, "You sure?"

I hastily stepped backwards and tried to lean casually against the counter. "Yeah, of course, why wouldn't I be?"

"I guess you just don't seem like the clumsy sort, that's all," he said, taking another step towards me.

"Hey, well, it happens to the best of us, you know. Can't always depend on those cat-like reflexes." I laughed weakly as I took another step back.

"Why do you keep doing that?" he asked as he advanced another step.

"Doing what exactly?" I continued to back away.

"That." He pointed to my feet. "Why do you keep backing away from me like that?"

"I have no idea what you're talking about," I said, shaking my head.

"Right." He moved towards me really quickly and I jumped backwards, trying to stay out of his reach. Unfortunately, I crashed right into one of my dining room chairs, lost my footing, and ended up on the floor, but not before taking the chair clattering down with me.

I lay on the floor with my eyes closed, panting for breath as my entire body went up in mortified flames. I began praying to whatever gods were listening that this would turn out to all be just a terrible, bad dream. The succubus version of showing up at homeroom in your underwear.

I opened my eyes to find Kane staring down at me with a worried expression on his face.

"So, are you going to tell me what's going on here? Or should I just give you a minute?"

"Umm, maybe just give me a quick moment. This floor should be opening up beneath me any second now," I groaned, slapping a hand over my face to cover my eyes.

I peeked through my fingers to see him holding a hand out to me. With a deep sigh, I reached up and grasped it, allowing him to pull me onto my feet.

"You bruise anything?" He stepped closer to brush some lint from the arm of my sweater. Inhaling deeply, I held my breath, waiting for him to step back again, but after a moment, he still hadn't moved, or taken his hand away from my arm. I released my breath and risked looking up into his deep brown eyes.

"I'm not bruised," I finally answered, unable to pull my gaze away.

"Good," he said as his hand moved down my arm and wrapped around my back.

"Vanessa?" his voice was low and rough as he tugged me gently closer, his eyes never leaving mine.

"Hmm?" I felt like I was floating, awash in the low, buzzing hunger.

"I'm going to kiss you now."

"Okay," I whispered, closing my eyes as his mouth pressed against mine.

The hunger slowly rose and flowed through me as Kane's other arm came up and wrapped around me. I wound my arms around his neck and surrendered to the soft flow of energy between us. So different from the usual raging hunger, I felt as if I were being swept away on a low, warm tide. My actions felt thick and heavy, like I was moving in slow motion and I heard myself moaning, as if it were coming from someone else. He angled my head in order to make the kiss deeper.

A few moments later, we broke apart, but continued to stand there in each other's arms, waiting to fully return to our senses.

"I'm sorry," he said after a moment. "I'm not quite sure what just came over me."

"Don't apologize, it was probably my fault. I was hungry." I released him and slightly retreated, while adjusting my shirt. "Why don't I get you that beer?"

"That would be great, thanks," he paused and looked around. "So, does that kind of thing happen to you often?"

"What do you mean?" I opened the fridge and pulled out two cans of beer, handing him one.

"Getting swept up like that," he explained, popping the tab on his can. "I mean, that seemed totally different from what I saw at the meeting. Maybe it was different because I wasn't just watching this time, but..."

"No, you're right," I shifted uncomfortably. "That was... different somehow. It's not just that I wasn't in control. I feed differently when it's passion instead of fighting. But the energy was just... different somehow. I've never felt anything like it."

"Is that good or bad?" A wry expression crossed his face.

"It was good," I smiled shyly and looked away, "It was just... unexpected. That's all."

"Vanessa, I want you to know that's not why I came over here tonight. I hadn't planned that, or given it any thought beforehand. I really did just want to spend some time with you."

"Don't worry about it." I smiled and patted his chest as I took a long pull from the can. "Why don't we finish these off and see if we can work up a sweat?"

I froze, suddenly mortified at how that sounded. "Umm, you know, pummeling some bad guys and what have you..." Turning my back to him, I slapped my hand over my face before finishing off my beer in a few large swallows. "Okay," I brought the can down hard on the counter and turned around to face him again. "Why don't we get the hell out of here before I make a more complete ass of myself tonight, yeah?"

Kane brought his drink to his lips and finished it off just as quickly before setting his can down next to mine. Sweeping his arm open wide, he gestured for me to lead the way.

There weren't many people out on the streets as we worked our way through the dark alleys of the city. The previous warmth of the day had long since fled once the sun went down. The wind that whipped through the streets, tossing wrappers and discarded trash in its wake, was a firm reminder to anyone stupid enough to be outside their warm homes at this hour that it was unmistakably fall. In the summer, Silver Lake caused the temperature and humidity to rise to scorching highs, but the wind coming off the lake now made anyone that felt its bite consider themselves whining hypocrites for complaining so loudly just a few months earlier. *God help us all when the snow finally falls.*

"So you never did tell me why you wanted to hunt in the city tonight. I thought you would stick to hunting the woods around your own lands?"

"We don't normally hunt in the city. Before this

started, we never had any reason to. We co-existed in peace. But I caught the scent of whomever was snooping around our lands, and I'm hoping if I spend some time in Silverlake, I might be able to identify the vampire to whom the scent belongs."

"So, if you smell him or her again in the city, you may have a better chance of finding them?"

"Exactly. Maybe find where they are staying, or even come across them in person."

"And if we can find them this way..."

"Then we won't have to go through with the plan, that's right."

For the first time since the meeting, I had a shred of hope that we could catch the Renegades.

"That's a great idea," I told him.

Kane stopped walking and smiled at me with warmth in his eyes. "I'm glad you think so."

I smiled back and felt the familiar tug of desire as he looked at me. I took a step towards him when I heard a soft sound coming from behind us.

Spinning around, my hand flew to the hilt of the dagger on my hip, only to find William standing a few feet from us.

Kane raised his face to the sky for a moment before turning around slowly and crossing his arms over his chest. "Evening, William."

"Kane. What brings you out to the big city tonight?"

"Just thought I'd do a bit of hunting and see if Vanessa here wanted to join me."

"I don't blame you. I love it when she has my back... and I have hers." He cocked a half smile and came towards us.

"Don't you look pretty tonight, love?" He wrapped me in his arms to hug me, briefly pausing with his face in my hair. He pulled back, frowning, his nose wrinkled and a sudden tightness in his jaw. "Sorry, pet, but you seem to have gotten the smell of dog on you some-how..." I bit my tongue and stepped back as William straightened and turned slowly towards Kane. "I wonder how that happened?"

"No idea," Kane said with a blank face, staring William down.

I had no idea how ugly it could get if a werewolf and a vampire came to blows, but that was sure as hell not the time to find out.

"So, William." I pulled on his arm, distracting him from Kane. "What brings *you* out here tonight?"

William dragged his cold eyes away from Kane's to look at me. "Well, since I had no plans, I thought I would come out and look for a bite to eat."

Kane snorted and rolled his eyes.

"Is there something you want to say to me, dog?" William asked slowly.

"Oh, there are a few things, but now isn't the time."

"And why not?"

"Because I think we're about to have company."

I turned to look down the street in the direction Kane was pointing, but couldn't see anything. The three of us stood in silence, waiting, and then I started to see them. Three shadows were moving along the tops of the buildings, jumping swiftly from roof-to-roof.

"Do you think they've noticed us yet?" I asked as the shadows came closer and started to solidify.

"If they haven't sensed us yet, they will soon," William said.

"How did you know they were coming?" I asked Kane as I slid the stake out of my jacket sleeve.

"The smell. We can smell the grave on vampires from blocks away."

"That must be convenient," I said as I continued to watch the shadows coming closer.

Kane glanced at William and caught his eye before turning back to the rapidly approaching vamps. "Well, it means that a vampire will have a hell of a hard time sneaking up on me to stab me in the back."

I caught the ghost of a smile playing over William's face before it disappeared. "Here they come."

The vampires came to an abrupt stop on the building next to the one we were standing in front of and looked down at us. A woman and two men, all three dressed head-to-toe in black leather and looking as if they had just stepped out of an eighties punk music video.

In a flash, they were off the roof and standing in front of us on the sidewalk, the petite female in the middle stepping forward on her spiked heels and sneering at us.

"Look at this, boys, when's the last time you saw a vampire running around town with a mutt and a human?" She swayed up to William and put a hand on his chest. "Is this your pet and your lunch then?" She turned and flicked her light brown eyes over me. "She doesn't look like much."

Tightening my grip on the stake behind my back, I fought the desire to plant my fist in her overly made-up face.

"Well, at least, I don't look like a reject from a Billy Idol music video," I replied sweetly.

"What did you just say to me, bitch?"

"Really? Are you deaf as well as blind? I mean, you'd have to be blind to leave your house looking like..." I waved my empty hand to encompass her entire outfit, "that."

Lunging, she grabbed me by the collar of my leather coat. I watched her fangs descending as a calm settled over me. She brought her face right up to mine. "How would you like it if I sucked you dry and let my boys play with whatever's left?"

"Okay, first of all," I said as I tilted my head to look at the two vampires behind her who were laughing and exchanging high fives, "I'm pretty sure that she just called you guys necrophiliacs. And secondly," I continued looking her straight in the eyes as I allowed my hunger to crash over me. "You were only right about two things. He's a werewolf and he's a vampire. But me?" I grabbed her by the shoulders and kissed her, pulling her energy inside me. Her fangs bit down into my lip and I cried out in pain as she struggled to get away, but I didn't let go even as my mouth started to fill up with blood. "I'm a succubus, bitch!" I shoved her back and she stumbled, falling weakly to her knees before getting up again.

"What the fuck did you just do to me, you freak?" she screamed, weaving back and forth, trying to regain her balance.

The other two vampires moved forward to help her, but she jerked out of their grasp. "What the hell are you idiots waiting for? Get them!"

I snorted and stepped towards her as her thugs circled around, blocking her from me. "I bet *my* boys will kick your boys' asses," I said as Kane and William stepped up to flank me.

"Kill them..." she panted as she fell against the wall. "Kill them, but leave her for me."

"Yeah," I taunted, "good luck with that."

The two vampires charged me and I threw myself between them, diving into a somersault on the other side. A quick look over my shoulder told me they were giving the guys a decent workout. When I turned back to the female vampire, she was already up in front of me, looking much steadier than she had a moment ago. I jumped backwards, but not fast enough and her fist came up and landed solidly on my torn lip where she bit me and knocked me off balance.

"Looks like you didn't drain me as much as you thought, doesn't it?" she taunted, her face smug.

Bending over, I licked the blood from my lip and spat the blood that was pooling in my mouth onto the ground before whipping up and returning the strike, causing her to stumble backwards a few steps. "Looks like I drained enough."

I ignored the loud grunts and crashing coming from behind me as I advanced on the vampire. I swung out with the stake in my hand, but she bent backwards and caught my forearm, using my momentum against me and pulling me forward. As I tried to regain my focus, she backhanded me across the face and shoved me backwards reverse, knocking me off balance.

"Where's your smart mouth now, freak?" she sneered as her leg came up before she deftly kicked me in the side.

Blocking her next blow, I stepped closer and tried to use the opportunity to stake her again, but only hit air; she moved too fast. For some reason, even though I just fed, I couldn't seem to get a handle on my powers. I was moving too slowly even with her being freshly drained.

"Well, look at this." Her voice came from behind me and I spun around to find her reaching for my dagger. The moment her hand came into contact with it, she started to scream. She did not expect it to be plated with silver.

Taking advantage of her distraction, I plunged my

stake into her chest just as she sliced out with my knife, catching me in the side.

I cried out as the searing pain went through me. The stake and knife clattered to the ground before the vampire turned to ash. My hands flew to my side. She stabbed me inside my open jacket, and my torn shirt was warm and rapidly becoming soaked with blood.

I fell to my knees and squeezed my eyes closed as my head started to spin.

"Vanessa!" William cried out before his strong hands picked me up off the pavement.

I opened my eyes to see I was pressed against his chest.

"Meet us at her apartment," he yelled at Kane before I was forced to squeeze my eyes closed once again as the streets went by in a rush.

A couple of minutes later, I felt my bed softly giving beneath me as William gently lay me down on top of my comforter.

"Vanessa, can you hear me?" he whispered, his voice full of worry. He pulled my jacket away from my injured side.

My eyes were hot with tears and I cried out as the fabric of my shirt left the wound when he moved it up out of the way.

"I know, love, I know, I'm sorry," his voice was tight as he looked at the puncture.

My front door crashed against the wall when Kane tore into the room.

"Is she all right? What the hell happened?"

"She... she got me with... my dagger," I panted as I cried. "I got her back good though. Bitch."

"Shh, don't talk," William said. "It doesn't look too deep. No internal organs, but it's too big for me to heal with only my saliva."

I caught the look of disgust that crossed Kane's face and, despite the pain, I couldn't help but smile. "I know, it's totally gross, but it actually works," I said slowly.

"You'll have to feed from me," William said, pulling off his jacket and sliding out of his shoes.

My eyes flashed over to Kane whose expression was alternating between worry and irritation at William's suggestion.

"When was the last time you fed?" I asked William as he went to work on the buttons of his shirt.

"That doesn't matter."

"Yes, it does, I could kill you, William. I've never healed anything this way before."

"I don't care. Now shut up, love, we don't have time to argue."

"I'm not going to risk your life," I protested as I shook my head.

"What if you were to feed from both of us?" Kane asked.

I looked at him in surprise and then back at William who stopped undressing, now pausing with his hands on the buckle of his pants.

"You must be joking," William said, his eyes narrowing as he studied Kane.

"Like you said, we don't have time to argue about this." Kane grabbed the bottom of his sweater and pulled it up over his head, revealing well defined abs.

I looked back and forth between him and William, but couldn't seem to find my voice.

"Well? What are you waiting for?" Kane asked him as he undid the button of his jeans.

Snapping back into action, William undid his belt and pants and finished pulling off his shirt as he stepped towards the bed.

I tried to sit up, hissing in pain at the movement, but the familiar hunger kept growing inside me as Kane and William supported me and pulled off my jacket.

I braced myself when the bed dipped beneath their combined weight. Kane moved around to my left side and held me up from behind as William leaned forward and took my chin gently in his hand, tilting my head back slightly. He paused there for a moment, his eyes flicking over to Kane's and holding his gaze briefly before coming back to me and taking my mouth with his.

I opened my lips to him, and tried to push back the pain. The cool touch of his skin was a stark contrast to the warmth radiating off Kane, and I felt safe and secure in the familiarity of his iciness. I pulled the energy from William as slowly as possible, lest I risk losing control and taking too much.

Kane swept my hair away from my shoulder and pressed a firm kiss on my neck. One of his warm hands came up around me to cup a breast as the other took my face and pulled it away from William, replacing William's mouth with his own.

The energy flared between us and my hunger flared as Kane succumbed to his need and kissed me more forcibly. The pain in my side started to fade to a dull ache and I reached out for William, stroking his chest.

I pulled back from Kane and winced slightly, shifting myself into a kneeling position with them, both now at either side of me. I took a deep breath and allowed the craving to overtake me when I saw their fervent desire mirrored in their eyes.

"Buckle up," I said. I grabbed William's shoulders and pulled him towards me. Our mouths crashed together and I shoved my tongue against his as I dragged his energy into me in one long pull. My head spun from the rush and I shoved him away before I could take too much.

I turned to Kane and grinned, "Come here, wolf boy." I wrapped an arm around his neck and dug my nails into his upper thigh as I bit his lip and thrust my tongue inside his mouth. Both of his arms wrapped tightly around me and he hung on for the ride as my hunger raged through me and I extracted the energy from him.

I released his mouth and rode the high as the energy rolled over my skin, completely engulfing me.

The cut in my side burned with a sharp frigidity before fading away and I fell backwards onto the bed, panting.

"Are you guys okay?" I pushed myself up onto my elbows to see them both propped against the pillows at the head of my bed.

"I'm okay, just need a minute," Kane reassured me.

"We're fine, love, but how are you?" William gave my foot a squeeze and sat up a little straighter.

"Much better." I lifted the bloody, torn shirt and examined the smooth, soft skin of my side. "Damn, that's some trick."

I turned myself around and scooted up to join them on the pillows before snuggling down between the two men.

"Thank you. Thank you for risking yourselves like that to save me. I was stupid and didn't have full control of my powers; I could have gotten myself killed. I was so damn cocky."

Kane took my hand and gave it a comforting squeeze, but didn't release it. Instead, he let our hands remain linked on my lap. "We're just glad that you're all right."

"Maybe next time, pet, you could do a little less taunting, and I a little more fighting. See if you can get out of the fight in one piece," he snapped.

I looked at William in silence, studying his face. The deep lines of worry were still etched in his brow and at the corners of his eyes.

He would have given his life for me. The thought came

as a swift shock. I never took the time to fully think through William's actions before. From the very start, he was there for me. Even if he had been under orders, I counted on him and had actually grown to trust him, despite my reservations. And tonight, he would have let me drain him even if it meant healing a wound that wasn't life-threatening.

I wanted to say something to him, and try to explain just how much his offer meant to me, but I had no words.

I propped myself up and leaned over William, hovering there for a moment and staring into his bright green eyes before I kissed him gently. "I'm sorry," I whispered in his mouth, planting another kiss on his cheek before lying back down.

My heart suddenly felt heavy as I lay resting between them. William and I were friends, good friends, and while we had warm feelings for each other, we never discussed what those feelings might mean.

No matter how I felt about him, I couldn't deny my growing attraction to Kane. And did I need to? *William and I never discussed our relationship, or any desires for monogamy. For all I knew, I was reading way too much into this.* It just wasn't a conversation that I was ready to have any time soon.

CHAPTER 15

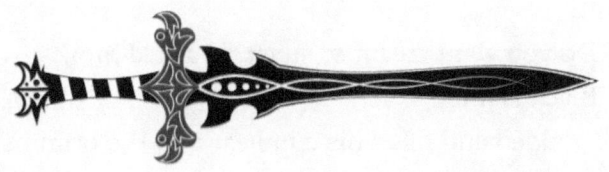

W hen I woke up the next day, I found myself alone, both men having left at some point during the night. *Without even so much as a goodbye, huh? Oh well, at least I didn't have to deal with any super awkward breakfast conversation this morning.*

I stretched and padded down the hall in search of life-giving coffee, but stopped short at the living room when I saw Kane, stripped down to his boxer shorts. He was sprawled out on my leather couch. He continued to snore softly as I tiptoed past him into the kitchen. *Maybe I'll have to prepare a side of small talk with my eggs after all.*

"If you're making coffee, I'll love you forever." Kane's sleep-filled voice came from the couch, and I almost dropped the mug that was in my hand.

"Don't *do* that! God, you're so big, you think a guy

like you would make some noise. Clear your throat, or something, before you give me a heart attack." I pulled a second mug down from the cupboard and inhaled deeply as my kitchen filled with the scent of French roast.

"Do you want cream or sugar?" I asked him.

"Black is fine."

I nodded and filled his cup nearly to the brim before taking it over to him.

"So." I curled up in the chair across from him. "How are you feeling this morning?"

"Not bad actually, just a bit tired still. Like I could sleep for a week." Kane stretched and took a deep swallow of the hot liquid.

"I'm glad it's nothing worse than that."

"I was surprised, you know. I thought you were going to have to take a whole lot more than you did."

"I'm still trying to figure things out myself." I shook my head. "Sometimes, my powers seem so sporadic. Like with the fight last night. I can't always count on them to come through the way I want or expect. If I had only fed off one of you, there was a good chance that you might have been killed or seriously hurt. Thankfully, I had already fed before the fight."

"Off me," Kane said, putting his coffee down on the table.

"Yes, off you." I looked at him and nervously brushed my hair behind my ear.

"Vanessa—" he started.

"Kane—" I interrupted him, but he held up his hand to cut me off.

"No, just listen. I know there's something going on with you and William. He's made that pretty clear. But last night, you kissed me. And maybe it was just a succubus thing, but I don't think it was. I like you, and I think you like me too."

"I do like you, but I barely know you." I stood up and tried to put some distance between us, but he grabbed my hand to stop me from leaving.

"So... get to know me then. Where's the harm in that?"

"Kane, I can't answer that. I like you, I do. But this, if we do this, things could get really messy real fast."

"Well, what's life without a little risk, right?"

"I just don't think the risk would be all that little."

"Vanessa..." He tried to pull me closer, but I yanked my hand out of his and wrapped my arms tightly around myself.

"I'm sorry, Kane, but I'm going to need a little time."

He sighed and nodded, relaxing back into the couch. I was grateful he didn't try to push the issue.

Kane's cell phone rang and I sent a quick thank you to the heavens for the timely distraction. Using the opportunity to get dressed, I was anxious to put some breathing room between us.

When I came back into the living room, Kane was off the phone and already dressed.

"Who was that?" I asked as he walked over to the front door and started pulling on his shoes.

"That was Sheena, she said the scent of vampires was detected in the area again last night. Not right on the lands, but close enough. I have to get back there and find Lena. I have to make sure she's ready for tonight. This may be the only chance we get to try our plan."

"I'm coming with you," I told him as I ran back to my room for my weapons. I strapped on my guns, knife and stakes before pausing at the bottle of colloidal silver. "Better safe than sorry," I mumbled softly as I shoved the bottle in my pocket.

"You ready?" he asked from my bedroom doorway.

"Yeah, let's go."

When we pulled up in front of Kane's house, I watched Sheena running down his front steps towards the truck. She pulled open the driver side door before we even came to a complete stop.

"Kane, you have to get inside," she demanded as she hauled him out of the truck.

"What is it? What's the matter?" Kane took the front steps two at a time and ran into his house with me close behind. I ducked as a lamp came flying at my head before crashing into the wall behind me.

"Lena is freaking out. When I told her we were

going to proceed with the plan tonight, she just snapped," Sheena explained.

"Lena," Kane called, walking slowly towards the living room and poking his head around the corner to see where she was. "Lena, do you want to talk about this?" he asked, his voice low and even.

"No! I don't want to talk about this, Kane," Lena snapped at him. "What we're doing is too risky, it's just too damn risky! I know I volunteered, but I hate you for putting me in this position. You're asking me to risk my son, Kane, *my son!* How am I supposed to explain that to Christopher? He won't understand what we're asking him to do. He's too little."

"He's a wolf, Lena, he'll be strong," he tried to reassure her.

"He's a pup, Kane, and he's my pup. What if something goes wrong? How could I have ever agreed to do this? What was I thinking?"

Kane took a deep breath and moved into the open doorway to get a good look at her. I admired his bravery even as I inched backwards to watch from a safe distance. There was no way I intended to be within striking distance of an angry werewolf mother. Call me a coward, but I preferred to keep at least some of my skin intact that week.

"Lena, you were thinking this was our best way, our *only* way, to protect the rest of the children and our Pack from whatever these vampires have planned for us."

"But he's my son, Kane, *my son*," Lena's head dropped to her chest and her shoulders shook.

Kane walked towards her slowly and put his arms around her, saying, "We can do this, Lena. We can, but it has to be tonight, or we may never get a second chance."

"It's too soon," she mumbled into his shoulder.

"I know." He squeezed her and stepped back.

"Lena, we'll make sure that everything goes okay. You know I love Christopher as if he were my own son." Sheena took her turn hugging her sister.

My heart went out to Lena as I watched her drying her eyes and collecting herself. I wanted to offer her comfort, but I didn't know how well it would be received. The wolves were suspicious of vampires at best, and right now, I couldn't be certain exactly how much distinction she would make between us.

Just then, Lena looked up and spotted me over Kane's shoulder, her entire body going still at the sight of me.

"What's she doing here?" Lena growled.

"I'm here to help," I said, walking forward to join the three of them in the other room.

"I don't want your help!" Lena snarled as she turned her back on me.

"Look, Lena, I know you don't have any reason to trust me, but you have to believe that I'm on your side. I want to get these guys, probably even more than you do. They've taken too much from me already. People that I care about, even someone that I loved. I'll do my part to keep your son safe. Christopher, right? I'll help you. I'll help you protect him, but you have to turn around and start trusting me. Otherwise, this plan is doomed to fail. We have to work together," I said as I held out my hand.

Lena turned to face me and looked down at my hand, considering my statement before she clasped my hand in hers and shook it.

"You'll do whatever it takes to keep him safe?" she asked me.

"Whatever it takes, Lena," I promised, "you have my word."

Sheena stepped forward and put a hand on her sister's arm, "Why don't we all go and see Chris? Vanessa can meet him and they can get to know one another," she suggested.

Lena nodded. "Okay, I'd like to spend some time with him before tonight."

The ride to Lena and her sister's house seemed strangely quiet. Only Kane and I rode in the truck after Lena's emotional outburst. The sisters took their vehicle, leaving us together again for the short trip over.

"Where's Christopher's father?" I asked in a desperate attempt to shatter the silence.

"What?" Kane said. He seemed slightly puzzled for a moment, having become lost in his own thoughts. "Oh, he was killed a few years ago. He was out running one night and got attacked by some rogue vampires. Having the upper hand, they killed him."

"Oh, my God, that's terrible! I'm amazed that she agreed to work with us at all. Did they ever find the vampires that killed him?" I wanted so badly to hear that his killers eventually met their own justice.

"No, we scoured the area, but by the time we found his body, they were long gone. Ian was a great friend to me, and a faithful husband to Lena. He would have made an amazing father if he had only gotten the chance. He seemed like a great dad for the short time that he was with them," Kane said sadly.

"You sound like you still really miss him." I squeezed his arm and he smiled sadly at me.

"I do. We were best friends for as long as I can remember. Completely inseparable. That is, we were until Lena came along and stole him from me." He grinned at the memory. "Lena's a great mom to the kid. She used to smile and laugh a lot more, but from what I've seen, she never lets Chris see her when she's really down."

"That's so brave. When my mom died, I never saw my dad any other way except completely depressed," I sighed.

"Your mom's dead?" he asked, surprised. "I'm sorry. I didn't know."

"That's okay, it was a long time ago, and now my dad's dead too," I shrugged.

"Wow, any brothers or sisters?"

"Nope, just me. All alone, treading this lonely succubus road." I smiled at him.

"Well, you're not alone anymore." He looked into my eyes and squeezed my hand before turning his attention back to the road.

"No, I guess I'm not."

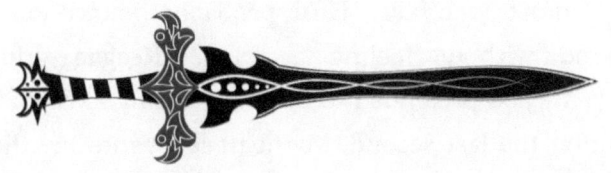

CHAPTER 16

When we got to Lena's house, a young, dark-haired boy was playing in the yard with Keegan. As I walked closer, I could see bits of leaves trapped in the ragged mop of hair, and the answer to how they got there became abundantly clear. The boy took a running jump at the larger man and tackled him to the ground with an accompanying high-pitched squeal.

I stood there grinning as I watched Keegan hauling the boy up by the waist and tossing him over his shoulders before spinning him about.

"Upside-down, Uncle Keegan!" the boy yelled, laughing as his arms flailed wildly.

Keegan grabbed the young boy by his ankles and dropped his shoulder, rolling the boy off and letting him swing freely upside-down.

STEPHANIE MARKS

"Keegan, don't you dare drop Chris on his head!" Lena called to him, trying to smother a laugh of her own as she hiked across the yard.

"Don't worry, the boy's got a hard head on his shoulders, don't you, kid? He'd probably bounce on the ground without feeling a thing." Keegan grinned wickedly and pretended to drop Chris only to catch him again at the last second. My heart leapt into my throat as I watched them play. This was a side that I never expected to see from the gruff, unkempt man.

"Well, how about not testing that theory right this moment, hmm?" Lena patted Keegan on the cheek and stepped back, giving him room to set her son on the ground the right way up.

"But, Mom," Chris pouted as he bounced up and down on the balls of his feet, his sparkling eyes wide and pleading. "I'm fine, and it's fun!"

"Well, why don't we find you something fun to do that doesn't involve crushing that cute, little head of yours? I've grown quite fond of it the way it is," she said.

Chris let out a deep, put-upon sigh and shot Keegan a look, requesting backup.

"Don't look at me, kid, you're on your own with this one. You're seven now, time to buck up and be a man," Keegan said, holding his hands up and backing away from the other two.

"If I stop, will you make me a grilled cheese?" Christopher asked his mom.

I covered my mouth with my hand, trying to hide my grin. *You had to respect the kid's negotiation technique.*

Lena pretended to take her time thinking about the offer before saying, "Deal." She ruffled Christopher's hair and turned to look at us as they walked towards the front door. "You guys want some grilled cheese sandwiches too?"

"That sounds great," Kane said.

"I would love one," I said, laughing as I headed with them into the house. I looked around for Sheena, but she was nowhere to be found.

Their ranch-style home felt cozy and warm after standing around outside. It was amazing how kids always seemed completely impervious to the freezing temperatures of fall and winter. Christopher barely seemed to mind that it was so cold outside, even though you could see his breath. Of course, perhaps as a wolf child, he was like Kane and just didn't feel the temperature changes to the extent that I did.

"Why don't you guys take your coats off and hang out for a bit while I get this started?" Lena said as she helped Chris take his coat off.

"Do you want some help?" I offered.

Lena froze and looked quickly at her son before giving me a sharp nod. "Sure, okay. The kitchen is this way."

It wasn't long before the whole house was filled with the scent of sizzling butter and rich, tomato soup. I stood at the stove, stirring the thick, red contents of the saucepan to ensure the soup didn't stick to the bottom and burn.

"Christopher is adorable," I told Lena while I kept one eye on the pot and the other on the guys in the next room.

"He's my whole world," she said with her back to me. She was looking out the kitchen window over the small vegetable garden in their backyard. "When Caleb died, my entire world was shattered. I harbored a lot of anger and hate for a long time. But Sheena, Kane and Keegan really helped me through. The whole Pack was there for me, of course, but I never would have made it to the other side without the three of them. They managed to make me see I couldn't give into my anger, or indulge my desire for vengeance. It would not only be virtual suicide, but also extremely selfish. I had Chris to think about! I didn't have the luxury of surrendering to some blind vendetta."

"Wait, I thought the vampires who killed your husband were never found."

"They weren't, but that didn't matter to me at the time." Lena turned around to face me, the dim rays of sunlight streaming through the window behind her and highlighting her in a soft glow. "I hated all vampires; it didn't matter to me if they were the ones that took my mate from me or not. I wanted to hunt down and kill any and every one that I could find. I was prepared to walk into the very heart of the Silverlake Coven, itself, if necessary."

"But that would be—"

"Suicide, exactly," she finished, nodding. "I was out of my mind with grief."

"The alliance with the Task Force must have felt like such a slap in the face to you," I said, turning back to the soup and giving it another stir.

"I was so angry with Kane when he called the Pack together to tell us about it. I demanded to be a part of the team. I wanted to see for myself who these dead bastards were that would presume they could involve themselves in Pack business. And I wanted to be in a position to keep my eye on all of you. I don't hate them now as broadly as I used to, not any longer. Time tempered the edge of that outrage, but I know I could never trust them."

"Completely understandable. I would probably have felt the same way."

Lena shook her head, and stared at me silently before whispering, "You, though, were a surprise."

"Me? Why?" I asked with sincere curiosity.

"Because before we saw you with our own eyes, none of us believed that you, or your kind, actually existed. Succubi are the stuff of legend, even for us. We were sure that Kane and Michael must have made a mistake, and that you were some sort of very clever vampire. But when we saw you, heard your heartbeat, and witnessed what you did to Keegan, we knew there was no mistake."

"Are succubi really so rare as all of that? I mean, I

always thought I was the only one, but it never crossed my mind that vampires or werewolves existed either. So for all of you to look at *me* like I'm an urban myth come to life is extremely bizarre."

"I don't know a single person that has met a succubus before. At least, no one that lived to mention the encounter." She shook her head and walked over to the stove to flip the sandwiches in the pan, the bread now a deep golden brown. *No wonder she stuck me on soup duty.*

"Elizabeth once told me that she met a few of them over the years. That was how she managed to recognize me for what I was," I told her.

Lena tensed up at the sound of Elizabeth's name and I watched her struggling to keep her face calm, even as the corners of her mouth nearly curled up into a snarl.

"I think the soup is done," I said, flipping off the heat and changing the subject. I didn't want to make Lena more uncomfortable than she already was.

"Well, then, let's get this dished up before the boys decide to start a riot," she said, the tension slowly leaving her shoulders as she opened the cupboard in search of plates and bowls.

After lunch was finished, Lena, Kane, Keegan and I were sitting in Lena's living room when Sheena walked into the house. Christopher was confined to his room to play with his toys for a bit while the adults took a few minutes to discuss the final strategy.

"Everything looks good for tonight," Sheena announced as she removed her coat and dropped into one of the worn armchairs. "The scout team and I found some good spots to watch from. All the members of the Pack that aren't directly involved in the plan tonight are ready to lock themselves inside come sundown, in order to protect the children. The last thing we need is anyone other than Chris running around out there."

Lena nodded at her sister and took a sip of whiskey to steady her nerves. "As long as all eyes are on Chris at every second, that's all I care about. We catch them and we make them talk."

Keegan wrapped an arm around Lena's shoulders, "That's right. If we get one of them to talk, we can get the children back and this unthinkable sacrifice will all be worthwhile. Our little Chris will become a hero." Keegan frowned. "Let's not tell him that though. There'll be no living with him after that."

Lena let out a shaky laugh and squeezed the hand Keegan had resting on her shoulder. "You're right. It would probably go straight to his head."

Keegan's face softened at Lena's touch, and watching them together, I wondered if Lena had any conception about the extent of Keegan's feelings for her. That was definitely a man in love.

"I sent everyone on the Task Force messages when Kane and I were on our way out of the city. They should all be here shortly after sundown. I'll send them another message asking them to be sure and let me know when they're getting closer. The last thing we need is for one of the wolves to get trigger happy at the smell of them, or attack our own team members by accident."

"I can't promise that it would be an accident," Keegan said gruffly.

"You see the crappy thing about that, Keegan, is that I know you're absolutely right. Too bad. It won't do a damn bit of good for vampire-werewolf relations, now will it?" I snapped at him, then sighed. "Sorry, I'm feeling a bit tense, myself. I just want this over and done, with as few fuck-ups as possible."

"I can totally agree with you on that," Keegan said.

I bit my tongue to hold back a biting retort. *Just breathe Vanessa, just breathe. Deep, cleansing breaths. A few more hours and this will all be over.*

"Lena, why don't Vanessa and I go back to my place for a bit so you can spend some time with Chris? It will be easier for us to surround your home if we don't all meet up here anyway," Kane suggested.

"Thank you, Kane. I really would like to spend some time alone with my son," Lena said.

"Well, then, we'll get out of your hair. Vanessa?" He looked at me.

"I'm coming." I stood up and walked over to Lena. Before she could object, I bent over, wrapped her in a tight hug and quickly released her. "We'll see you in a bit," I said, leaving quietly with Kane.

CHAPTER 17

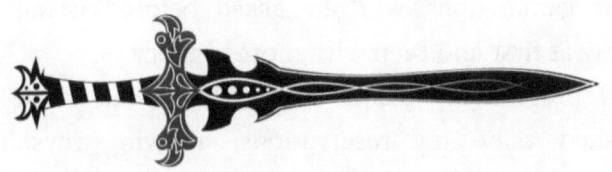

I leaned against the rail post on Kane's front step and watched the sun slowly setting behind the trees. It wouldn't be long now before the vampires showed up. With a little bit of luck, our vampires would arrive before the Renegades. But when was luck ever on our side? There was no point in trying to count on it now.

"Are you ready for this?" Kane asked from the porch swing.

"Yes, I am. When it comes right down to it, this is just another mission," I said. "I have to remember that," I added under my breath.

"Come here," he said, sliding over to make space for me on the seat next to him.

The bench was warm where he was sitting and I tried to relax and appreciate these last few minutes of peace, but the moment I got settled, Kane turned my face to his.

"Kane," I warned him.

"Hey, we want to make sure that you're at the top of your game, don't we?" he asked before kissing me, softly at first and then with more urgency.

I pressed my palms against his broad chest and pushed aside my reservations, allowing myself to simply enjoy the moment. No matter how confusing my feelings were, I couldn't deny how much I loved being held in his arms.

"That had nothing to do with the fight," I said after a few minutes, pulling back from him.

"You're right, it didn't. And since you obviously saw right through me, I might as well tell you that neither does this." He grabbed me, crushing me into his chest, and forcing me onto my back as he took me again. I arched beneath him when his hands flew all over my body.

Moaning into his mouth, I opened myself up, pulling the energy inside me and wrapping my leg around his waist, holding on as the wave of pleasure rode over me.

My hunger soon subsided, and I lay on the swing, panting, my shirt damp against my chest, the heat radiating off him and warming me completely through. For the first time in weeks, I was actually thankful for the cold snap we were enduring this fall.

Kane pushed himself up off my chest and took hold

of my face, forcing me to look him in the eyes. "I know that you aren't ready to talk about it yet. And right now sure as hell isn't the time, but make no mistake, Vanessa, we *are* going to have this conversation," he promised, his golden eyes glowing.

I swallowed and nodded, "I know."

I checked the sights on my guns one last time before placing them back in my holster vest. The sun had fully set over a half-hour ago, and the rest of the team was scheduled to arrive any minute.

The flash of headlights crossed the large living room window and I looked out to see Thatcher's truck pulling up to the house.

"The team's here," I called out to Kane as he walked down the stairs to the foyer.

A moment later, there was a firm knock on the door before William, Thatcher and Anastasia walked through without waiting for Kane to open it.

Anastasia, looking flawless as always, was dressed head-to-toe in tight leather. She smiled widely at me before rushing over and wrapping me in a tight hug. A soft, icy, floral scent floated from her as her waist-length, pure white hair swung forward in my face. All the female vampires I ever met had a flawless beauty about them, but Anastasia's beauty stood apart. Tall and willowy with sharp European features, even I, a succubus, still had moments when her looks made me fight the urge to claw her eyes out in envy. It was impossible to hate her once she opened her mouth and revealed how nice her personality was. Besides Elizabeth, Anastasia was the only person I knew who could put Thatcher in his place without simply resorting to staking him out of sheer annoyance.

"Vanessa, I think you may be spending too much time out here." she said with concern. "You're starting to smell like a dog."

"Yeah," I said evenly, trying not to look at Kane. "I've been hearing that a lot lately."

"Hmmm," she said, releasing me, her eyes flicking to Kane and then back to me again.

"So are we doing this, or what?" Thatcher barked.

"Yes," Kane told him. "We're leaving the cars here and heading over to Lena's house. She and Chris are going into the woods where she will separate herself from him; and then after that it's all about waiting."

I tried to swallow the rising bile in my throat at the thought of Chris's terror at being alone in the woods, lost without his mother, and my concern must have shown on my face for Kane to see.

"Don't worry, Vanessa, Chris won't be afraid. Those woods are his home, he's spent more time exploring those trees in his brief seven years than you probably have in your entire life. He'll try to find his mom, and if that fails, he knows how to make his way home. I know it's hard for you to see since he's so young, but he's not your average seven-year-old boy. The forest at night won't frighten him in the least."

I nodded as I wrapped my hand around the hilt of my dagger, squeezing it tightly.

"Okay then," Kane continued, satisfied, "let's head over. Vanessa, will you be able to keep up?"

I opened my mouth to answer him, but William cut me off, answering for me. "I'll carry her. Sorry, love, but we don't have time to see if you have enough control over your powers to move as fast as we can right now."

I ground my teeth in frustration at being spoken to as if I were the weak link. "Fine," I ground out. "Let's go! We're wasting time."

We spread out in the driveway and William scooped me up into his arms like he did in the alley the night before. I wrapped my arms tightly around his neck. Looking over William's shoulder, I watched Kane stripping off his shirt before undoing his pants, and I didn't fail to notice Anastasia eyeing his chest in open appreciation.

"I'll be right behind you," Kane said.

"Don't let me go," William told me, and I closed my eyes as he began to move.

The wind whistled in my ears as we moved smoothly through the dense trees. It wasn't long before William came to a stop and set me down. The woods were dark around us and I could just make out the spattering of stars through the tops of the trees. Peering into the dense night, I couldn't see or hear any of the others. William and I were already completely alone, the team having spread out at some point during the run.

"Anastasia was right, you do smell like dog again," William said, his voice devoid of all emotion.

"It seems to me that's bound to happen when you hang around werewolves all day," I said casually.

"Especially when one can't seem to stop rubbing himself all over you," William said, leaning against a tree.

"What?" I choked.

"Come on, love, did you really think I couldn't smell you all over each other? He sure as hell knows that I can. He wants me to know."

"Oh, for fuck's sake," I spat and stormed away a few feet, cursing a certain sneaky werewolf to the sky. Whether I was ready to talk about it or not, Kane was determined to make sure the situation was front and center in everyone else's mind.

"Don't be mad at him, love," William said, wrapping his arms around me. "If I were he, I would have done the same thing. In fact..."

I gasped as William spun me around and shoved me against the nearest tree, lifting me off the ground and forcing me to wrap my legs around his waist for support.

"Why don't I just remind the dog who had you first?" He grinned wickedly and nipped at my jaw.

"Damn it, William, this isn't a contest. I'm not some

prize for the two of you to fight over and try to win like a pair of goddamned hyperactive kids at a theme park," I hissed. I was struggling against my growing desire for him when one of his hands vanished up my shirt and squeezed my breast as he ground his pelvis into mine.

"But you are, love," he whispered, flicking his tongue against my bottom lip. "You're my greatest prize, and I'm not about to let you go so easily."

"Well, maybe I don't want to be your damn prize!" I snapped, hitting him in the shoulder with little effect.

"Are you sure? Maybe it's because you do that's pissing you off so much. Hmmm? Maybe that's the real problem here." His fangs flashed as a cocky smirk crossed his face and he grabbed a fistful of my hair. "Maybe you're just afraid of losing that control, succubus," he growled as he pressed me harder into the tree. He bit down on my lip before forcing my mouth open and taking what he wanted.

I resisted for a moment, feeling furious at him before I lost the battle against my need. I kissed him back just as passionately. The energy tore through me, and when I opened my eyes, the edges of my vision were tinted red. The hunger raged inside me and I took all he offered, filling myself before being pried away.

With a final, swift kiss, William set me down and smiled, satisfied with himself. "There she is, all dressed up for the party," he said, grinning.

"Hell, yeah!" I snarled, adjusting my gun holster, "Thanks for the boost."

"Anytime, love." He turned to examine the trees for any signs of Renegade movement. "Anytime."

William and I walked silently through the forest, listening intently for any strange sounds and trying to sense the presence of any vampires in the area.

Two hours dragged by and my holster was starting to feel more uncomfortable with every step. *Someone had better show up soon so I can shoot it. This is getting ridiculous!*

William reached out and grabbed my wrist, and I jumped and almost cried out. I was so intent on sensing any other presences that I forgot about him for a moment. He moved silently through the trees about twenty feet from me.

"Someone is coming," he whispered in my ear while pointing over to the right.

I nodded and adjusted the grip on my gun before indicating I wanted him to take the lead and let me cover him. We had gone less than five steps in the direction of the incoming vampire when a shrill scream pierced the night, sending a flock of birds right out of the trees.

"Who the hell was that?" I whispered loudly.

"I don't know, but we can't let this one get away!" he snarled.

"Go! Get him, I'll see who that was," I said, turning in the opposite direction.

"Be careful."

"Just go!" I yelled before tearing through the trees.

I pushed myself to move faster, clearing my mind and forcing the energy to move through me. I was pressing myself forward until the trees started to blur and I knew I was gliding between them too quickly to be seen.

Another scream tore through the night, followed by another and another. I slammed to a halt and turned in a circle, trying to judge where they were all coming from. *Oh, my God! The houses!*

I took off toward the heart of the Pack lands at full speed, desperate to get to the small cluster of homes. While Kane's house sat on a more private patch of land, and away from the others, most of the weres preferred to live close to one another, enhancing the Pack sense of community.

As I came up on the security perimeter that was set up, I saw the bodies of werewolves. They were torn apart, and their bloodied, broken carcasses littered the ground everywhere.

My eyes landed on the remains of a young female, torn almost completely in half mid transformation. I doubled over and vomited. The lower half of her body was still human, and the vampires had gotten to her just as her snout began to elongate. The oversized fangs were still protruding from a lifeless, far too human jaw. One or more vamps even risked getting close enough to tear open her throat, but failed to get away intact. The long, sharp claws of the werewolf's hand were still dripping in blood.

After I emptied the contents of my stomach, I wiped the back of my shaking hand across my mouth and took a look around to see if anyone was still moving, but they were all dead. There was nothing I could do there and I couldn't waste anymore time.

I ran the rest of the way to the houses and my eyes opened even wider at what I found there. The yards were teeming with dozens of vampires fighting were-wolves. Two of the houses were burning. *They aren't here for just one or two children. It's a fucking harvest festival!*

My mind raced as I looked around for Lena's son, but I couldn't see the little boy anywhere.

"Christopher!" I yelled as I ran through the mess. "Chris!" A loud bark came from a giant, pale gold wolf in front of me and I skidded to a stop as it lunged straight for me. Ducking down, the wolf sailed over my head and landed with a crash behind me. I turned and found it snapping its jaws down on the vampire that was coming at me from behind. The wolf brushed its giant head against my hand and looked me in the eye.

"Sheena?" I asked uncertainly, but the color of her fur looked familiar. There was no way Lena would waste time saving my ass, not with Chris missing.

The wolf let out a short bark and I knew I was right.

"We have to find Chris. I don't know where the Task

Force is; I think they're all fighting in the woods," I yelled over the noise of vampires and wolves screaming and dying.

The sound of an engine drew my attention when a large, cube truck turned the corner. A vampire hopped down from the driver side and went around to the back. He opened the door and six vampires jumped out and sped off into the houses.

"Stop them!" I screamed to Sheena as I tore off after one of the vampires. I got to the front door of the house just as he returned from inside, dragging along a struggling were-girl. He was so focused on getting her out of the house despite her grabbing hold of every passing doorframe that he didn't see me in the entryway.

Without thinking, I raised my gun and shot him in the head. As soon as he dropped the girl, I pulled out my stake and stabbed it as hard as I could into his heart.

I looked down to see the little girl shaking and crying, curled up on the floor. I couldn't leave her there alone, but I couldn't take her with me either.

A crash came from the front door and I spun around with my gun raised as a woman rushed into the house.

"Sarah!" she roared, coming at me.

"Mommy!" the little girl at my feet shrieked, and I quickly held my weapon up with both hands in the air over my head.

"I'm here to help!" I yelled, hoping that my words would make sense and defuse the woman's rage.

The little girl wrapped her arms around one of my legs just as her mother swung at me with her vicious claws, causing her to pause.

Looking down at her daughter, she saw the pile of ash on the floor behind me and scooped the little girl up into her arms.

"Thank you," the woman said, fresh tears streaming down her face.

"Hide her!" I commanded before running back out of the house.

Two children were being loaded into the truck when I got outside. Enraged, I started towards them, but a vampire stepped in front of my path.

"Oh, fuck off!" I shot the vampire in the face and kept running. I didn't have any time to waste.

A blur came out of nowhere from the side and the wind was suddenly knocked out of me when something hard drove itself into my fist, knocking me off my feet and onto my back.

I smashed the back of my head into the hard-packed ground and my vision swam. A blonde blur hovered over me; and when my sight cleared, my breath caught in my throat. I looked up into Colleen's sweet, cherubic face.

"What... the... hell... Colleen...?" I panted, trying to catch my breath. *So this is what it feels like to be clothes lined at vamp speed. It's not much fun being on the receiving end.*

It had been months since I last saw her. After I failed in my mission of keeping her safe, which resulted in her being turned by Merrick. And even though I watched her kill John, the detective on my stalker case, and for a short while, my friend, my mind couldn't connect that monster with the face of my former best friend, now staring down at me. Even though she had just violently knocked me off my feet and onto my ass.

"You have a bad habit of getting in our way, Nessa," Colleen said, pouting at me.

Sitting up as my wind returned, I dragged myself onto my feet.

"Well, that's the kind of shit you have to put up with from me now that you're a crazy vampire bitch, Coll. Looks like we're both a little disappointed at how this friendship turned out."

She giggled, her high, tinkling laughter a jarring contrast to the violence and pain surrounding us. "You always were funny, Vanessa. I miss that."

"And I miss you having a pulse and a conscience," I replied, shrugging. "But none of that will stop me from kicking your ass for trying to take these people's children."

"But, Vanessa, you know how much I love kids. They're so cute and fun to play with."

"Yeah? Well, get a puppy," I snapped.

The smile fled from her face and her cold, black eyes

bore into mine, lifeless and devoid of everything that was once familiar. "But that's exactly what I'm doing."

Furious, I lashed out at her with my stake, aiming for her heart, desperate to destroy the sickening creature that wore my friend's skin.

I could no longer stand the venom pouring from her mouth. Whatever this thing was, it walked and looked like Colleen, but my friend was dead and this thing was no more than a grotesque imposter.

Colleen dodged my blow just in time, and the stake tore a ragged line in the skin of her chest, but missed her heart.

Screaming, she attacked me, her fists flying as I dodged out of the way again and again, returning her blows with my own.

I risked a peek over her shoulder to the truck, and saw that it hadn't left yet. If she were still with Merrick, the others probably wouldn't leave her behind. I just had to keep her distracted long enough for the rest of my team to show up and get all the kids. *Where the hell is everyone?*

"Chris!" Lena's scream shattered my concentration, distracting me as I looked around for the little boy.

A vampire ran out of the woods with a thrashing Christopher over his shoulder. A large, pale gold wolf ran behind him, rapidly closing in. The vampire looked back to his detriment as the wolf crashed into him, knocking the boy out of his grasp before he could reach the safety of the truck. The wolf wasted no time closing its giant jaws around the vampire's head and crushing it beneath its massive teeth. A moment later, the vampire's body exploded into dust.

In that moment, I forgot about Colleen; my only thought was of Christopher and getting him to safety as quickly as possible.

Colleen took advantage of my distraction, grabbing my arms and driving her fangs into my shoulder.

I cried out in pain as she released me, laughing, "Oh, God, Vanessa, the look on your face. It's almost as funny as the one you had when I tore John's throat out right in front of you."

I ignored the burning pain in my shoulder as the blood flowed freely. I tightened my grip on the stake, trying to keep my emotions under control.

"Don't think that I don't have plans to make you pay for what you did to him," I said, sliding my hands into my jacket pocket and wrapping my fingers around the bottle inside. I carefully positioned my finger on the top.

She smiled, licking my blood off her lips. "You taste better than he did, you know that?"

"You know what else I am?" I asked, preparing to make a run for it.

"What's that?" she asked me, almost bored.

"Cuter than you." I whipped the bottle of colloidal silver out of my pocket and sprayed it at her face.

Colleen screamed as the liquid burned like acid and

ate away her face. The skin peeled away in patches, revealing bubbled, angry-red flesh.

I ran past her to where Chris was lying in the dirt, knocked unconscious due to falling from his captor's arms. Lena was now surrounded by vampires. They were all biting her in their attempts to get to him. She was slowly starting to lose ground as the fight was now five-to-one in the vampires' favor.

I reached out for the hunger, letting it rise up and overtake me. As I encountered the first of Lena's attackers, I tore his head back and covered his mouth with my own. The energy came out of him so fast, the power almost knocked me out. A moment later, his skin was covered in black veins and he started foaming at the mouth before turning to ash. It all happened so fast, it took the other vampires a moment to notice that one of their own was dead. By that time, however, I was already plunging my stake into the back of the second vampire as deeply as it could go while still keeping a firm grip on it.

As he crumbled to dust, the remaining three finally realized how rapidly their numbers were dropping.

The surviving werewolves chased the few straggling vampires into the trees. Hopefully, the wolves would dispatch them before they got away.

Lena swiped out with her massive paw and sent one of the last three vampires attempting to get to Chris crashing into a tree. She did it with so much force, I could hear the trunk cracking.

"Vanessa!" Colleen's yell echoed through the night.

I turned to face her just as an arrow bolted past me and lodged deeply in Lena's side. The wolf let out a piercing yell and stumbled when a second bolt struck her, sending her to the ground.

I ran to Lena's side and glimpsed the blur of a vampire passing behind her before grabbing Chris's limp body from the ground.

"No!" I moved from Lena's side to stop the vampire, but something blunt and heavy landed on the back of my head.

"I'm not going to kill you tonight, Vanessa," Colleen's sweet voice whispered in my ear as the world started to go black. "But I *am* going to take the boy. And then I'm going to make you pay for what you did to my face."

My head exploded with pain as the hard object was brought down on the back of it again. I did a faceplant into the dirt. I turned to look at the blurry vision of Colleen's retreating back as the vampire that grabbed Chris placed his limp body in her arms. Fading into darkness, I could only recall hearing the heartbreaking sound of Lena's pained howl as it echoed in my ears.

CHAPTER 18

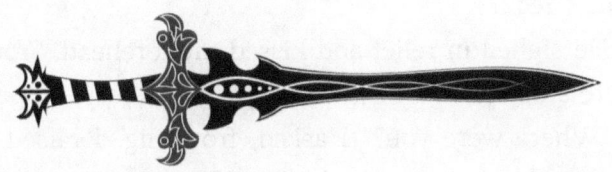

I awoke with a moan to find myself cradled tightly in a pair of strong arms. I slowly opened my eyes to see William's drawn face above me. I tried to turn my pounding head to look around, and spotted Kane just in front of us. He was carrying Lena. Her eyes were still shut and I couldn't tell if she were dead or just unconscious.

The men hurriedly carried us into Kane's house and I was surprised to find Anastasia and Thatcher already inside. Neither Sheena, Michael nor Keegan were with them. Where the hell were they while we were getting overrun?

"Put Vanessa on the couch there," Kane told William, "I'm taking Lena upstairs."

The bright lights in the living room burned my eyes, now extra-sensitive from the blow to my head, and I shut them against the painful glare.

William set me down gently and brushed the hair back from my face.

"Vanessa?" he whispered.

I blinked up at him and tried to work up a small smile, "Yeah?"

He sighed in relief and kissed my forehead. "You've got to stop scaring me like that."

"Where were you?" I asked, frowning. I raised my hand over my eyes to shield them from the lights.

"Anastasia, will you please turn the lights down?" William asked when he noticed my discomfort.

Anastasia nodded silently and moved to the switch on the wall to turn off the overhead lights, leaving only the warm glow of the floor lamp for illumination.

Her usually confident, graceful stride was hampered by a painful-looking limp, and she held her right arm across her chest.

I looked at Thatcher, slumped in an armchair without any of his usual, insulting, snappy retorts, and started to panic about the whereabouts of the wolves missing from the room.

"William, what happened to all of you?" I asked again.

"They were well prepared for us," he said, kneeling beside the couch.

"There were so many of them," Anastasia added, "and they just kept coming."

William nodded, "They kept coming out of the trees. Every time we defeated a group, and tried to head towards the houses, more Renegades came to stop us and hold us back. Because we were all spread throughout the woods, it wasn't too difficult to over-take us. It wasn't until we managed to make our way back to one another that we could regroup and reach you."

"But by then, they'd already gotten what they came for," Thatcher grunted, shifting uncomfortably in his seat.

"Christopher! They took Christopher!" I closed my eyes as the blurry memory of him being carried away by Colleen returned to me with a vengeance.

"We don't know how many others they took as well," said Anastasia. "The rest of our group are trying to find out from the Pack how many other little ones are missing."

"Why are they doing this?" I looked at each of them, trying desperately to see the answer on their faces, hoping that one of them could make sense of it where I could not. "None of the other Packs were attacked like that. They came here, planning to take them all. Why did they suddenly need so many?"

"Maybe..." Anastasia paused, thinking it through, "maybe because they are running out of time for what-ever they need them for?"

"Or maybe they knew that after they hit a few packs, it wouldn't be so easy to get to the kids anymore," Thatcher suggested. "They knew the werewolves would start to expect them, and thus, be on their guard."

"Do you think there's a chance they will be hitting other packs this hard soon? They suffered a lot of casualties tonight," I said.

"It depends on how many people they have turned, and how quickly," William said as he took my hand. "Right now, there's no way for us to know before it's already too late."

"We have to get them back, William. All of them!" I told him.

William nodded. "We'll think of something; and we'll get them back. But for now, you need to rest, as we all do."

"We can't waste time! We have to follow them! We have to know where they're going! We may never get another chance like this. Tonight can't be for nothing," I groaned.

"We won't let it be for nothing, love," William reassured me. "We can track them. There were so many of them here that we'll have no trouble hunting them down. But we can't do much more tonight. We have to feed and rest, and then tomorrow, we will hunt them right into the ground."

"She can stay here tonight," Kane said as he stepped into the doorway. I never even heard him come down the stairs.

"How's Lena?" I asked him.

"Physically, she will be all right. The arrows went deep, but I managed to remove them without too much damage. The wounds will heal fairly quickly. That's one of the benefits of being a wolf. I'm more worried about the damage that was done to her mind. She hasn't woken up once yet, and I fear she may have slipped into a comatose state caused by the loss of losing Chris. I'm going to keep a close eye on her."

"Vanessa should go home," William told him.

"Not with that blow to her head, she shouldn't. Look at all the blood in her hair! She's not going anywhere tonight," Kane told him, coming forward to point at my head.

I lifted a heavy hand and touched my hair, which I found sticky and matted. Whatever I got hit with must have split the back of my head open. My head was still spinning and I couldn't stomach the idea of having to take the long, winding trip back into the city. Not in my condition.

"I'll be okay here, William, I don't think they're going to come back tonight," I said, squeezing his hand.

"Don't you dare let anything happen to her," William told Kane.

"I won't. She'll be safe with me. She just needs some sleep after I take a closer look at that cut." Kane eyed me with a mixed expression of tenderness and worry, and I knew that I would be safe with him for the night.

William cupped my cheek and kissed me gently on the lips, lingering there for a moment before pulling away. "We'll be back as soon as possible tomorrow," he promised me.

"Please be careful tonight, all of you." I bit my lip as Anastasia limped over to me.

"You too," she said, smiling down at me. "Come on, William, we have to go." She placed a hand on his shoulder, but he hesitated for a moment before finally standing.

"Promise me that you will rest tonight," he said.

"I promise," I tried to reassure him, but I seriously doubted that my night would be very restful.

I watched the vampires walk to the door, clouded in an air of frustration and defeat. As I listened to the sound of their vehicle starting up and reversing out of the driveway, I suddenly felt very much alone. Even though I knew I could trust Kane to keep me safe, the vampires had become my family. And no matter how much pain I was in, I felt like I belonged with them after the night we just had.

"I'll be right back," said Kane. "I have to clean that wound."

He left me for a few minutes before returning with a steaming bowl of water and some hand towels.

"Can you roll over so I can examine the back of your head?" he asked.

"Okay." I shifted slowly onto my side and faced the back of the couch.

I hissed as the warm, damp cloth touched the back of my head. The contact stung and I tried not to flinch away.

"Are you all right?" he asked me, moving the cloth away.

"I'm fine." I exhaled and tried to relax my tense muscles. *Just being a big baby*.

"I'm sorry I wasn't there to help you tonight."

"You had your own problems, Kane. I didn't expect you there to protect me and do all the heavy lifting."

"Maybe not, but I should have had your back. If we had gotten there sooner, perhaps we could have stopped them."

Water sloshed in the bowl and the cloth was pressed to my head again.

"You don't know that," I told him. "There's no point in speculating about it now; it's just going to drive us crazy. All we can do is pick up their scent tomorrow, hunt them down and make them pay."

Kane ran his fingers gently through my matted hair, getting the locks wet and rinsing out the blood.

"How is it looking back there?" I asked.

"Not too bad. Head wounds tend to bleed a lot, but you should be fine."

"Am I going to need stitches?"

"I don't think so."

"Well, thank God for that, at least! I really don't fancy the thought of you shoving a needle repeatedly through my scalp."

"I don't blame you," he said, "especially since I've never stitched a wound before in my life. I've never needed to."

"Are you sure you know what you're doing back there?" I asked him nervously.

"Don't worry, Vanessa, I think I have enough skill for this at least."

We sat in silence as Kane finished cleaning the blood out of my hair and examining my scalp. His gentle ministrations were soothing and I could finally relax, and enjoy the tenderness of his kind touch.

"There, you're all done," he told me as he stood up from his spot on the floor.

"Were you hurt at all? Is there anything that I should look at for you?"

I'm fine," he said as he picked up the bowl. "My injuries started healing a short while ago, I'll be fine by tomorrow."

I rolled onto my other side so I could look up at him without craning my neck. "Are you sure? Your injuries really shouldn't go unchecked. I promise to be gentle."

I sat up slowly and reached for him, but he took a step back beyond my hand. I looked at him, puzzled, but he just shook his head at me and walked out of the room.

Well, what the hell was that?

I stood up from the couch and the room tilted beneath me. I grabbed for the arm of the couch to steady myself, and took a few deep breaths before letting go and trying to stand up straight again. Once my head started to clear, I tried out a few tentative steps towards the door to follow Kane.

Shuffling my way into the kitchen, I found him emptying the bowl of bloody water and loading it into the dishwasher.

"What are you still doing up?" he demanded when he heard me behind him. "You should be resting."

"So should you. What's going on?"

"Nothing," he replied without turning around to see me before he started wiping down the counter instead.

"Hmm, I wonder why I don't believe that?"

"I couldn't tell you," he said, throwing the dishcloth into the sink and grabbing the counter with his head bowed.

I walked over and placed a hand gently on his back only to feel him instantly tensing up beneath my touch.

"Talk to me, Kane, you can't just bottle it all up inside."

"We completely failed tonight," he whispered, his voice hoarse.

"No, we didn't. If we completely failed tonight, all of the children would have been taken, and most of your Pack would be dead. Maybe this wasn't the glowing victory that we hoped it would be, but we did some good here tonight."

"Our Alpha should be here, leading our Pack; it shouldn't be me. I shouldn't be the one making these critical decisions right now. I'm not making the right ones; and now so many of our dead are littering the ground, and I don't know what to say to my people. I should be out there right now, *doing* something. But instead, I'm in here, doing what? Cleaning the kitchen?" He snorted in disgust.

"No, Kane, you got Lena and me to safety. Are the bodies of your dead still lying out there right now?"

"No, they've been collected. I delegated some people to gather them all together so we could give them a proper burial tomorrow."

"Then there is nothing more you can do. Tomorrow, we will lay them to rest, but tonight, you have to find a way to get past this. You have to be strong for them. I don't know why your Alpha isn't here. I don't know what could be so important to keep him away from all of you at a time like this, but that is none of my business. I'm not part of your Pack, and therefore, I'm not owed an explanation. But I do know that you *are* the one in command around here right now, and no amount of wishing it weren't so can change that. It's only going to get harder from here, Kane, so you'll have to make peace with that."

"I was prepared to make the tough choices, I just didn't expect I'd have to look them in the face if I failed. I never allowed the idea of failure to enter my head."

"I saw them out there tonight, Kane, and they're strong. They can handle this."

"They shouldn't have to handle this! This shouldn't be happening! This vampire uprising, this revolution, we shouldn't have any part of it. We just want to be left in peace."

"I know, but you *are* part of it. So we need to stay

focused on what comes next. Now is not the time for throwing a pity party."

Kane spun around and scowled at me. "Is that what you think this is? A pity party?"

I held my ground and looked straight into his angry, golden eyes. "I think you're hurting right now and just exhausted and confused. I think that you don't know how you will face Lena in the morning. And yes, I think you're feeling a bit sorry for yourself at the moment. Honestly, I don't blame you for that one bit. But right now, the Pack needs you, and I need you to be strong."

He sighed and wrapped his arms around me, pulling me into a tight hug. I inhaled deeply, drawing comfort from the smell of the forest that still clung to him.

"I will be strong for them, and for you, come morning. I promise. I just need some sleep. And maybe when I wake up tomorrow, the best way for me to get through this will be a little more clear," he said into my hair.

"I know it will," I said, squeezing him tightly.

"Come to bed with me," he said quietly.

I froze and started to release my grip on him.

"I didn't mean it like that," he said, letting out a low chuckle. "It would just be nice to have you there, that's all. It will comfort me not to be alone. I promise not to lay a finger on you."

"All right," I agreed, taking his hand and letting him guide me up the stairs to his bedroom.

CHAPTER 19

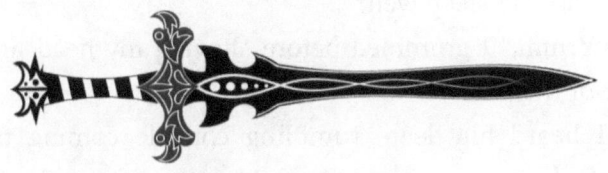

I pulled the thick quilt over my face to block out the morning sun that streamed in through the window and snuggled against the warm, human furnace snoring softly behind me. Kane's arm wrapped around me sometime during the night, and I sighed contentedly as he held me tightly next to him, his heat radiating through the large t-shirt that I borrowed to wear while I slept.

Closing my eyes, I tried to go back to sleep. I was not yet ready to face the day that awaited us. *God, it would be wonderful if I could just spend the next three weeks like this.*

The snoring stopped and Kane scooted himself more tightly against my back. A moment later, I felt the rough tickling of his morning beard growth nuzzling into my neck.

"Good morning," his muffled voice floated over the pillow.

"Mrnnnn," I mumbled back, refusing to believe it was time to get up.

"Did you sleep well?"

"Yrnnn," I grumbled before shoving my head under one of the pillows.

I heard his deep, rumbling chuckle coming from somewhere above me, followed by the soft touch of his large hand as he ran it down my spine.

"We have to get up," he said apologetically.

"Maybe you have to get up," I said, lifting a corner of the pillow in order to be heard, "but I'm not going anywhere. I've decided that I'm staying right here, now and forever."

"Well, now, while you know I don't mind the idea of you spending forever in my bed, we can't start now. There's too much to do today." The mattress shifted as he sat up before getting out of bed.

I dropped the corner of the pillow back down and crossed my arms over it, holding it tightly against my head.

Kane's hand ran down my backside, and over my thigh to my calf, where it continued down until his fingers wrapped around my ankle. Suddenly, with a heave, he pulled me down the bed.

I let out a yelp and released the pillow as I found myself half off the end of the bed with a laughing Kane standing above me.

He bent down and picked me up by the waist before tossing me over his shoulder.

"Where the heck do you think you're taking me?" I asked as he walked us into a beautiful, white marble en suite bathroom with a giant, claw-foot soaker tub.

He set me down on the bathroom counter next to the sink, stole a quick kiss and winked at me.

"Why don't you wash up first and get dressed while I start breakfast?" he suggested. Then he walked out of the bathroom, closing the door behind him.

I sat on the cool counter, unmoving, and simply stared at the bathroom door. Kane dutifully kept his word, and his hands never ventured to my side all night. But just then, I couldn't help wishing they had.

The bathroom was a beautiful combination of light pine and white marble. I filled the soaker tub and slipped into the steaming water, savoring the precious few minutes I had to myself before the day properly started.

My throbbing headache from the night before was gone, and a gentle probing of my head revealed that my scalp wound had finally stopped bleeding.

After my leisurely soak, I climbed out of the tub and went to search for my clothes from the night before. While my pants weren't too much of a mess, my shirt was not only torn, but also caked in sweat and vampire dust. Tossing it aside, I decided to borrow one of Kane's plaid, button-down, flannel shirts instead. It looked ridiculously large on me and I had to roll the sleeves in multiple folds, but it was serviceable. Besides, I had no plans to enter a fashion show anytime soon.

When I opened the door to the bedroom, the air in the landing was filled with the scents of sizzling bacon and pancakes. My stomach growled loudly and I hurried downstairs to find Kane.

"I love your bathtub," I told him in greeting as I slid onto one of his wooden kitchen chairs.

"I'm fairly partial to it, myself. It was hard to find something big enough for a guy my size to get a proper soak in."

I looked him up and down and nodded. "I don't doubt it."

"I see you also found something to wear," he said, nodding at the shirt I had on.

"Yeah, I hope you don't mind. Mine was in no shape to be worn again without a serious wash and mending first."

"No problem. Help yourself to anything you need around here."

I smiled at his generous offer. "Thank you. I really appreciate that. So what's for breakfast? It smells delicious in here."

"Bacon, eggs, pancakes and some fruit. I thought we could use a good start today."

"Sounds amazing, I'm starving," I said as he placed a heaping plate of food in front of me before joining me at the table.

"I checked in on Lena this morning," he said while

taking a bite. "Her wounds are healing nicely, but she's still asleep. Her breathing is holding steady, although I'm still worried about her."

I put my fork down and frowned at my plate. "I can't imagine what she's going through right now. I think we should let her sleep for as long as possible. She needs the rest. I want to be able to offer her something concrete when she wakes up. I only hope we have some sort of answer for her."

Kane reached across the table and squeezed my hand, "We will. After we eat, we'll go see the others; and when she wakes up, we *will* have something solid for her."

There was a knock at the door and Kane got up to answer it. I smiled when I looked up to see Keegan, Michael and Sheena walking into the kitchen.

"I'm so glad that you guys are okay," I said, getting up from the table and rushing over to embrace them all in turn. Sheena and Michael were quick to return my embrace, and after a moment, even Keegan relaxed a little and gave me a hug.

"Grab something to eat," Kane told them, "there's plenty in there."

The three newcomers filled their plates and eagerly joined us at the table. I noticed Keegan's eyes darting to the upstairs every few minutes and I smiled at him.

"She's still sleeping," I told him, "but Kane says the arrow wounds are looking much better."

He grunted and nodded before going back to shoveling the delicious food into his mouth.

Well, I can't expect to be his favorite person in the world, not after putting him on his ass the first time we met.

After that, we ate in silence, developing our plans for the day ahead as we fueled our bodies. Once the plates were scraped clean and the dishwasher loaded, we moved to the living room to get the meeting underway.

"The very first thing we need to do this morning is bury our dead," Kane told us. "They all deserve a proper burial."

"Keegan and I gathered them all last night. We stayed up digging the graves in the woods," Michael told him.

"Thank you," Kane told his brother. "How many are there?"

"Six. All six of the perimeter guards are dead. Others were injured, but the Pack held their own last night. No others died," Keegan told him.

Kane sighed with relief. "That's better news than I could hope for."

"We've always been a match for those bloodsuckers," Keegan spat out derisively.

"Yes, we have, but we haven't needed to be in a long time. I wasn't sure how we might fare under an ambush attack after being so long at peace," Kane told him.

"A wolf is a wolf," Keegan sneered. "We never forget how to defend our own."

"What is the count on missing children?"

"Four," Sheena said sadly. "They managed to get four of the children. The families are inconsolable. Pretty much everyone is out for blood."

"We'll get them back. We'll get them all back," I said.

Sheena nodded, "I know we will. I've never been more certain of anything in my whole life. I'm just worried about Lena."

"We all are," Kane said, "but we'll get her through it."

"After the funeral, I want everyone to start picking up their trail," Michael told him.

"We will as soon as it's over," Kane agreed. "Now come on, we have family to bury."

We stood in the woods with the wind blowing through our hair. The entire Pack was huddled together, leaning on each other for support as we lay their loved ones to rest. The ground was covered with six large heaps of fresh dirt. It must have taken Keegan and Michael hours to dig the graves last night, excavating through the hard-packed, frozen ground.

The tears ran freely from their bowed heads and all fists clenched with rage as the promise of retribution was vowed one-by-one. The grieving people turned from the graves and headed back to their houses. Kane,

Michael, Keegan, Sheena and I stayed until the very last mourner left.

"Their sacrifice won't be in vain," I whispered into the wind. Wrapping my hand around my dagger, I squeezed it tightly before stroking the butt of one of my freshly loaded guns. The weight of them against my side felt strangely reassuring. *I'll take Colleen's head, myself.*

Kane squeezed my free hand and turned to look off into the trees. "We need to get started." Facing us, he ordered, "Spread out and find me something. I want every square inch of these woods covered until one of us picks up a usable trail. If you smell something, send up a howl and the rest of us will join you. Vanessa, you're with me."

I averted my eyes as they all started to strip naked before shifting into wolf form. Even though I knew they wouldn't attack me, I couldn't help holding my breath when I found myself surrounded by four wolves the size of fully grown lions.

Closing my eyes, I tried to regulate my breathing, reaching down inside myself to summon my power forward. I needed to keep up. The energy rolled over my skin, raising the hair on my arms and I nodded to Kane. He bumped his large head against my hand once, and took off into the trees with me following close behind him.

We sprinted through the woods and eventually came around to meet up with the main road that ran past the Pack lands. With his nose to the ground, Kane picked up a scent and followed it away from Silverlake for a good fifteen minutes before he stopped. Sitting back on his haunches, he released a long howl.

We sat together just off the road, under the cover of the trees and waited for the others to join us. Kane curled the soft, warm bulk of his body around me to keep away the chill, and I busied myself by rubbing his pelt and scratching behind his ears. I never had a puppy when I was growing up, no matter how many times I begged my father for one. It was hard for me to remember the grown man behind what was essentially a giant dog.

I looked up suddenly as the trees rustled behind us before the wolves poked their heads out of the bushes and swiftly disappeared again. Kane and I rose, following them deeper into the trees. Sheena shook as her body started to change and shrink, returning to its human form. She was soon standing naked in front of me.

After a moment to stretch and relax, while I tried to keep my gaze focused on her eyes, she said, "They thought you might be more comfortable if I were the only one to change back for this."

"Oh, well, thanks, guys," I said as I continued to rub my hands into Kane's thick, dark brown fur.

"Kane says before we follow the trail any further, we should go back and get a truck. There's no telling how far they've taken Chris; and now that we have a solid trail, the travel will be much easier with a vehicle."

"Let's go get a truck then," I agreed, "but shouldn't one of us stay behind, you know, in case Lena wakes up?"

Sheena bit her lip, furrowing her brow as she struggled with a decision. "I'll stay behind with her. She's my sister. If she wakes up, I should be able to handle her."

"Okay then," I nodded, "let's do this!"

CHAPTER 20

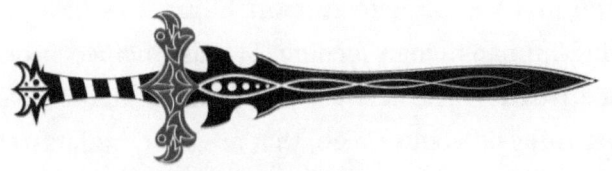

W e followed the highway two hours east of Silverlake, with Kane stopping the truck every few miles so they could get out and smell the air. We had to make sure we were still following the trail.

After three hours, we took the exit off the highway and found ourselves entering the city of Hollowind. Smaller than Silverlake City by half, Hollowind was still rather large, and home to about a million people.

"Are you guys getting anything?" I asked as I watched people hurrying up and down the sidewalks to their appointments.

"I smell vampires," Keegan growled. "I just don't know if they're the ones we're looking for."

"Well, right now, finding any vampires is a start," I told him. "Does Hollowind have a coven as well?"

"Yes," Kane said, "but a much smaller one than

Silverlake, and from what I've heard, they aren't nearly as... friendly."

"So they kill people?" I asked through gritted teeth.

"Caleb, the leader of the Holloway Coven, was one of the first vampires to support Elizabeth's idea of not killing humans when feeding. He also helped broker a peace treaty with the werewolf packs, but I've heard... other things... about Caleb, that are a bit.... distasteful."

"Are you going to tell me what those things are?" I asked him.

Kane looked over at me and opened his mouth before closing it again. "No," he said simply.

I raised my eyebrow at his choice to shut me down, but didn't probe any further. If we had to hunt Renegades in the Hollowind Coven's territory, then I was about to meet Caleb and find out for myself soon enough.

"Do you know how to find Caleb?" I asked him.

"I've heard he has a club, where he can usually be found most nights," Kane said reluctantly.

"Okay... and do you know where this club is located?" Kane's reticence to answer my questions was really starting to worry me.

He sat silently, navigating the city streets before finally answering. "I'm not positive, but I can find out."

"Well, do you have any idea where we are going now?" I asked as we rolled to a stop at a red light. I looked out the passenger side window and through the glass doors of a fast food chain selling fried chicken. *I can't believe these guys can actually smell anything over the scent of delicious, greasy chicken parts.*

My stomach grumbled loudly and they all turned to look at me.

"What?" I demanded, my face growing warm. "You guys don't get hungry? Give me a break, I saw how high you piled those plates this morning," I pouted.

There was a pause before they all erupted into loud laughter.

"Oh, shut up!" I snapped. I crossed my hands over my chest, slumping down lower in my seat; but I couldn't help smiling as well. The next thing I knew, I was laughing along with them.

"Kane, I can't smell anything anymore," Michael said. "I mean, I smell something, I just don't know where it's coming from, or who it belongs to. I think we might have lost them."

"We can't give up yet," Kane said as he turned another corner and stuck his head out the window for a long inhale.

"We can't just drive around in circles," Keegan said.

"Do you have a better plan, Keegan?" Kane snapped. "Because I would really love to hear it."

"Okay, how about we all just take a breather before anyone says something they really don't mean?" I said, holding up my hand. "First things first, let's get a hotel room."

They all stopped and stared at me again, but I just rolled my eyes.

"Oh, ha, frigging, ha. The succubus suggests getting a room. How about you guys get your minds out of the damn gutter! Look, you guys lost the trail, right? I mean, the trail disappeared. And Kane said this city has its own coven, which means: we have to play by their rules. Before we can go tearing apart Hollowind, we have to talk to this Caleb guy. The last thing we need is to make enemies of the local coven by roughing up its members tonight. Elizabeth would have my head."

"Huh," Keegan grunted.

"What? What is it now, Keegan? Please, don't hold back on my account," I said sarcastically, twisting around to look at him in the back seat.

"Not bad," he said begrudgingly.

"Oh... well, thanks." I smiled before turning back around to face forward.

"Let's get a hotel then," Kane agreed.

I fished inside my jacket pocket for my cell phone and brought up William's number.

"Who are you calling?" Kane asked me.

"Just sending a text message to William for when he wakes up. I'm pretty sure he won't be in love with the idea that not only did we start tracking the Renegades without the rest of the team, but we also ended up so far away."

Kane growled low in his throat, but I couldn't make out any words.

I sighed as I typed my message into my phone. "You don't have to love him, Kane, but he's a valuable asset and you know that. The entire Task Force is, otherwise you never would have agreed to team up with us in the first place." *God save me from temperamental werewolves.*

"He wasn't bad last night, for a leech," Michael commented graciously.

"Why, Michael, I believe such high praise coming from you is bound to make him blush," I said. "I'll be sure to let him know you said so."

"Don't you dare!" Michael shouted.

"Hmmm," I said noncommittally.

We pulled into the mostly empty parking lot of a small budget motel and hopped out of the truck.

"I'll go get the room," Kane said, "and you take a look around.

The motel was painted a deep red with off-white, yellowing doors, and had two levels. A couple of half-empty vending machines flanked the outside entry of the manager's office.

Rat-bag motels not being my usual haunts, I wasn't in any rush to find out what kind of horror show might be going on behind the door to our room.

Every late night expose on hotel rooms, written by undercover reporters with black lights, flashed through my mind all at once, and I tried to repress an instant shudder.

"It ain't the Ritz, princess, but you might as well get used to it," Keegan laughed as he patted me hard on the back.

"You know, Keegan, you and Thatcher should spend

more time together. I bet the two of you could become the *best* of friends," I said between clenched teeth.

"Don't even joke about that," Keegan said, looking horrified.

"Why not? I'm sure stranger things have happened," I laughed.

Kane came out of the manager's office and tossed Keegan the extra room key before leading us to a room located on the second floor.

I closed my eyes and held my breath as Kane unlocked the door to our room and let us inside. Once the door was open, I risked taking a peek, surprised to find the room looking so clean and tidy. Two double beds were neatly made, covered with a blotchy red, orange and yellow floral pattern. The pea green carpet felt thin beneath my boots, but other than a few questionable stains on the floor, which I refused to examine too closely, the lodging didn't seem that bad.

I went to the bathroom and flicked on the light switch. As the yellow fluorescent lights came on, the bathroom fan choked and sputtered to life as well. I made the mistake of glancing into the mirror and slammed the light off instantly. I was brashly greeted by my hollow-eyed, washed out reflection. No succubus should ever be seen like that, *not ever*.

Hurrying out of the bathroom and closing the door behind me, I sat cautiously on the edge of one of the beds.

"Are you okay?" Kane asked.

I nodded before shaking my head. "I need some fresh air."

I walked out the door and leaned over the railing outside, taking a few deep breaths.

Fluorescent lights are the spawn of the devil! Fluorescent lights are the spawn of the devil! Repeating the mantra over and over in my head, I inhaled deeply through my nose and exhaled through my mouth.

Being a succubus meant I was born beautiful. Everything about me was created to be enticing and seductive to all the people around me. Of course, I've had my share of bad hair days, but even those weren't actually *that* bad on the grand scale of things. Prior to that horrible moment, I had never seen myself look anything but beautiful, and what I just saw in that mirror scared me. Right to my very core. I never stopped to wonder what could happen if I were suddenly unable to feed. If something happened to me, and I could not entice people anymore. A hungry succubus was a dangerous thing. Elizabeth had often warned me about the dangers of going too long without feeding. The violence and madness that awaited me if I weren't careful. Hell, part of the reason I kissed Kane so willingly the first time was because I was careless and went too long without feeding. The thought of something happening to me that would make it difficult to find willing people to feed off scared me to the bones. *I will definitely be peeing in the dark while we're here.*

I heard movement behind me and knew it was Kane even before he wrapped his arm around my shoulders.

"Are you sure you're all right?" he asked me again.

"Yeah, I'm fine, just a bit shaken up, that's all. No big deal. It'll pass."

"If you're sure." He squeezed my shoulders and kissed the top of my head.

"Yeah, you know what though? I've got to run an errand. Do you mind if I borrow the truck for an hour?"

"I don't like the idea of you going anywhere by yourself. I'll come with you."

"No." I shook my head and held out my hand for the keys, "It's just something I have to do really fast. For me. I promise it's safe, and I won't be gone long."

Kane looked me in the eyes for a moment, tacitly questioning my motive before dropping the keys into my palm. "If you take too long, we'll search for you," he warned.

"I know you will, and I won't. I swear." I stood on my tiptoes and he bent down so I could give him a kiss on the cheek before I ran down the stairs.

Hopping up into the driver's seat, I put the truck into reverse and backed out before heading towards a mall that we passed on our way to the hotel.

The mall's parking lot was full as I maneuvered into one of the last available parking spots. I sat there briefly with the engine idling as I collected myself.

If I had to meet the head of the Hollowind Coven

tonight, there was no way in hell I intended to meet him looking the way I did.

CHAPTER 21

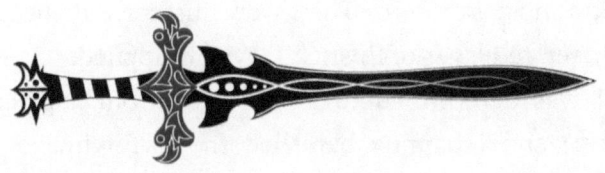

I t was fast approaching eight PM and the guys were getting restless as they waited for the last members of the team to show up. Michael argued that we were wasting valuable time, but I refused to walk into a nightclub run by vampires with nothing but werewolves for backup. Not that I didn't trust them to be on their best behavior, but it seemed prudent to make sure we brought a few actual vampires with us to a vampire club.

"What the hell is taking them so long?" Michael demanded as he paced back and forth across the worn hotel carpet.

"They'll be here soon. William texted me and said they were only a few minutes out. Will you please stop pacing? You're making me antsy," I said. I piled my hair high on the back of my head and pulled it through my hair elastic, creating a long, thick ponytail.

Flipping open the compact I bought earlier at the mall, I applied another thick coat of mascara to my eyelashes and studied my reflection in the mirror. The deep smokiness of my eyeshadow made my blue eyes look almost sapphire. They were further enhanced by the deep red layer of lipstick I lavishly applied.

I was determined to go in there from a place of power; and I happily banished the awful image that shook me up so badly to the back of my mind. *I don't know what I'm getting into tonight, but insecurity won't help me keep my powers at their highest potential.*

I placed my hand over the lace, cut-out pattern that ran down the outside seam of the legs on my new skin-tight, black pants. Then I adjusted my cleavage in the cropped, amethyst tank top.

I giggled at the memory of Kane's mouth dropping open when I walked out of the dark bathroom after getting changed. The shirt was so tight, it seemed painted on. I had to jump and down in the change room for three minutes to make sure my girlie parts would stay in their proper place during a fight. Presently, I was certain I made the right choice.

I put down the mirror and stood up, shooing Michael out of the way. He blushed and moved swiftly, tying not to look directly at me. Grabbing my last shopping bag, I upended it and shook the large box out onto the bed. I flipped back the lid to reveal a beautiful pair of knee-high, lace-up leather boots. Sliding them on, I pulled up the zippers on the backs of them and broke into a wide grin.

"I am so ready to do this," I said to no one in particular.

"Glad to hear that, love," William replied.

William was leaning casually against the door frame of the motel room with Thatcher and Anastasia behind him.

"You clean up nicely," I said with a whistle at the sight of him. He wore slim, black jeans and a pure white, turtleneck sweater.

"So do you, pet, so do you. Give us a twirl then," he said spinning his finger in a circle.

I stood up and did a slow rotation on the spot, showing off my new purchases.

He came forward and gathered me into his arms. "Just beautiful," he said before letting me go.

My eyes went wide as I looked around him to see Thatcher. "Holy crap, Thatcher! What are you wearing?" I asked, my mouth agape.

Thatcher strode into the room in a dark denim jacket, light green. silk shirt and dark wash jeans. Even his boots looked like they might have actually known the rare touch of a polishing cloth.

"What? You don't think I know how to dress up for special occasions, girlie?" he retorted gruffly with a sneer.

"I'm sorry, Thatch, but I'm going to have to revise

everything I thought I knew about who you are," I told him.

"You don't know nothing yet, girl, but give it time." He cleared his throat and grunted again.

"Enough about them," Anastasia said, her lyrical accent preceding her as she sashayed into the room to join us. "What about me, darling?"

"Holy crap..." I said, completely lost for words. When Anastasia intended to make a statement, the girl didn't mess around. Her long, white hair fell over one shoulder in a single, thick, waist-length braid. She pulled it nicely back from her face to emphasize her razor-sharp cheekbones.

Her tall, willowy body was clad in a skimpy, silk, fire engine-red dress with thin straps that crossed in the back. It exposed miles of pure white leg before ending in four-inch, spiked heels, which made her almost the same height as Kane.

"Ana, you look... unbelievable," I breathed. "But umm... how do you plan to fight in that?" I asked, dying to know her answer.

Anastasia shot a look at the men before taking me by the arm and pulling me into a corner of the room. She whispered into my ear, "Spandex shorts."

I laughed and hugged her. She really was brilliant.

"Is there a reason you all look like you're getting ready for a damn photo shoot?" Keegan asked, eyeing the vampires with undisguised disdain. The were-wolves were still wearing the clothes they wore to bury the deceased Pack members this morning. They also still looked distinctively rumpled from the nap we took earlier to conserve energy for the long night ahead.

"Didn't anyone tell the dogs this was a party?" William asked with a sneer.

"What the hell are you talking about?" Michael asked him.

"Oh, good God," Anastasia groaned, covering her eyes delicately with her hand and shaking her head slowly.

"It's called protocol, pup," Thatcher said to Michael. "You might want to look it up before you go shoving your nose into places where you shouldn't. Less likely for it to get bitten off that way."

"Hey!" Michael yelled.

"Enough!" Kane shouted at them, holding up both hands for silence.

"Will someone please explain what the hell is going on? And why does it feel like the plan has changed, even though you weren't even here today?"

"Because it has," Thatcher shrugged.

I looked at William with alarm, and he sighed, rolling his eyes at us.

"You, the whole lot of you, are ridiculous. Did you really think you could visit Caleb without Elizabeth finding out? No. She has to sanction a move that big, especially when it has the Silverlake Task Force name slapped all over it. We told Elizabeth of the plan. She, in turn, called Caleb to inform him to expect our arrival his evening. That way, we can get out of this ordeal with a greater chance of keeping our heads. I don't know a whole hell of a lot, but I have grown quite partial to mine over the centuries."

"Won't this ruin what little element of surprise we might have previously had?" I asked.

"Surprising Caleb is not the best of plans, love. He's not like Elizabeth," William said.

"What do you mean?" I asked.

"You'll find out soon enough. Just try to keep that sharp tongue of yours under control tonight, all right?" He winked at me, but didn't smile and I sensed real worry behind his words.

Now both Kane and William had warned me about Caleb. I really wished I had some idea of what to expect.

"So where are we going tonight then? Where's this club of his?" I asked as I slipped on my leather jacket.

"The Devil's Garden," William and Kane replied in unison.

The front of The Devil's Garden nightclub was a plain black wall, with the name of the club spelled out in bright red, block letters above the door. The front door was guarded by two large bouncers. Both had the smooth, flawless good looks and pale skin that would easily have given them away as vampires, even if I weren't able to sense it, myself.

"We're here to see Caleb," Thatcher told them. "He's expecting us."

One of the bouncers whispered something into the small headset in his ear before nodding to his partner.

"Go on in," the partner said, opening the door for us before turning his back and dismissing us just as quickly.

The energy in the club pulsated as a mass of bodies gyrated on the dance floor. Humans mingled unknowingly with vampires in almost every corner.

"Are they all part of the local coven?" I whispered into William's ear.

He shook his head no. "The Devil's Garden sees a lot of nomads as well," he told me, scanning the crowd and taking it all in.

I could hear Michael growling deeply in his throat, and I placed my hand gently on his arm. "Hey, it's all right. Just relax."

"I'm fine," he said pulling away. "I just don't like being outnumbered like this."

"I don't blame you, but if you don't ease up, people are going to start thinking that you *want* a fight," I told him.

We started heading deeper into the club when we were approached by a short, female vampire. Even in her spiked heels, she was a couple of inches shorter than me. She was clad in a black leather bustier and short, leather miniskirt. A row of earrings traveled down her ear, highlighted by her short, spiky haircut.

"Caleb, will see you now, if you'd like to follow me," she told us before turning and walking away without waiting for an answer. *I guess people don't reject the opportunity of seeing Caleb very often.*

We were led past semi-enclosed VIP rooms that were separated from the main club by drawn back curtains. A peek inside showed patrons guzzling alcohol of all kinds and varieties. I looked away quickly and watched a pretty blonde trying to subtly snort a line of cocaine before handing off one of her keys.

My eyes flickered to Anastasia who, also having seen the movement, rolled her eyes at me and shook her head.

The vampire led us through an unobtrusive, black door at the back of the club before going down a long, wide corridor that was lit only by dim, red wall sconces.

At the end of the hall stood a large set of double doors, which she knocked on. She waited for a beat before opening them a crack and sticking her head in.

"Your guests are here, Caleb," she announced.

"Excellent, that will be all, Seline," a soft, low voice came from inside.

Seline nodded and opened the door wider, gesturing us in before closing it again once we were all inside.

The office was done in Halloween chic. Dark red walls, draped with heavy, black velvet curtains and electric sconces that were shaped like ornate candelabras graced the walls. After the old world elegance of Elizabeth's manor, and the modern style of William's condo, it amazed me to see how any vampire would choose to decorate his office in such a painfully clichéd style.

"Ah, welcome. Please come and sit. I am Caleb, and it is a pleasure to make your acquaintance this evening."

I shuddered slightly as a thick, greasy energy rolled over me and slid down my spine. Drawing my attention away from the décor, I slowly studied our host.

I had to stop myself from taking a step backwards in retreat as my eyes met his. Even though he addressed us as a whole, his eyes remained entirely focused on me, pulling me in. I stood frozen, locked in the bottomless gaze of his hypnotic black orbs.

I wanted to run from him as far and as fast as my legs could carry me; but at the same time, I felt compelled to approach him. I even felt the urge to kneel before him and bow my head. I fought the strange impulse to swear my life to him, and offer him my body to use in any way he wished. My stomach rolled and the taste of acidic bile climbed up my throat as my instincts warred with the foreign compulsion. Just when I thought I would scream, I was suddenly freed from his gaze.

Caleb held out his hands to us and gestured toward the seats gathered around his desk in preparation for our arrival. He politely asked us to sit with a large smile and soft, warm, brown eyes.

My heart was pounding in my chest and I was breathing way too quickly. I tried to regulate my breathing and plastered a smile on my face, but every person in that room was equipped with supernatural hearing. I'm sure they could hear everything that was going on inside me right then.

I walked forward with all the confidence I could muster and chose a chair between William and Kane, drawing comfort from having both of them at my sides.

None of the others seemed to take any notice of what happened just moments before. Caleb somehow shielded the entire thing from all of them. That meant I had to be extremely careful. I may have just met the first vampire that actually possessed the strength and power to glamour me.

"Now, why don't you tell me what has brought this unusual union of vampire and werewolf to my door? And please know," he added, addressing the Pack members, "that all kinds are welcome in The Devil's Garden. We do not allow any discrimination here."

"Thank you for your hospitality," Kane began, "Unfortunately, however, we are not here for the entertainment. A serious crime has been committed by the vampires against the Silverlake Pack and we have tracked them into this territory. We come to you now and ask your permission to hunt these Renegades inside your city."

"Renegades? Ah, yes, Elizabeth's minor disciplinary

problem from the summer. And you believe they're here?" he asked.

"At least, a few of them are here; although we don't know how many. We tracked them here earlier today after they attacked us last night," Kane explained.

Caleb sat up in his high-backed, ornate chair and steepled his fingers beneath his chin. "The pact between our two kinds is still new and too tenuous to allow this sort of trouble to go unchecked. I have nothing to gain by barring you from hunting those few vampires in my territory. But if I find or hear that you are causing trouble for the Coven, I will command you to cease all action immediately."

Kane nodded. "That's more than generous, and we thank you for your help and permission."

"Of course, of course," Caleb said with a grin. "We all just want to get on with our lives, or after-lives, as the case may be. Blood feuds are bad for business."

"We just want to get back that which was taken from us," Kane told him.

"Well, then, I wish you luck in retrieving your stolen property. Hopefully, you will find it undamaged." Caleb stood up and showed us to the door.

"Now, if you'll excuse me, these contracts won't read themselves. Just one of the many annoyances of running a legitimate business in this millennium. There always seems to be an abundance of paperwork for me to do."

"Thank you fer takin' the time to see us," Thatcher said, dipping his head quickly.

I almost tripped over the carpet at his words of respect to the older vampire.

As I walked past Caleb to get to the door, I tried to put as much distance between us as possible, but he reached out at the last moment and grabbed my hand.

"Ah, yes," Caleb said as his thumb caressed the palm of my hand. "You must be the succubus I have heard so much about. Rumors of your presence in Silverlake have even traveled all the way out here."

Breaking into a cold sweat, I tried not to snatch my hand away from him. I was supposed to be on best behavior after all, and any trace of my revulsion toward our host wouldn't earn us any favors.

"I'm surprised people don't have better things to gossip about," I laughed weakly. "Whatever happened to the classics, like the weather, or sports?"

"Ha!" he laughed freely, throwing his head back. "And quite the wit to go with such beauty. It's a shame that you ended up in the Silverlake Coven instead of mine. Elizabeth is quite fortunate to have encountered one so rare as you."

Caleb's eyes flashed black before returning to their normal light brown, and I quickly removed my hand from his icy grasp.

"Well, thank you," I said, forcing my voice to stay level. "I'll be sure to tell her that you think so."

I felt that same oily energy rolling over me again as

he smiled at me and inclined his head. "It was a plea-sure to meet you tonight, succubus. I'm sure we will be seeing each other again very soon. I hope you all have a wonderful time here and satisfy your collective curios-ity. And please, for those of you that still drink alcohol, the drinks are on the house."

I hastily left his office with the others and had to resist the incessant urge to race down the entire length of the hall, and straight back to the main club.

Bursting through the door, I was greeted by the thumping bass of house music. Inhaling deeply, I bent over and placed my hands on my knees, trying to extri-cate myself from the residual tendrils of Caleb's energy that still curled around me.

When I stood up again, the entire group was looking at me with varying expressions of worry and confusion on their faces.

"What the hell happened in there?" William demanded.

"Nothing," I panted, shaking my head before I made my way towards the exit. Caleb could take his free drinks and shove 'em where the sun don't shine.

"It sure doesn't look like nothing," Kane said, grab-bing my arm and pulling me to a halt.

I scanned the bar and shook my head before quickly bringing my finger to my lips and starting towards the door again.

No one spoke until we were standing in the parking lot next to Thatcher and Kane's trucks.

"What happened in there, love? I thought your heart was going to explode," William said.

"That's probably because it almost did. We have a problem. I don't know what kind of treaty Caleb and Elizabeth signed when starting these covens, excluding the provision not to kill the humans they use for food; but let me tell you something, Caleb is evil. Right to the core. And it gets worse," I took a deep breath and pinched the bridge of my nose before dropping my hand. "I think he may also have the power to glamour me."

CHAPTER 22

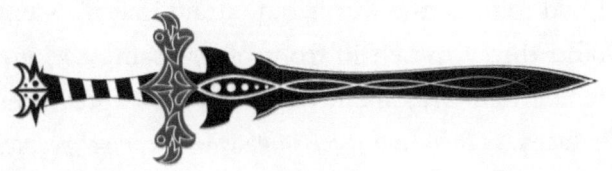

I never had so many blank faces staring back at me at once before, which made me increasingly more uncomfortable. I instantly understood just how quiet a place had to be in order to hear a pin drop. When a group of supernatural creatures didn't so much as blink an eye, the ensuing silence became almost overwhelming.

"Are you sure about that?" William asked slowly. His eyes narrowed as he glanced over his shoulder towards the club.

"Am I sure if he actually can? No, I don't know if it would work. But I'm sure that he tried. I could feel his energy rolling over me, and something tugging at me from deep inside, urging me to do things I would never consider," I said, shivering.

"Urging you to do what kinds of things?" Kane demanded.

"I can't explain it, I sorta wanted to..." I looked away in shame, "give myself to him, I guess? Not quite sexual, but just, become his. Let him own me, or possess me."

I had to force the words out, afraid that if I stopped, I would throw myself in front of a passing car, just to avoid the embarrassment of seeing the expressions on their faces. *Is this what it feels like when I compel people? Do they feel as sick inside as I do now? No one ever seemed to mind my small glamours, but how could I ever really know? The whole point of a glamour is to influence a person's will. I don't even know if the people I glamour ever remember what they've done.*

"Don't worry, Vanessa," Anastasia said as she wrapped a long, slender arm around my shoulders. "Caleb may be powerful, but he will never get his hands on you. Elizabeth would not take kindly to him even trying. You may not be a vampire, but you are a part of this Coven, and that makes you family now."

I smiled at her in gratitude, but couldn't bring myself to reply. The truth of the matter was: she couldn't promise me anything. And while Caleb may not have been able to take me by force, there was a good chance he could *make* me simply choose to go to him.

"I'm not surprised," Thatcher grunted. A coven leader with a reputation like his? Owning a place like this?" He nodded towards the large, black building.

"Having a succubus would be like winning the damn lottery!"

"I don't understand? Do you mean because I can glamour people into spending more money? Like a hostess bar? Don't the vampires that already work there just do that anyway?" I asked them.

Thatcher suddenly became engrossed in the chipped paint on the side panel of his truck, and seemed unable to look me in the eye.

"Kane? You were mentioning something about him earlier, what did you mean?" I asked.

Kane shuffled uncomfortably and cleared his throat. Their evasiveness was verging on ridiculous.

"It's a brothel, love," William said, looking distinctly bored.

"Say what?" I looked at him, then toward The Devil's Garden, then back to William again. "But, how? It's a nightclub."

"Right," he drawled, "and beneath the club is a brothel. Everyone that works there is a paranormal."

"Well, you seem to know quite a bit about it. Come here often, do you?" I raised my eyebrow at him and he offered me a half smile.

"No, pet, I don't. But our community isn't so large that news about something like that wouldn't get around quickly. Even the dog here knows, isn't that right?" he asked Kane.

Kane glared at him, but nodded, refusing to rise to the bait. I was starting to think William antagonized him not so much out of actual dislike, but simply as a way to relieve his boredom. What an annoying way to get his jollies off.

"Anyway, if he's running a brothel in there, that would explain why he wants a succubus in his harem. It would almost be too perfect, wouldn't it? What a creep!" I spun on my heels and walked to the door of Kane's truck. "The important thing is that he gave us the go-ahead to hunt in his territory, so let's go beat the shit out of some people and get Chris back."

A phone rang and I looked around the group, wondering which one of them just destroyed a great exit line. Kane pulled his phone out of his pocket and read the display.

"It's Sheena," he told us. "How is she?" he asked Sheena.

I strained my ears, trying to hear what Sheena was saying, but I couldn't make out her low voice on the line.

Kane nodded a few times and hung up the phone. "We have to go back," he said as he hurriedly jumped into his truck.

"What do you mean, go back?" Michael yelled at him. "We're here, and we haven't done anything yet. We can't just go back. Who the hell knows what's happening to Christopher!"

"I know, Michael, but Lena woke up and she lost it. Losing Chris was too much. She's not in her right mind and raging out of control; I have to get back there and make her submit before she gets herself killed, or something worse. Now get in the goddamn van!"

I hopped in the Task Force van next to Kane in an instant. I never heard him yell like that before and it seemed so out of character. I wanted to save Chris, but running around in the middle of the night with no real leads, while his mother was in dire need of us, wasn't the best use of our time or energy.

"Did you want us to stay behind and keep searching?" William asked him in a rare show of solidarity.

Clenching his teeth, Kane shook his head. "No," he said, "I hate to say it, but I may need your help. Lena is strong, much stronger than she looks. And if she goes rabid, I'll need all the help I can get just keeping her under control."

"Can we please hurry up and get the fuck out of here now?" Keegan shouted at us, banging his hands on the back of Kane's seat.

Kane threw the van into reverse and sped out of the parking lot, the tires squealing on the pavement as he hit the main street and headed for the highway. I held on as tightly as could to keep myself from being thrown around as he took a sharp turn. Kane was determined to get us back to Silverlake as soon as possible, and I only hoped he could also get us back in one piece. We would be no good to Lena if we all ended up dead in a ditch somewhere. Whatever Lena was going through was serious enough to terrify her Pack mates, and I prayed we reached her in time.

We made it back to the Pack lands in record time, with Kane breaking every speed limit along the way. He slammed the van into park at the top of the driveway and we all jumped out and ran up the steps of his house before bursting through the front door.

I looked up at the sound of crashing and a long, gut-wrenching cry of frustration.

"Lena!" Keegan yelled, shoving past me and running up the stairs.

Kane and Michael tore after him and I followed behind, taking the stairs two at a time and sprinting down the hall.

"Oh, my God," I gasped as I reached the doorway to the guest bedroom.

Lena stood in the middle of the bedroom, trying to break free from the grip of the other wolves. Sheena and Michael each had her by an arm while Keegan stood behind her with one arm around her waist and the other across her throat, struggling to keep her contained.

"Get off me!" she roared, kicking out towards Kane anytime he got too close, although he continued to inch towards her. "Get the fuck off me! My son! I have to get my son!"

Her eyes had changed to those of a wolf and glowed like bright embers, filled with so much pain and fury, it tore me apart inside.

William wrapped a hand around my arm and I jumped. In my hurry to get upstairs I forgot all about them.

"Don't get too close," he said, pulling me back a step. "If she gets loose and attacks you, I don't know what a werewolf bite might do to a succubus, love; and I don't want tonight to be the night we find out."

I swallowed and nodded, taking another step back. I wasn't in any hurry to find out either.

"Lena, Lena! I need you to calm down," Kane said in an even voice as he deflected another of her kicks. Stepping in to grab her face with his two hands, he forced her to look into his eyes.

"They took him!" she screamed. Tears poured down her face as her fingers started to elongate and her nails turned into sharp claws.

"Lena, stop!" Sheena begged her sister. "You have to stop. You can't do this, you might not come back from it this time."

Sheena started to cry as well, holding onto her sister even tighter. She dug her nails into Lena's arm and refused to let go.

Lena pulled her head from Kane's grip and turned towards her sister, her jaw starting to elongate into a snout. She snapped her jaws viciously at Sheena's face.

Sheena squeezed her eyes shut and leaned back to avoid her sister's sharp teeth. With a heave, Lena threw Sheena off her and hard against the wall. She landed with a crash and slid to the ground, falling forward on her hands and knees.

William moved past me in a blur and grabbed onto her, taking Sheena's place before Lena had a chance to free herself from the other three.

"Hold her! Get her onto her knees!" Kane yelled, stepping back and tearing off his clothing. I watched wide-eyed as he shifted from a man to a giant wolf while the three men pulled Lena to the floor and wrestled her down to her hands and knees.

Even while she was being taken down, the muscles in Lena's back began to roll, and her clothes started to split before she grew larger, shifting into a wolf.

Before she could complete her transformation, however, Kane leapt forward and closed his jaw around the back of Lena's enlarged neck. Placing a large paw on her back, he shoved her lower, right onto the floor. I watched, horrified as Lena's body halted mid-transformation and she let out a pained howl from her half-formed wolf jaws before going limp.

The room was dead silent as she lay on the floor. Then slowly, her body began to shrink; and a few moments later, Lena had returned to her fully human form.

Kane backed away from her gradually, followed by Michael and William releasing her as well. Keegan lifted Lena gently into his arms and placed her back in the bed before covering her with the blankets.

I wrapped my arms around myself and fell back

against the wall. Exhausted, I suddenly felt like I had just run a marathon, and I didn't even participate in the rescue.

William came out of the room and put a hand on my shoulder, giving it a light squeeze.

"Are you all right?" I asked.

"I'm fine." He looked over his shoulder at Kane who had changed back and was finishing getting dressed. "He handled that well, it could have gone a lot worse. If Lena had fully changed and gone rabid, we would have had to kill her."

"What?" I hissed in shock, looking past him to the bed. Lena lay silent, her face even more pale against the dark green pillowcase. All signs of the violent outburst were now gone. How could they even suggest killing her?

"Once a wolf goes rabid, there's no coming back from it, Vanessa," William told me in a hushed voice. "We got here just in time."

I clenched my jaw and nodded sharply. Kane and I needed to have a long talk later about what exactly "going rabid" meant and how it happened, but now definitely wasn't the time.

Michael helped Sheena up. He supported her weight with his arm around her waist as she limped out of the bedroom. She hit the wall hard, which resulted in a large hole, more evidence of her sister's excessive strength when fueled by fury.

Keegan stood by the bed with his arms crossed over

his chest. He watched Lena while she slept, and his drawn face was almost as pale as hers, emphasizing the dark circles under his eyes.

"Did you want me to bring you anything?" Kane asked him.

Keegan shook his head, but didn't say a word as he continued to watch the sleeping form of the woman he loved. Kane patted him solidly on the back and left him to his vigil, joining the rest of us in the hall and closing the door behind him.

"That was... intense." I glanced at Kane from the corner of my eye and then looked down at the floor. There was definitely a reason he was left in charge of the Pack in their Alpha's absence. What he just did upstairs was no less than impressive.

"We were lucky," Kane said, falling back in his chair, utterly exhausted.

Back down in the living room, each one of us was still reeling over what almost happened upstairs. We could have lost Lena. And although I hadn't known her very long, I would have grieved for her if William were right and Kane had been forced to kill her.

"We need to go back to Hollowind tonight," I told them. "We're running out of time. I know we had to come back here tonight, but we have to stay focused on our mission. We have Caleb's blessing to hunt in his territory, so that's what we're going to do. We'll tear that city apart if that's what it takes to find Chris and any of the other kids."

"Speaking of Caleb, love, I don't want you going anywhere near him again," William said with a deep frown on his face.

"Trust me, I don't want to ever speak to that creep again either, if I don't have to," I told him.

"I love your enthusiasm, girl," Thatcher said roughly, "but I'm not actually hearing much of a plan in all that bold talk."

"You want a plan?" I asked him quietly, standing up and crossing the room to where he was leaning in the doorway. I stood so close to him that the toes of our boots were touching and I brought my face within a few inches of his.

"Fine. Tomorrow night, we're going back to Hollowind and we'll be packing heat. A shit ton of heat. Then we're going to find some vampires and I'll shoot them full of silver until they tell me what I want to know. How's that for a plan?"

I turned my back on him to face the others. "I don't care who we have to kill, torture, or maim to get this done. You guys thought I was soft for not endorsing this plan in the first place, right? Well, fine, the time for being soft and any reasons for my hesitation are gone."

"Vanessa, no one thought you were soft," said Anastasia.

"Yes, Ana, you did. I know you did. And you know what? Maybe I was. But it doesn't matter anymore. Now we need to face the consequences of our actions.

I'll need to get a lift back into the city with you guys. There are a few things that I'm going to need."

Kane looked at me with sadness in his eyes, but I shook my head ever so slightly. I couldn't stay there with him again.

Eyeing the vampires, I cocked my head toward the door.

"Let's go."

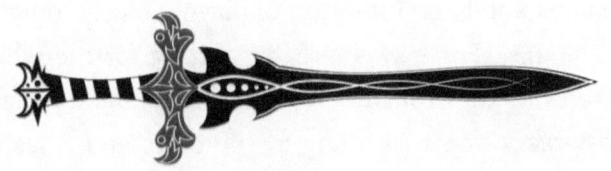

CHAPTER 23

Standing in the kitchen, I was staring at all the weapons lying on my kitchen counter. After the Task Force dropped me off at home that morning, I stripped down all my guns and cleaned them thoroughly before shooting a few rounds of dry fires to make sure they were operating in pristine condition.

I dressed and prepped in complete silence this time, in contrast to the usual ear-bursting music that I preferred to listen to in preparation for a hunt. With every movement, I remained focused completely on the night ahead.

I slid my arms through my double chest holster and clipped myself in before loading it up with my guns and extra magazines. I strapped my dagger to my hip and my fingers twitched when they touched it, eager to use it on the first idiot that got in my way. Bending down, I slid a short, throwing knife into my boot, then strapped a stake to each forearm. Finally, I wrapped a three-foot-long silver chain around my wrist a few times before clipping it so that it looked like a cuff around my wrist. I had absolutely no intention of playing nicely tonight.

The Task Force was already waiting for me when I walked out the front doors of my building. The large, glossy-black van was idling at the curb, and Anastasia slid open the back door for me to climb in.

"You ready to do this?" Thatcher asked me as he pulled into the street, merging into traffic at top speed.

"You know it," I told him.

I caught William's eye in the rearview mirror and gave him a silent nod. I was so ready to do this.

As we sped past the Pack lands, Kane, Michael and Keegan were waiting for us on the side of the road. We barely slowed down long enough to give them time to jump into the van before speeding off again down the highway. We were in such a hurry to get to Lena the night before, we left the truck behind in Hollowind. It had probably already been towed away.

Keegan sat in the back, staring at nothing with a grim expression on his face.

"How is she?" I asked him.

Keegan turned to me and blinked slowly a few times, as if unsure that I actually spoke to him.

"She's a mess," he said hoarsely, turning his face away from me, and obviously not wanting to speak anymore about it.

"We'll make this right, Keegan," Michael said to him. "Don't worry, we'll make this right."

"I don't care about making it right," Keegan whispered. "I just want to make them pay."

We rode the rest of the way to Hollowind in silence, each one of us lost in our own thoughts.

"Where should we start?" Michael asked as we exited the highway to enter Hollowind.

"The same place we'd start if we were looking for vampires back home," William told him.

"Hunting grounds," Thatcher answered.

"Well, if we're going clubbing, you guys will need to do some serious glamouring. I'm sure I'll set off every metal detector within twenty feet," I told them.

"With what we have planned for tonight, we'd be more worried if you didn't, love," said William.

We sped towards downtown, searching for anything that looked like a large bar or dance club.

"Up there," said Anastasia, pointing out her window. I looked over to see a huge crowd of people standing in line outside of a place called "Passion."

"Passion, huh? That sounds like a good place to start."

Thatcher parked on the side of the street a block away from the club and we doubled back on foot, then ignored the line and walked straight up to the bouncer.

I watched, fascinated, as Anastasia put a hand on the large bouncer's chest and leaned into him with a small smile on her lips and an intense look in her eye. A moment later, she dropped her hand and simply walked past without speaking another word.

It was the first time I had ever seen her use her glamour on anyone, and I was impressed. Maybe it was just because she was so gorgeous, but watching her, you could almost mistake her as part succubus, her glamour was so sensual.

We all walked past the bouncer and I breathed a sigh of relief when there were no metal detectors on the other side of the door.

"You know the game plan," Thatcher said to all of us, scanning the interior of the large, one-level club.

"Find a vamp, then beat 'em bloody 'til we get what we want?" I asked.

"Shit, yes," he said with a nod as he stalked off.

"Let's go then," said Michael, shoving past me and disappearing into the crowd.

Kane turned to me and gave my hand a squeeze. "Watch your back," I told him.

"You too," he said. He looked over my shoulder to William and gave him a sharp nod before walking off.

"I'm going to find someone fun to play with," laughed Ana with a wicked glint in her eye as she sashayed off.

Keegan said nothing, but simply slipped away from the rest of us.

"Don't die," I told William as I started to walk away, but he grabbed my hand and pulled me back.

I tilted my face up to meet his as he lowered his head for a kiss. Ignoring the flare of hunger that surged within me, I simply took a moment to savor the taste of him, then I pulled away.

"Like I said, don't get killed," I repeated before being swallowed up by the crowd.

The rhythm pounded from the speakers and I tried to ignore the rock music and swelling energy of the crowd that threatened to consume my senses. I concentrated exclusively on trying to pick out any vampires in the crowd.

Standing in the middle of the dance floor, I went completely still, except for my chest, which rose and fell in time to my deep breaths. They were here somewhere, and there had to be at least one. I just had to find them.

But I sensed nothing.

God damn it! What was wrong with me? This was not the time for my powers to take a nap, or go on holiday, or whatever the hell they were doing. What was keeping me from sensing any vampires? I couldn't even sense my own team.

Someone bumped into me and I spun around with a few choice words to complain about such rude clumsiness, but they died on my lips when I saw the offending klutz.

"I'm so sorry," she said, flashing me a megawatt smile, her eyes glazed.

"No problem," I replied, stepping closer.

The pert brunette was wearing a silver minidress that dipped low in the front, and barely grazed the top of her thighs as she tottered drunkenly on sky-high heels.

"Want to make it up to me?" I asked, wrapping my hand around her waist and pulling her closer.

"Umm..." she said uncertainly.

"Of course, you do."

I captured her mouth with mine and kissed her deeply, letting the hunger emerge from me. Pressing her body tighter, I ripped the energy from her until I felt her starting to go limp in my arms. Then I pulled back.

She blinked up with a blank expression on her face for a moment before her eyes rolled up in her head and she passed out.

I held her as I panted heavily and struggled to get myself back under control. Grabbing the arm of the man dancing next to me, I pulled him around to face me, then shoved the passed out girl into his arms.

"What the hell?" He looked at the unconscious girl with utter confusion.

"Help her, she's only—" I stopped abruptly, sensing something near.

That's more like it. All I needed was a little boost.

I slid off the dance floor, moving slowly between the dancers and hunted for the vampire. Scanning the faces of the patrons, it didn't take long before I saw a flash of black eyes in the face of a tall, slim, blonde man. If I hadn't been looking for it, I would have missed the change completely. His eyes were soon back to normal with no sign they had ever changed.

I slid up beside him and pressed the side of my body along his.

"Hi, there," I said to him, flashing a seductive smile.

"Hi, yourself," he replied, grinning.

"This place is totally dead tonight, isn't it?"

He looked out toward the packed dance club and then back at me as I touched his hand lightly.

"Yeah," he agreed, "there's nothing going on here tonight."

"What do you say we go find a better party?" I asked, trailing my finger up his wrist and never taking my eyes from him.

I didn't have to glamour him to get him out of there, I just needed to act like an eager, willing woman.

"I've got a place not too far from here..." he trailed off and raised his eyebrows at me, being a little more direct.

"Sounds like fun. Let's go."

I proceeded with him through the building and out the door. I looked for the rest of my team and caught Michael near the entrance. He was standing off to the side, watching the vampire. He blinked slowly before walking out the door.

"It's this way," said the vampire. He put a hand on the small of my back and led me down the street. "Let's go through here," he said jerking his thumb in the direction of an alley. "It's a bit faster."

"I don't know," I said hesitantly, hanging back and feigning fear.

"Hey, don't worry. It's perfectly safe, I promise."

I let him tug me into the alley, listening behind me for footsteps. I didn't know if Michael had continued to follow us out of the club, or was hunting for some of the others first.

"You sure it's safe down here?" I asked timidly.

"Oh, yeah. No one's going to bother us, I swear."

"Good," I said, my voice low and cool. I was smiling as he turned to me with a curious expression on his face. "Because I have a couple questions and this would go a lot faster and easier for both of us if you could just tell me what I want to know instead of making me beat the answers out of you."

He tore his hand away from mine and stepped into my space.

"Who the hell are you?" he snapped.

"Like I said, I'm just a girl that needs to ask you a few questions. Think you can provide some answers for me, stud?"

"I think I'd rather eat and run," he snarled, leaning in to bite me.

I slapped a hand on his chest and stared him in the eye.

"If you even think about coming anywhere near me with those fangs, I promise you will not like the turn this conversation will take. So why don't you just put your fangs away and tell me what I want to know?"

The vampire stood there sneering down at me for a moment before letting out a sigh and stepping back.

"So what do you want to know?" he asked.

"We're looking for some vampires. You may have seen them around, or heard about them. They like to kill their feeds, and they're turning new vampires at a crazy rate. Oh yeah, and they're also kidnapping were-children."

The vampire's expression stayed blank throughout the entire description, but I noticed a slight tic at the corner of his eye at the mention of the kidnapped weres.

"Sorry, can't help you."

I tilted my head and looked him dead in the eye.

"Okay, see? Now I know you're lying. Why would you want to lie to me like that?"

With a sigh, I whipped out my gun and shot him in the kneecap.

"You crazy bitch," he snarled, as he lunged at me.

I jammed the muzzle of my gun beneath his jaw, pointing up into his head and he froze.

"Now, I'm sure that the burning in your leg tells you that these rounds are fortified and come with an extra surprise. So unless you want hot silver searing through your brain, I suggest you calm the shit down." I emphasized my point by pressing the gun deeper into his jaw.

"I should tear you apart," he spat.

"Yeah, well, get in line. Now, what do you know about the kids?"

"Not much."

"Well, why don't you just tell me what you *do know* and I can take it from there?"

"Look, I don't know anything solid; just that were-kids have been disappearing. You hear whispers, you know?"

"Any place in particular that you're hearing these whispers?" I asked.

"You hear all kinds of shit when you hang out at The Devil's Garden. You get people from all over. They like to talk."

"One last question. You ever hear of a vampire named Merrick?"

He thought for a moment, then nodded his head. "The name sounds familiar. I think I heard someone at the Garden mention it before, she may have worked there."

"Can you remember why she would have mentioned his name? Or what she was talking about?"

"How the hell should I know? That was weeks ago. You expect me to remember something that far back?"

"Try. Harder," I said through gritted teeth, moving closer to him.

"I don't know. It sounded like the guy was supposed to be there or something. Maybe he was running late. That's all I know."

Damn it! I really wasn't looking forward to returning to that place. I didn't want to get within a hundred feet of Caleb if I didn't have to, but it looked like I was out of options.

"Thanks for the help," I told him. "Now run along, and don't even think about trying anything.

"If this is how you pry information from the vampires at The Devil's Garden, you're going to be dead soon enough anyway!" Laughing, he abruptly turned and disappeared into the shadows.

"You get what we need?" came William's voice from behind me.

I turned around and holstered my weapon.

"Yeah, I've got a lead, but you're not going to like it."

"Come on, the others are waiting for us back at the van," he told me.

"Back at the van? What if my lead doesn't pan out?" We headed out of the alley and down the street.

A puzzled expression crossed his face and he looked down at me.

"It's happening here too. None of us could sense any vampires in there. Maybe you really did find the only one, but not even the wolves could sense him. Whatever is blocking the Renegades from being sensed in Silverlake is out here as well," he said.

"Shit. If that guy was blocked, then..."

"Then he probably knew more than he let on."

"I knew I should have just shot him."

"He didn't give you any reason to."

"No." I looked over my shoulder and back down the street. "I don't suppose he did."

CHAPTER 24

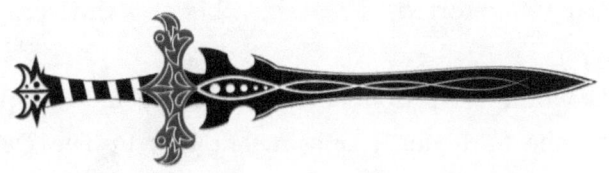

"I don't like this plan," said Kane as we pulled up to The Devil's Garden for the second night in a row.

"Plan? What plan?" asked Michael. "There's no plan, there's just us walking in there and hoping to find... what? Some server or bartender that may or may not have mentioned this guy, Merrick's name, weeks ago?"

"Yeah," I said, "that's pretty much the plan."

"I don't like it," Kane repeated, shaking his head.

"You don't have to, but it's the only plan we've got." I raised my eyebrows at him. "Unless you can come up with something better?"

He glared at me in silence.

"I didn't think so," I said.

I unclipped my holster and slid out of it. There was no way I could pass through the doors of a vampire-owned nightclub with all my weapons on me.

"It will be all right, Kane," said Anastasia. "We will

simply go in and listen. Maybe ask a few questions. There will be no," her gaze slid over to me for a moment and then back to him, "jamming guns into anyone's face while we are there."

"Hey," I retorted, "I was in a bit of a time crunch, okay?"

"I would have done the same thing in your position," she told me. "I only meant that in The Devil's Garden, more finesse will be required from all of us if we wish to avoid angering Caleb."

"If we're lucky, he won't even know we're there," I said hopefully.

Thatcher let out a rough bark of a laugh. "Now, girl, I know you ain't that stupid!"

"Excuse me for trying to think positive," I snapped at him.

He laughed again and shook his head. "Girl, you've strolled right on past positive thinking and straight into dreamland! Might as well ask for a pink pony while you're at it. The moment we start asking questions, he'll know. Hell, the moment you step one foot across the threshold, you can bet your ass he'll know. He wants something from you, girl. There ain't no way he won't have all eyes on the lookout for you, just in case you come back."

I shuddered and stared out the window at the passing lights. Thatcher was right. There was no way we'd be able to get in and out without Caleb knowing we were there. We just had to hope our poking around wouldn't piss him off too badly.

But Merrick's name was mentioned in his club, *by his staff.* If Caleb was somehow mixed up in all of this, then we were in way over our heads. It was one thing to try to take down Merrick and his cronies, but something else altogether if we had to go through a coven leader to do it.

"You know what, Thatcher? You've got a point," I told him. "Kane, I need you to come with me. Everyone else, wait here. This shouldn't take very long."

"What's going on?" William asked.

"I've got a new plan." I opened the door and hopped out, Kane following close behind.

"You gonna let us in on the plan, or should we just sit here and paint our toenails while we wait for you to come back?" Thatcher snorted.

"Caleb will know it the moment I walk in there, right? So why play games? He wants something from me and we need something from him, so I'm going to ask him for a favor," I shrugged.

"I think I should be the one to go with you," said William, "you should have a vampire in there."

"No," I shook my head, "this is about the werewolf children so I need Kane to come with me for this one."

"You'll be safer with me," William said, stepping toward me.

"You don't think I can take care of her?" Kane growled, stepping in front of William.

"Get out of my way, dog," William said quietly.

"Don't talk to my brother like that," said Michael, his fist clenched in anger as he went over to stand beside his brother.

"We don't have time for this shit!" Keegan yelled at them.

"To hell with this," I sighed, throwing up my hands and walking away, leaving them to argue among themselves.

I was halfway to the club doors before Kane caught up with me.

"Vanessa?"

"I don't want to hear it," I snapped. I kept walking, refusing to slow down.

"I'm sorry."

"Do I look like I care? I am so sick of you two and your macho bullshit. Let's just get this done."

We walked up to the bouncer and he opened the door the moment he saw me.

"Looks like Thatcher was right," I said, walking inside.

Kane and I headed straight for the door at the back of the club that led to Caleb's office. We were almost there when a sweet-faced girl with soft, Asian features and a flowing cloud of silken, black hair stepped into our path.

"He's waiting for you," she told us. She led us the rest of the way to Caleb's office.

Knocking once before opening the door, she ushered us inside.

Caleb stood in front of his desk with his hands clasped behind his back. My stomach roiled in protest when his eyes landed on me. I had to fight the urge to flee.

"Thank you, Lily, that will be all."

The Asian girl nodded and backed out of the room, closing the door behind her.

"Vanessa, Kane, it's nice to see you again so soon. Please sit. To what do I owe this honor?"

"I've come to ask you a favor," I told him as I took a seat.

"A favor? How interesting. And what may I possibly do for you?"

"You seem like the type of man that knows everything there is to know about what's going on in his city. And if you don't know it yet, you can find out, and quickly."

Caleb narrowed his eyes at me and lifted the corner of his mouth in a slick, half smile.

"You seem to have formed quite the opinion of me."

"Well," I leaned back casually in my chair, slowly crossing one leg over the other, "no man, and especially no vampire, can achieve all that you have without completely controlling everything that's going on around him. And that's why I need your help finding a vampire that may have been seen inside your city."

"And does this vampire have a name?"

Kane opened his mouth to answer, but I held up my hand to stop him.

"Merrick," I told Caleb, watching his face closely.

"And this Merrick, is he part of your Renegade problem?"

"Yes, he is. And we are willing to tear this city apart to get to him if that's what it will take. But of course, we would very much prefer to avoid making that kind of mess, especially in your backyard. I would be very grateful for your help in finding him. It would be a huge favor, and I would be forever in your debt."

"Now, that is a tempting offer. I can think of all kinds of ways I could make use of a succubus that owed me a favor." Caleb leaned back against his desk and crossed his arms over his chest. "Unfortunately, I've never heard of this Merrick."

"No?" I lifted my finger to my lips and gave him a puzzled look. "That's too bad, because I was sure that if anyone could find him, it would be you. And I could have sworn I heard one of your bartenders say his name last night, but she disappeared before I could ask her about it."

"I'll be sure to look into it for you," Caleb said, his eyes narrowing slightly

"Thank you, I would appreciate that."

I stood up and walked to the door. When he opened it, Lily was still on the other side.

"Lily will walk you out," he told me.

"That's all right, we can find our own way."

"No, please," said Lily, "it is no trouble. If you would follow me?"

"I look forward to seeing you again soon, Ms. Kensley. I hope that I can provide something of use for you."

As soon as the door shut, Lily's hand shot out and took hold of my wrist, squeezing it tightly. Her finger flew to her lips, and she gestured for us to be silent before she let me go and walked quickly ahead of us.

I looked at Kane in confusion, but he just shook his head. He had no idea what it was about either.

As we walked past the dance floor, she stopped suddenly, causing me to stumble into her.

"1350 Canal Road," she whispered quickly while I was pressed up against her. Then she began walking again as if nothing happened. It took only a few moments.

I waited until we got outside and were far enough away from the bouncers that I didn't think we could be overheard.

"I don't know what the hell that was in there, but tip or trap, we have to check out that address."

"What address?" Kane asked.

"1350 Canal Road. That girl, Lily, said it to me when I bumped into her. That's all she said, just 1350 Canal Road."

"And you think it's a trap?"

"It could be. Why would she help us?"

He shook his head, "I don't know."

When we got back to the others, everyone was

sitting silently inside the van, not speaking to one another.

"I don't know if this is better or worse than the fighting," I told them as I climbed in. "For a bunch of supernatural badasses, you guys could give toddlers a run for their money at the Sulking Olympics, you know that?"

"What did you find out?" Keegan asked.

"Not much, just an address," I told him.

"1350 Canal Drive," said Kane.

"What is that?" asked Anastasia.

"I don't know," I told her, "but we're going to find out. Thatcher?"

"Already got it on the GPS," Thatcher told me. "Let's go."

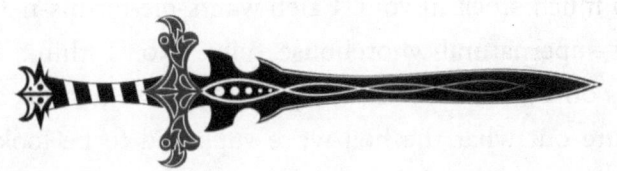

CHAPTER 25

U sing GPS, we drove deep into an industrial part of town and slowly passed the shadows of a large mill that dwarfed the van. I looked up at the huge, dormant smokestacks and wondered what kind of business Merrick could possibly be running out there.

"What kind of mill is this, do you think? Anastasia asked.

"I have absolutely no idea," I told her as Thatcher put the car into park.

"Lots of places you could hide for an ambush though," Keegan said as he turned around, trying to get a better look at the area.

"If we were being set up for a trap, why not just kill me when I was right there in his office?" I asked him. "Why go through all of this trouble just to get me out here?"

"He may not want *you* dead, love, but I'd be willing

to bet he doesn't feel the same way about the rest of us," William said. "Finish us off and it's a whole lot easier for him to get to you."

"You know what? I think you guys are putting way too much stock in your 'Caleb-wants-me-for-his-nefari-ous-supernatural-whorehouse' plot. No, I think Lily was on the level about this place. Now we just need to figure out what the hell we're supposed to be looking for."

I jumped out of the van, feeling much more prepared now that all my weapons were back in their proper places. After the things I'd seen over the past few months, I didn't think I would ever be able to walk down the street at night without at least one sharp, pointy object strapped somewhere on my body. Looking back on it now, it amazes me to have spent so many years walking around the city blissfully unaware, when the whole time I was being viewed as a walking, talking happy meal.

"All right, if we're going to do this, let's be smart about it," barked Thatcher. "Keegan, you're with me. William, go with Michael. Ana, Kane and Vanessa, you guys are together. Let's cover as much ground as possible. Meet back here in thirty minutes whether you find something or not. Got it?"

We all nodded.

"Good. Now move your asses!"

We split up, each group branching off in different directions. We inched our way around the building, scanning the windows for movement and pulling on the handles of every door we came across, but all of them were locked up tightly. The mill was silent, with no other sounds than those of our own footsteps.

"Does anyone else have the feeling this is one long, wild goose chase?" grumbled Kane.

"I think I have to agree with you," sighed Anastasia. "There is nothing here, Vanessa; and we have to be getting back soon. Our time is almost up."

I shook my head and pressed on. "No, there has to be something here," I told them stubbornly.

"Vanessa, there's nothing here," repeated Kane.

I spun on him in anger, jabbing my finger into his chest. "Look, if you want to give up, you can, but I'm not leaving until I've searched every inch of this place. Lily gave me this address for a reason. I'm not going anywhere until I find out why. Now are you coming with me, or not?"

He grabbed my hand and lowered it gently, then tugged me closer so there were only a few inches between us.

"All right," he said quietly, "let's keep going."

A soft cough made us look over to catch Anastasia rolling her eyes at us.

"If you two are going to kiss, will you please be quicker about it? We still have work to do."

Embarrassed, I stepped back and pulled my hand from Kane's. "No, we're not. Let's go."

It wasn't long before my tenacity paid off and we

found an unlocked side door. The un-oiled hinges squeaked loudly in protest when we opened the door and I cringed at the sound.

"Let's just hope if anyone's here, they're too far away to have heard that, yeah?"

"I'm pretty sure that screech was audible in every corner of this place," groaned Kane.

"That's the spirit," I said sarcastically, patting him on the back. "Way to think positive."

We followed a long, empty corridor with metal pipes that ran along the ceiling until we reached a wall. Our only option was to go left or right.

"Which way?" asked Anastasia.

"How do you guys feel about splitting up?" I asked.

"Never gonna happen," said Kane.

"Didn't think so," I sighed. "Well, I suppose Rock, Paper, Scissors is also out."

"I think we should go left," said Anastasia, starting down the hall without us.

I looked at Kane and raised one eyebrow. "I guess that settles it then."

We caught up with Anastasia and continued down the hall together, keeping our eyes alert to any activity ahead. The door we came through was the only open one we found inside the entire mill. I highly doubted it was unlocked by accident, which meant that whoever left it open was probably still around.

The last thing I wanted was someone sneaking up on us, but the deeper we went into the building, the more the others seemed right. This was starting to look like a set-up. One that would place us far away from any means of escape.

"Do you hear that?" asked Anastasia.

At the same time, Kane asked, "What's that?"

"I don't hear anything," I told them, straining to listen.

"There are people up ahead," said Ana. "Vampires."

"How many?" I asked. Sometimes it really sucked being the only one without supernatural hearing.

"I'm not sure," she told us. "There could be four, maybe five?"

"Do you think they know we're here?" asked Kane.

"I'm not sure, but I doubt it."

I pulled out my stake and crept forward with the others beside me. Once we got close enough, I spotted a side door that was slightly propped open and I could finally hear the voices inside.

"If you aren't more careful with those boxes, I'm going to tell Caleb to hire himself some new errand boys," snapped a female voice.

"You think you're hot shit, don't you?" sneered a male voice. "What makes you think he'll listen to a word you say?"

"He won't have to so long as I can offer proof of your utter stupidity. And the more I watch you slamming those boxes around, the surer I am that I won't have long to wait."

"You know you've got a big mouth on you for such a little girl," said another voice.

"And yet, I'm sure no one would be the least bit surprised to discover my dick is bigger than yours as well. Now watch it with those damn boxes! Or I'll carve you out one for your very own."

I slapped my hand over my mouth to keep from snorting. *Damn, if only she wasn't one of the bad guys, I probably could have really liked her.*

Kane turned and glared at me, but I just shrugged. I couldn't help it. He had to admit the girl had style.

Taking hold of the doorknob with one hand, I held up my fingers with the other and counted to three, before whipping the door open and walking in.

"Who the hell are they?" asked one of the four vampires inside. He stood frozen, looking at us, agape, while holding what looked like a Styrofoam box out in front of him.

"Are they with you?" asked another. She was addressing the striking, blonde woman.

"Werewolf," snarled the third man, stepping forward and sneering at Kane.

"Well, that guy's obviously the smartest of you three," I said, pointing to them. I turned to look at the blonde female standing across from the men and eyeing us suspiciously. "Don't you just cringe every time you have to work with these guys? I mean, can't you feel yourself getting more stupid? I swear, I must've lost at least fifty IQ points just by walking into this room."

She crossed her arms over her chest and tilted her head, scanning me up and down.

"I like to think of it as my own personal challenge. Will I be able to make it through these nights without waking up the next morning only to discover that reading a *See Spot Run* book is suddenly extremely difficult?"

I sighed and shook my head. "I knew I would like you. It really sucks that I'm going to have to mess up that pretty face of yours."

She stepped forward and nodded her head. "Yeah? I was just thinking the same thing about you."

Launching herself at me, her fist aimed for my face, but I managed to block it before returning the blow. She was a skilled fighter, swift in her movements and slick, smooth and calculating. Although she was fast for a human, she was strangely slow for a vampire. Either she was newly converted, or Anastasia must have gotten it wrong.

"Ana, grab him!" I heard Kane shout as I spotted one of the vampires running for the door.

Ana dispatched the vampire she was fighting and took off after the one trying to escape. The vampire Kane was sparring with slipped away from his grasp and followed Ana out the door.

"Get him!" I yelled to Kane as I swung for the blonde.

"Where are the kids?" I demanded, pulling her forward by the shoulders, and preparing to plant my knee deeply into her stomach. She blocked the move at the last moment, deflecting some of the force into her arms instead.

"You're here for kids?" she laughed. Raising her arms and breaking my hold on her, "Look around you!" she yelled. "Do you see any kids here?"

She shoved me backwards, but didn't swing for me again. Taking a step back, her chest was heaving.

"Open your eyes, succubus. You're in way over your goddamn head," she told me.

I lifted my hands, and fisted them in front of me, ready for another attack.

"How the hell do you know who I am?" I demanded.

"You think one of your kind can walk into The Devil's Garden without us finding out about it? You're the only phenomenon everyone there's talking about right now." She crossed her arms over her chest and laughed. "You could practically see the drool on Caleb's chin today. You'd better believe he's got plans for you."

I narrowed my eyes at her and slowly lowered my hands, then mirrored her stance by crossing my arms over my chest.

"So I keep hearing. He can drool all he wants, he's never getting his hands on me."

"Good, because that's the last thing you want."

"Why the hell are you telling me all this?" I asked her.

"Because things are heating up, and it's time to start picking sides. I may have to do some shady shit, but when it comes right down to it, I wake up every day wishing Caleb chokes on his next meal."

"So why do you stay?" I asked her.

"You think I have any choice?" she shook her head. "Just because I'm out here instead of in the club doesn't mean I'm not equally as trapped as the rest of them. No. We're taking a big risk by contacting you this way."

"We?"

"Myself, Lily, the girl that sent you here tonight, and... another. I saw you the first night you met Caleb. I knew you would be back."

"Well, I'm here now, so why don't you tell me something I can use?" I asked her.

"I can't. You think Caleb would trust me with his secrets? No! I don't know what's in these boxes, and I don't want to know. I'm just supposed to make sure they get transferred safely. When I go back empty-handed, my punishment will be severe; but I have to believe it will be worth it."

"If you don't know anything about the kids, what do you know about Merrick?"

"I know he's been in the club. He has business with Caleb, but I haven't been able to figure out what it's about.

"They've been kidnapping werewolf children over the last few months. We're trying to get them back."

Her eyes went wide at hearing that and she sneered.

"I'm not surprised to find out it's something like that. I wouldn't put anything past him."

I heard footsteps scurrying back down the hall and she tensed as Anastasia and Kane rushed in, both heading straight for her.

"No, stop!" I yelled. "She's on our side."

"And you believe that?" said Kane, eyeing her suspiciously.

"Yeah, I do."

"Look, handsome, I know you've got no reason to believe me, but I mean what I say, and Caleb needs to be taken down," the blonde told him.

"But how did you know you could trust us?" asked Anastasia, her eyes narrowing.

"I waited and watched that first night you came. I saw Vanessa's reaction when she came out of the hallway. Something was very, very wrong. I overheard Caleb talking on the phone later, mentioning something about a succubus that was in the club, and when he described you, I knew."

"Why do you want him to pay so badly?" I asked her.

"That's my business. All you need to know is: I want him to feel severe pain even more than you do."

"I seriously doubt that," snarled Kane.

"Whatever," she said, dismissing him. "I'm not really down for a game of 'Who's Got The Biggest Grudge?' right now, okay? Just know that you aren't the only ones out for his blood. If Merrick has been taking your kids, then you can bet your ass Caleb is in on the whole thing too. He's probably the one that gave the order. Unfortunately for you, he's pretty much untouchable."

"So then, what the hell do you suggest we do?" I asked.

"Open the boxes. Don't open the boxes. Whatever. Figure it out. Whatever is in there is very important to him. Maybe it will help you and maybe it won't; but it will give you more ammunition to use against him."

"Are you going to stick around and see what's inside?" I asked her.

"No way in hell!" she told me, shaking her head. "I don't want to know. I can't know. I can't run the risk."

"But you're willing to let us burn?" Kane said coolly.

"In a heartbeat. You're on the outside. You can take the extra risk, I can't."

"So what is your part in all of this then?" asked Anastasia. "You've hardly told us anything useful."

"You guys seem to be under the mistaken impression that I'm here to help you. Wrong! I brought you here because I need you to help me."

"We don't have time for your problems," I told her. "We have plenty of our own."

"They aren't mutually exclusive. You want Merrick? Well, I'm here to tell you he's protected by Caleb. You want to know where your kids are? I have no doubt that Caleb knows exactly where they're hidden. But Caleb is a coven leader and you will never, ever, be able to get the answers you're looking for from him. I'm willing to help you find a way to get your kids back if you promise me one thing."

"And what is that?" asked Ana suspiciously.

"Promise me you will help us take down Caleb."

"Done," said Kane.

"No," she said shaking your head. "I don't want *your* promise, I want hers." She stepped so close to me, we were almost touching as she looked me in the eyes.

"Promise me that when the time comes, we can count on your help," she whispered.

"I promise. Caleb will pay."

She smiled and her eyes flashed a brilliant blue. It was gone so fast, I stood frozen, unsure of what I just saw. I reached out and grabbed her arm, digging my fingers into her flesh.

"He doesn't know?" I hissed.

She shook her head ever so slightly.

"Lily and the other one?" I asked frantically.

She nodded her head almost imperceptibly.

"Rose," she whispered. "Her name is Rose."

"But... how?"

"The witches," she said simply. "They're good at cloaking things that need to be kept hidden."

She stepped back and I dropped my hand from her arm.

"What's your name?" I asked, my voice sounding tight and rough.

"Iris."

She stepped around me and walked to the door.

"I'll try to find out what I can about the kids," she said, and her voice returned to normal volume.

"How will we get hold of you?" Kane asked her.

"You can't." She turned back to me. "But if you give me your number, I'll get in touch with you if I find anything."

She passed me her phone and I quickly programmed my phone number into it.

She turned to leave, but Anastasia stopped her.

"Wait, you shouldn't go out there alone. There are more of us, and Caleb's men are most likely searching for us now."

"Ana's right," I agreed. "They are probably trying to find us by now and if they see you first, they'll take you out without stopping for any witty banter."

We walked with Iris from the building and headed toward the van.

"So how are you going to explain losing the shipment?" I asked her.

"I'll just tell him the truth. I'll say that the hand-over was interrupted and I barely escaped."

"And you think he'll believe that?" said Kane.

"He will when I show up with a pretty new shiner to prove my story."

She turned to me and raised her hands, waving me forward. "Come on, let's do this."

I hesitated, not wanting to hit her.

"Are you kidding me?" she asked with a harsh laugh. "You were ready to take my head off only a few minutes ago without a second thought. Now put on your goddamned big girl panties and take a swing at me!"

I balled up my fist and swung at her face. My punch connected and the force of it knocked her off her feet before she fell to the pavement.

"Vanessa!" William yelled from behind me.

He and Thatcher were next to us in an instant with Michael and Keegan close behind.

William's arm shot out to grab Iris, but I caught his wrist in time.

"No, don't touch her!" I told him.

He looked at me, confused, and I shook my head, bending down to help Iris to her feet.

"Are you all right?" I held her chin gently between my fingers and tilted her head.

The point of impact was already blooming into a large, colorful bruise and the side of her face was starting to swell.

"I'm so sorry," I said sadly.

"Don't go soft on me now," she chuckled. "It's better this way; believe me."

"What the hell is going on?" asked Keegan.

"Kane and Ana will fill you in," I said as I pulled Iris a few feet away from the group.

I knew they would still be able to hear us with their supernatural hearing, but at least, they weren't hovering as well.

"I'll be back soon," I told her. "Those kids are here somewhere. But if I'm not around, you can find me in

Silverlake." I gave her my phone number and she committed it to memory.

"You can't tell them," she said. "They can never know."

"I won't say a word. I promise."

"I have to get back to the club. If I'm gone too long, people will start to notice."

"Stay safe," I told her.

"You too."

I watched her as she took off and disappeared around the corner of the building.

Once she was out of sight, an overwhelming emptiness swept through me and I began to shake. Feeling light-headed, I sank slowly to my knees. I couldn't believe what happened. I finally met another succubus.

Wait a minute… Did she say witches?

CHAPTER 26

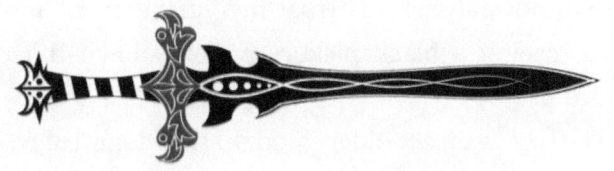

The next night, we waited for Iris in the parking lot of a dive bar just outside of town.

"Do you think she will have anything for us so soon?" asked Michael.

"I doubt it," said Keegan.

"She might, you never know. She seemed pretty determined to bring down Caleb. I doubt she's going to let this chance slip through her fingers. Besides, why risk meeting up with us if she doesn't have anything useful?"

"Trusting her is a bad idea," growled Thatcher. He spat on the ground and leaned against the van.

I looked away from them and back to the road, hoping to see Iris drive up soon. Her text message to me told us to meet her here just after sundown.

"Not everything is a trap, Thatcher," I sighed.

Thatcher barked a laugh and my shoulders tensed, knowing he was laughing at me.

"It amazes me how naïve you can still be, girl," he snorted.

"I'm not naïve, I just trust my gut instinct," I whispered, seeing a black pickup cruising down the road toward us.

The rig was an older model, two-door truck. Up close, I noticed the rust that was starting to form on the wheel wells, but the truck itself was spotlessly clean. Through the windshield, I spotted a flash of Iris's white-blonde hair. It was almost the same rare color as Anastasia's.

My heartbeat sped up as the driver side door opened and Iris jumped down. I approached her and my stomach clenched. Struggling to squash the urge to embrace her, I searched her face, wondering if she were fighting the same odd impulse. She was a stranger, I didn't know her, and despite what I said, I knew Thatcher was right; it would be stupid for us to blindly trust her. But I couldn't help myself. She was the only other succubus I ever met, and everything inside me insisted she could be trusted.

Iris and I stood facing each other without saying a word. Her eyes traveled over my face and I stood as still as possible as the tension arced between us. Finally, she held out her hand to me and I took it in mine.

I could feel the energy flowing from me, unbidden,

and wrapping around her. Her eyes widened and her mouth formed a surprised "O."

She laughed and squeezed my hand tighter. "I haven't felt that in a long time," she whispered, looking down at our joined hands. "I miss it."

Warily eyeing the others over my shoulder, who were waiting for us, she stepped back, removing her hand from mine.

"Follow me," she called out before climbing back into her truck and starting the engine.

"Let's go," I said, heading back to the van.

"What the hell was that?" asked Keegan guardedly.

"What?" I asked, avoiding their curious expressions.

"You guys looked like you were in some kind of trance or something," said Michael. "You get really weird around one another.

I shook my head and hopped into the van. "Don't know what you're talking about, kid," I replied dismissively.

I could see the others exchanging worried expressions from the corner of my eye, but I didn't say anymore.

They piled into the van and Thatcher followed Iris's truck out of the parking lot and down the road, further out of town. After a few minutes, the truck turned down a dirt side road and we trailed Iris into the dark shadows of tall trees that grew on either side of the road. Once we were well-secluded, the truck pulled off to the side of the road and killed its engine. We parked behind it and piled out.

"Looks like a good place for an ambush," said Thatcher to Iris, who was leaning casually against the side of her truck, waiting for us.

"It is, isn't it? It's also a good spot to talk without having to worry about being seen or overheard," Iris retorted with a smirk.

"So what have you got for us?" asked William, crossing his arms over his chest and glaring at her.

"Well, you're all business, aren't you?" Iris said, scanning him up and down.

"We don't have time to play games," William said coolly, "so tell us what you have, or we're leaving."

Iris raised one eyebrow at him and shrugged casually. "So go."

William shot me a look of pure annoyance and I held up my hands in surrender. "Don't look at me," I said, "you're the one throwing around ultimatums."

Keegan marched up to Iris and grabbed her by the front of her fitted, blue t-shirt, lifting her up off the ground and giving her a rough shake.

"Children's lives are at stake and you want to waste our time?" he growled in disgust. "Tell me why I shouldn't snap your neck right now."

I stepped forward to pull Keegan off Iris, but two hands clamped down on my arms and I found myself held fast between Kane and Thatcher.

"Let go of me," Iris said quietly.

"Tell us something useful first," Keegan countered, giving her another firm shake.

"The kids are still alive," she said.

"How do you know?" asked Kane. "Are you sure?"

She looked at him and nodded. "Yeah, I'm sure. We got it out of one of their guards. He's constantly sniffing after the girls at the club. One of the girls I work with managed to get him to talk last night."

"How do you know the information is good?" asked Anastasia.

"There's no reason for it not to be. Now, if you don't mind, I'd really love it if you would put me the hell down."

Keegan grunted and released his grip on her, dropping her unceremoniously.

"Such a gentleman," Iris said with a sneer, smoothing down the front of her top.

I pulled myself free and glared at Kane, ignoring Thatcher completely. Kane looked at me apologetically, but didn't say a word.

"Were you able to find out where they're being held?" I asked her.

"They're here, but they won't be soon. Caleb refuses to keep them in one place for too long."

"Less chance of getting caught," Michael spat derisively.

"Exactly," Iris said with a nod. "The guard told our girl that he wouldn't see her for a few days, and had to temporarily leave town first thing in the morning."

"Morning? So he's not a vampire?" I asked.

Iris shook her head. "No; that way they can move during the daylight. There will be at least a few of them traveling with him in order to avoid any problems."

"Oh, they're going to have problems, all right," said Thatcher.

"Did he say where they were being taken?" Kane asked her.

"No, I'm sorry, but she couldn't get that out of him."

"And we still don't know where they're being held," said William.

"No, we don't," said Iris.

"Well, then, we are barely better off than we were before," said Anastasia with obvious annoyance.

"Well, not quite," said Iris. "There was something else that I managed to get, something that we didn't have before."

"Oh yeah? And what's that?" snapped Thatcher.

"We know where the guard lives," Iris said with a smile.

"What?" I asked with unmasked surprise.

Iris's small smile grew into a wide grin. "I thought you guys might like to pay him a little visit before he had a chance to leave town."

Iris reached into her pocket and pulled out a piece of paper, which she pressed into my hand.

"You can find him here; his name's Cliff. I stopped by the place before I met you. Quiet area of town, nothing special. Old apartment block. I snuck in and heard sounds coming from the TV in his apartment. He might still be there. And if not, maybe you can find something else that might be helpful."

"You're not coming with us?" Kane asked her.

"No, I can't risk it. I've got to get back soon anyway. I really hope you guys find those kids." Iris turned to me and nodded. "It was nice meeting you, succubus."

"Yeah, you too," I said, my throat tightening.

"Try not to die, all right? Remember, you promised me you'd help us."

"Don't worry," I said, shaking my head. "I don't plan on dying anytime soon."

"Good, we've still got a lot to talk about."

"Yeah, we do."

Iris climbed into her truck and slammed the door before rolling down the window.

"Don't let him get his hands on you, Vanessa, no matter what happens," she said, and I could see the worry clouding her eyes.

"I'll kill him first," I said, and I meant it. An involuntary shudder went through me at the memory of his power when he was trying to pull me in.

Iris nodded, appearing satisfied. "Be sure you do. Good luck."

"So," I said, looking down at the small slip of paper in my hand. "Who wants to go pay this asshole a visit?"

∿

We sat quietly in the van as it pulled up in front of Cliff's apartment building. We didn't need to speak; we all knew what we were there to do.

Thatcher cut the engine and we hopped down onto the pavement and looked up and down the street. Thankfully, no one was around. Iris was right, it was a quiet area.

We all looked at Kane and he nodded, silently leading the way into the building and up the stairs to the sixth floor. The weight of our boots fell heavily as we ran up, and I sensed the buzz of energy swirling around me as we reached the landing. We silently spilled into the hallway.

Rushing down the hall without making any noise, we dared not alert the other occupants of the building to our presence. My entire body was shaking by the time we found ourselves in front of his door. I wanted to kick it in and storm the room, but the last thing we needed was someone calling the cops.

Kane held up his hand and counted to three on his fingers before turning the handle on the door. There was a moment of resistance, and then I heard the lock cracking as the door swung open.

The wolves and I rushed inside to find Caleb's guard passed out in front of the TV inside his cramped apartment, the remote control still loosely hanging in his hand.

"Well, he's no good to us asleep," I whispered before stepping up to the unconscious man in his armchair. I hit him across the face with the butt of my gun.

The pain of it woke him instantly, but before he could take stock of what was happening, I grabbed him by the front of his t-shirt and tossed him onto the floor. Stepping on his chest to keep him there, I pointed my gun at his head.

"Wakey-wakey, sleepyhead," I said with a smile as I cocked my gun. "We need to ask you a few questions."

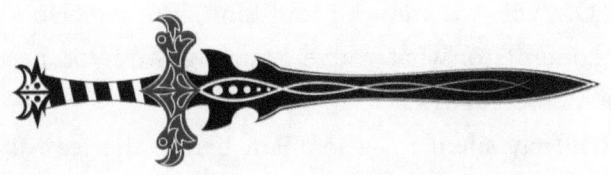

CHAPTER 27

"Vanessa, we need him alive," said William slowly from the doorway.

"No, William, we need him alive *for now*," I replied without releasing my gaze on the man, and emphasizing the last part. I never killed a human before, but I was suddenly ready and willing to make an exception.

"Look, I don't know what you guys want, but I don't have any money here. Just take whatever you like, okay? I'm not going to fight you. Just take it all," the guy said, his eyes darting frantically back and forth.

"We're not here to rob you, Cliff. It is Cliff, right?" I asked.

He nodded his head quickly, "Yeah, yeah, it's Cliff."

"Oh, good, because I'd really hate it if we had the wrong apartment," I said with a relieved sigh. "So here's the thing, Cliff. You work for a very bad man, who does very bad things, and now, karma's about to show you just how much of a bitch she can be," I told him.

"I don't know what you're talking about," Cliff said. "I'm just a security guard."

"Oh, yes, we know," I told him. "But we also know the contents of what you're guarding. And you need to take us there. Now."

Cliff lay silent for a moment before the fear on his face was replaced by a sneer.

"I ain't telling you shit," he said.

"Oh, ho! Thanks for dropping the act, Cliff, I thought I would have to hit you again. Not that I wouldn't enjoy it, mind you, but I'd hate for your nasty blood to get my pretty gun all dirty."

"You think you scare me? You don't know shit. If I talk, I die. So you might as well just shoot me now."

"Oh, I'm not going to shoot you." I took my foot off his chest and stepped back, keeping my gun trained him. "But you see, you've got their kids." I gestured to the werewolves who stepped closer. They were starting to transform, elongating their fingers while their nails grew into tapered, savage-looking claws.

"And judging by the looks of it, they'd very much like to have a word with you..."

I stepped out of the way and moved back to the doorway to stand beside Anastasia. Her face was blank as she watched Cliff cowering before the partially trans-formed wolves. Keegan grabbed Cliff roughly by the ankle, slicing through the skin as he dragged him across the floor.

Cliff's bravado cracked, and he started to yell out in fear while trying to grasp the legs of the furniture. Michael knelt down and tore Cliff's shirt off before gagging him with it. Then he, Keegan and Kane dragged Cliff into the bedroom to interrogate him further.

The vampires and I stood in the living room silently. The only sound, apart from the TV, was the low rumble of Kane's voice coming from the bedroom. Sometimes, it was punctuated by Cliff's muffled cries of pain that floated down the halls.

We were so close to finding the kids that the waiting was making me antsy. I wanted to go in there and wrench the answers out of Cliff, myself; but this was werewolf business and dealing with him was their right and privilege.

"This is taking too long," grumbled Thatcher, echoing my thoughts.

"Leave it, Thatcher," said William.

"Well, what are they doing in there? Tickling the answers out of him?" Thatcher asked.

"Thatcher is right," agreed Anastasia, "it would have been faster to simply glamour the guard for the answer."

"It's not about the answers," I said quietly as I listened to some more sickening thuds coming from the other room. "They know the kids aren't being moved until morning. They'll get the answers we need in plenty of time."

"They are currently wasting time," said Anastasia.

"They need this, Ana. They've been through so much. They need to make someone pay. They'll make everyone pay in the end. He helped abduct their kids. He forfeited his life the moment he agreed to do that. The guy's been living on borrowed time. He was just too stupid to know it."

Just then, the door to the bedroom opened and Keegan walked out first, wiping the blood off his hands onto what must have been one of Cliff's pillowcases.

Michael and Kane followed him out. They were supporting Cliff, who hung weakly between them, his arms slung across their shoulders.

"He's still alive," said William, surprised.

"We don't have the kids yet," said Kane. "If we kill him and his information is bad, we've got nothing. So he's coming with us."

Kane's face was grim, his lips pressed tightly together in a straight line as he and his brother hauled Cliff out the front door and towards the stairs.

My chest tightened as I watched him walking, his back ramrod straight before me, and his movements stiff and unnatural. I noticed it for just a moment when he came out of the bedroom. The flash of suppressed rage behind his eyes. I almost felt sorry for any of Caleb's people that Kane decided we didn't have further use for.

Werewolf or not, Kane had always seemed... gentle to me. I knew he could hold his own in a fight, but there seemed to be less blood lust inside him. He appeared to have very little love of the hunt, or the kill. But I could see it now. I could finally see his innate desire to tear through this city and every one in it until he had his people back safely at home.

"What is it, Vanessa?" I didn't even notice Anastasia sliding up silently beside me as we left the building.

"Nothing, I was just thinking that this town's vampire population is going to be seriously reduced by the time we're done here."

Anastasia's eyes flicked towards Kane and the other wolves before landing on me again.

"I believe you're right."

We piled into the van, dumping Cliff on his side in the back before tearing away from the curb.

"So what's the plan?" I asked Kane as Thatcher sped through the streets. We were heading towards the address the wolves managed to beat out of Cliff.

"We go in there, we kill everyone and we take the kids home," said Keegan, answering for him.

"Sounds like a good plan," I agreed with a nod.

"He tell you anything about what we're up against in there?" asked Thatcher with a quick glance into the back seat.

"The kids are being held together in a basement in one of Caleb's buildings. It's guarded by maybe half a dozen vampires at any one time," Kane replied. "Sometimes, Merrick is there too, overseeing things, and sometimes he's not."

"If we're lucky, he'll be there tonight and I'll finally get my chance to end him once and for all," I said as I tried to quiet my mind and focus on channeling my power.

"If we get a chance, we take him out. But the kids are our first priority," said Kane firmly.

"Don't worry, Kane, I know what needs to be done. We'll get your pups."

The location where the children were being held was an unassuming, one-level office building not far from the area where we met Iris the night before.

"We were so close to them," said Kane as he looked around. "How is it we couldn't smell them? Or sense them at all?"

"It's the same with the Renegades," William told him. "They can cloak themselves from our perception. Whatever is cloaking them must be doing the same to the little weres."

"Come on," said Thatcher, reaching for one of the heavy, double doors, and dragging Cliff along with him.

"Why is there no one out here?" I looked around, but couldn't see anyone watching the building.

"You're right, there should be someone here. They wouldn't leave this place so exposed," said William.

"Maybe everyone is inside, getting ready for the morning?" suggested Anastasia.

"Maybe..." I said, feeling even more uneasy.

Thatcher looked at us and nodded before opening the door and moving quickly inside.

"What the hell?" asked Thatcher.

Beyond the front door was a small rectangular room. It was barely ten feet wide and about five feet from another set of double doors. But unlike the door we just came through, this door was completely made of metal.

"I can't hear anything from the other side," he told us after listening for a moment.

A second later, there was a whoosh of air behind us and we all turned to find six vampires blocking our path back.

I felt William tensing beside me and preparing to attack when the massive, metal door creaked and opened.

The vampires that blocked our path pressed forward, herding us into the large, empty room behind the door. Inside the room were a bunch of empty cages, just large enough to tightly confine a small adult, or a child.

"Surprise!" shouted Colleen with a laugh. Around her stood roughly two dozen vamps, all sporting the same smug, self-satisfied expression.

"Looks like they were anticipating our arrival," I said, my voice tight as I viewed Colleen's smirking face.

"I knew she couldn't be trusted," said Thatcher.

"Shut up, Thatcher," I said under my breath. If they didn't already know about Iris's involvement in this, I didn't want to expose her.

"She set us up!" he continued.

"Shut up, Thatcher!" I hissed.

"We were starting to think that you guys would never get here. That would have made it, you know, pretty much the worst surprise party ever. Once we heard you guys were in town, we thought we should throw this little party for you. Just in case you discovered where we were." She cocked her head to the side and wagged her finger at Cliff. "Naughty, naughty, Cliff. Now you'll have to be punished. You should be more careful about who you go running your mouth off to. Don't you know that bartenders are awful gossips?"

Cliff blanched and tried to slink backwards, but his retreat was swiftly deterred by the group of vampires at his back.

It sounded like Iris's informant wasn't the only woman at The Devil's Garden whom Cliff was trying to impress the night before. I raised one eyebrow at Thatcher and he shrugged his shoulders in acceptance. Iris didn't betray us after all.

"Where are the kids, Colleen?" I asked, stepping forward. She raised her gun again and aimed it at my center. I stopped moving.

"The kids aren't here," she said. "Look around, do you see any kids here?"

"You expect us to believe that you're all here, but the children aren't?" Kane asked her. "No, they're around here somewhere."

"They're long gone. They were moved the moment we learned you guys found out and were getting too close. Seriously, Nessa, what is it about guys who always think with their dicks? A pretty girl smiles at them and BAM! They just blab, blab, blab."

She jerked the gun away from me and aimed it towards Cliff. It went off with a loud bang and I jumped in surprise as he collapsed to the floor. I looked down at him struggling to breathe, his hand shaking as he held it above the wound. She shot him right in the chest!

Colleen watched him die with a bored look on her face. "So now, what are we going to do with you?" she asked, focusing her attention back on the rest of us. "Oh, I know." She looked over her shoulder at the other vampires. "Kill them."

The Renegades rushed us, intent on tearing us to pieces, but I barely noticed them. I watched Colleen take the opportunity of instant chaos and confusion to slip out the door behind her.

I dodged the fighting around me, my eyes intently riveted on her. I couldn't let her escape again. The howls of the wolves and the grunts of battle grew faint in my ears as I ducked and wove my way across the room.

A hard, cold hand clamped down on mine, pulling

me back. Without slowing, I whipped out my gun and pressed it to the vampire's forehead before pulling the trigger. His head snapped back and he loosened his grip on me. I knew the shot didn't kill him, but I didn't care. He let me go and that was all I needed to get past the rest of them and slip out the door after Colleen.

I chased her down the hall and through a side door. I caught up to her on the a short flight of stairs that led to another door.

"Colleen, stop!" I shouted as she lay her hand on the release bar.

Colleen paused before turning around to face me.

"You're too late, Vanessa, the kids are gone. Just give up. You can't win."

"I'm not letting you out of here until you tell me where they are," I told her, moving to stand on the bottom step.

"You seem pretty confident about that. Almost as if there is something you can do. 'Sweet Colleen, always such a pushover,'" she mocked me in a sing-song voice.

"I never thought you were a pushover, Colleen. You were one of my best friends."

"Yeah? Well, now I'm something better than that."

"Oh yeah? And what's that?" I asked, climbing the stairs towards her.

"I'm the one that still has her hand on her gun," she said with a laugh.

My eyes flew down to the hand she held behind her, but it was too late. The sound of the gunshot echoed through the little space so loudly, it made my ears ring. The pain of the sound was nothing compared to the agony tearing at the center of my body. Sharp and burning like fire, I pressed my hand on the wound, and pulled it away only to find my fingers covered in blood.

"Bye, Nessa," Colleen said before shoving the door open and disappearing into the night.

I gasped for breath and my vision began to blur as I stumbled backwards. I lost my footing on the stairs and fell down, landing with a crash at the bottom of the staircase, and crying out at the jarring thump of my clumsy landing.

I stare up at the cracked ceiling, listening to the fading sounds of fighting only a few hundred feet away. There were so many Renegades; did anyone make it out alive?

I tried to begin healing myself, but the pain was too intense for me to concentrate properly. I couldn't think about anything except how cold I felt as my blood spilled out onto the hard floor, puddling beneath my body.

My breathing started to slow and my eyes grew heavy as I faded in and out, blinking up at the naked light bulb swinging above me.

I barely heard the sound of a door crashing open, but it seemed very far away, as if at the other end of a tunnel.

"Vanessa!" A worried voice called my name. "Oh, my God! Vanessa!"

Kane, the voice belonged to Kane. I wanted to answer him, and I tried, but no sound came; it remained trapped inside me.

"Oh, God, Vanessa, try to hold on."

My eyes were suddenly filled with the faded, blurry image of Kane's face as he leaned over me and pressed his mouth on mine.

"Come on, Vanessa, come on," he whispered urgently against my lips. "Take some from me, please. You have to heal. Please!" He kissed me again, more urgently. My lips felt numb, while his seemed scorching hot.

I tried to pull some energy from him, moving beyond the pain with all of my strength to draw some of his life force into me, and I could feel it beginning to stir. The smallest amount of energy slipped from him into me, but it wasn't enough. Not nearly enough.

"I'm getting you out of here," he said, sliding his hands beneath my body and lifting me up.

I screamed out at the extreme pain. The movement, alone, was enough to wrench agonized gasps from me.

He pressed his lips on mine again and I managed to pull a small amount of energy from him again before I completely blacked out.

CHAPTER 28

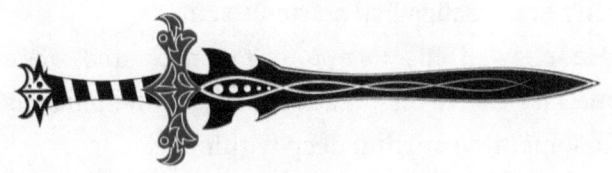

"Vanessa? Vanessa, can you hear me?" a frantic voice shouted at me as I struggled toward consciousness.

Groaning, I blinked my eyes open slowly to see Kane's worried face hovering above mine.

The air felt cold on my skin and it took me a moment to realize that Kane had removed my shirt.

"You're losing so much blood! You're losing so much blood!"

I looked down at my body to see him holding a towel, now bright red and soaked with my blood lying on my stomach.

"The only reason you're still alive is because of the energy you took from me. But that wasn't enough. Please, please! You have to take more, Vanessa. You have to try!"

I whimpered in pain, but nodded. I was so tired, and felt so weak, but I also didn't want to die.

Kane brushed the sweat-soaked hair back from my face and caressed my cheek, wiping away the tears that I didn't even realize had started to fall.

He nuzzled his face into my neck and placed a gentle kiss there, his breath feathering the tender skin. I felt something stirring deep within me.

Kane moved carefully around to my side, making sure not to jostle me as he kept one hand firmly pressed on my stomach to staunch the bleeding wound while he clasped the back of my neck with the other hand. I sighed as his lips trailed the line of my jaw before he captured my mouth with his.

Arousing me to life, he slipped his tongue inside my mouth and I felt the familiar tugging that launched me beyond the pain in my abdomen. Hunger stirred from deep inside me. I kissed him back with more force, allowing the electric energy to roll up my arms and over my chest. His hand left my neck and traveled down over my collarbone and then lower. It grazed lightly over my breast. I inhaled deeply at his touch and sensed the first heavy wave of energy flowing from him into me.

I reached up with my free arm and gripped his shoulder as the hunger began to overtake me, pulling even more energy from him. After a moment, the hunger took control and I could not stop myself. My body needed healing and went on auto-pilot. Suddenly, its only goal was survival. Somewhere deep in my mind, I knew I had to be careful, but I couldn't restrain myself. I needed more.

I bit Kane's lips and plunged my tongue deeper into his mouth, desperate to get even closer to him.

"Vanessa, wait! Wait! I think we need to slow down," he said, trying to pull away.

"No, no, it's not enough. It still hurts," I whimpered, tugging on his shoulder, trying to bring his face back down to mine. In my weakened state, however, he easily pulled away from me.

With a look of concern, he carefully removed the towel from my stomach in order to examine my gunshot wound.

"It's closed," he said with obvious relief. "It's not bleeding anymore."

"It still burns, and everything hurts," I panted. I tried to sit up, but the world spun and I collapsed onto the numerous pillows.

"Oh, God!" he said frantically. "Don't you dare pass out again!"

Kane gathered me to him and kissed me hard, as though he were determined to force the energy out of his body and into mine by the sheer power of his own will if necessary.

I kissed him back desperately, anxious to consume everything he offered. It wasn't long before I could feel my internal wounds healing as the soft tissue began stitching itself back together. I tugged his shirt up and over his head, hissing in pain at the movement, but not allowing it to slow me down. My hands roamed over the hard planes of his abdomen and down further, popping open the button on his jeans.

"More," I groaned into his mouth, "I need more."

Kane continued to kiss me as he tugged down my pants, removing his mouth from mine only long enough to lose his pants, leaving him naked. Then he eased off mine, taking my underwear with them.

My eyes traveled over the hardness of his body and lingered on the broad sweep of his shoulders as he moved closer.

"I don't want to hurt you," he said, covering my body with his.

"I'm already hurt," I replied with a shallow laugh as my hands freely roamed his sexy body. The hunger now roared from within me, and my need to feed lessened the previous pain I was feeling.

I opened my legs to accept him and he slid inside me with ease, joining us at last. At that moment, I lost all control of my hunger. My vision flared with red and I was instantly consumed by need. Tangling my legs with his, I rolled us over so I could straddle him and rode him wildly, tearing the energy from his body, heedless of the danger my feeding might impose to him.

His strong fingers dug into my hips as he thrust

into me like a piston, trying to match my pace. My body was feverish as the energy rolled over me, crashing through me and healing me from the inside, dragging me back from the verge of death.

"Vanessa? Vanessa!"

I looked down at Kane as he screamed my name and gasped. His skin had turned incredibly pale as he strained for breath before tiny, black veins began to form like a spider web on his body. Even though Kane was a werewolf, my injuries were so great that healing them must've drained him. Now, his whole life was in danger. His hands slipped from my hips as I leaned forward and wrapped my arms around his neck, riding him toward the finish. My body began to shake and I pressed my mouth on his, channeling the excess power right back into him. I pushed it with all my might, expelling it into him with all the force I could muster. I had never given energy before, but I had to try. I wasn't about to let him die for me. His back arched as he cried out, the color flooding back into his cheeks.

Flipping me over, and newly reenergized, Kane and I clung to each other. We strove to push each other over the edge in our shared finish, tethered together by the energy trapped between us. It didn't take long before we were crying out into the night. As I hit my peak, the energy exploded from me and engulfed both of us before slowly receding. Eventually, I regained my senses.

We lay together, panting. Kane's forehead was

pressed on mine as my thoughts became crystal clear again. Easing himself off me, Kane wrapped his arms around me and tucked me into the warmth of his body. Overcome with exhaustion, we fell asleep.

I re-taped the corner of the black tarp that covered the window and pressed down hard. No one else had returned to the motel room, so I made sure the sun couldn't shine in if any of the vampires arrived before we found them. I listened to the sound of the shower running in the bathroom and slipped a clean shirt over my head. After smoothing it over my newly flawless skin, the sun began to appear above the horizon. I was wide awake. I didn't have so much as a single bruise or scar, no trace or evidence that I was shot and almost killed the night before. Kane came out of the bathroom fully dressed just as I was tugging on my second boot.

"We have to hurry," I said, not quite meeting his eyes. "No one else made it back last night. We have to find them."

"Are you sure you're up for this?" His eyes traveled over me. I felt sure he was checking for signs that I hadn't healed properly.

"I'm fine," I told him, "are *you*?"

"Yeah."

"You could have died, Kane. Healing me like that should have killed you last night."

"I couldn't let you die, Vanessa. I couldn't. And it looks like you healed me too. So don't worry about it."

"It was still a stupid risk to take!" I snapped.

"Maybe it was, but it was *my* risk to take, my choice, so how about a thank you?" He looked at me with an annoyed expression on his face, crossing his arms over his chest while he waited.

"You're right," I said with a sigh. "Thank you. You saved my life, so thank you."

He came over and rested a hand on my shoulder, but I shrugged it off, slipping away and grabbing my leather jacket.

"Come on," I said, "we need to leave."

He stood there frowning at me, so I turned my back on him to head toward the door.

"Vanessa, what's wrong?" he asked.

"Nothing, we don't have time for this; let's go."

I opened the door, but he came up behind me and placed a hand firmly against it, shoving it closed again.

"What the hell is wrong with you? You think you'd be happy to even be alive today, so why won't you even look at me?" he growled.

"It's nothing, all right? Our people are out there somewhere and now we have to find them, on top of the missing kids, so why don't you just drop it, okay?" I knocked his hand away from the door and pulled it open, escaping as quickly as I could.

Once outside, I took a deep breath of the fresh morning air. The room was too confining, and I felt as though the walls were closing in on me. I desperately needed to get out before being crushed.

He should have just let me die, I thought to myself as Kane came out of the room behind me.

He walked past, and bumped me, but didn't stop. I stumbled before catching my balance and stared after him. With everything that was happening, I had no doubt the tension of his shoulders was due completely to me. A heavy weight of shame and regret settled in my stomach, but I tried to ignore it as I followed after him.

"How did we get back here last night?" Thatcher had been the one with the keys, and looking around, I didn't see our van anywhere in the motel's mostly empty parking lot.

"I stole a car."

I stopped in my tracks and raised one eyebrow at hearing that revelation.

"You stole a car? You never really struck me as the type of guy that knew how to hotwire a vehicle."

Kane walked around to the driver side of a gray, four-door sedan and leveled his gaze at me over the roof of the car.

"Well, it's not like you ever bothered to ask, is it?" he said before pulling the door open. Dropping down into the driver's seat, he slammed the door closed again.

Shit.

I opened the passenger side door and collapsed into the seat next to him.

Kane was silent as he put the car in reverse and headed out of the parking lot. He unexpectedly slammed on the breaks before we hit the street, and I was thrown forward before falling back again, held fast by my loyal seatbelt.

"Kane, what the hell!?" I shouted, turning in my seat to face him.

Kane was staring out the windshield, his chest heaving, and his face looked thunderous. He clenched the steering wheel so tightly, his knuckles went white. I was a little surprised it didn't simply crumble to dust in his crushing fists.

"Kane?" I asked quietly.

"Why are you doing this, Vanessa?" His voice was so soft, I barely heard him.

"Doing what?"

His hands tightened on the wheel and he closed his eyes, letting out a deep breath before turning to me.

"You won't even look at me. I saved your life!"

"I know you did. Thank you."

"So why are you treating me like I did something wrong?"

"You didn't," I tried to reassure him, but I couldn't hold his gaze. I dropped my eyes down to the dashboard.

He sat silently for a minute, contemplating me, then he reached out and took my hand.

"We made love," he said in a level voice.

I pulled my hand from his and stuck it in my lap.

"We had sex," I said firmly.

He didn't reply before nodding slowly. "So that's it. You're mad that we made... I mean, had sex."

I turned away and looked out the window, the sky was getting lighter by the minute. We didn't have time for this inane conversation. Why couldn't he just let it go?

"You can't just ignore that, Vanessa."

"And why the hell not?" I yelled, turning back to face him. "Why do we have to get into that? And why now? When our friends are out there, getting hurt or worse? Why would you want to get into that now?"

"Friends? You mean, William."

I didn't reply, but simply glared at him while struggling to regain my control.

"William, of course," he ground out.

"I didn't say that," I snapped and my voice grew tight.

"William and I aren't... we are, but it's not... shit!" I slammed my hand down on the dashboard. It felt so good, I did it a few more times before falling back into my seat and covering my face with my hands.

"You were dying, Vanessa, you had no choice," he answered coldly. "I'm sure he'll understand. Just tell him... tell him it didn't mean anything. I was just trying to make sure you didn't die."

"No, Kane, please, don't think—"

"No, you're right," he said swiftly, cutting me off. "We really don't have time for this."

"But—"

"Just leave it, Vanessa."

Kane threw the car in drive and pulled out onto the street.

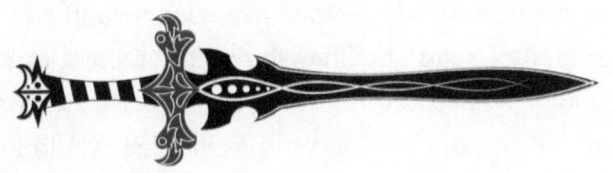

CHAPTER 29

"Can you sense the others?" I asked finally. Neither of us had spoken for twenty minutes while we drove around with the windows rolled down, Kane continuously sniffing the air, anxiously trying to pick up a scent.

"Yes, it's faint, but it's there. I can smell my brother and Keegan. Hopefully, the vampires will be with them."

"You can't smell the vampires?"

"No."

I bit my lip and held back the questions that were tumbling around my head. *Was he even trying to sense the others? Did he actually want to find William?* I watched him out of the corner of my eye, my doubt slowly creeping in.

Oh, God, I've been around killers for too long. There's no way Kane would let anything happen to William. He's not like that.

But Kane was speaking the truth before; I hadn't really taken the time to get to know him. What *did* I know about him? He seemed like such a solid guy, but what kind of solid guy knew how to hotwire a car? It's not like it was something that people just learned on a whim. What kind of guy could he be that would know how to steal cars?

"Son of a bitch," I swore under my breath as the scent trail led us right to the last place I wanted to be, The Devil's Garden. "There's no way they would have been stupid enough to bring them back here, is there?" I asked Kane.

"It doesn't make any sense. Caleb certainly wouldn't want to be tied to this. It would be much safer to just kill them all," he agreed.

We got out of the car and crossed the street to the entrance. Kane pounded on the front doors, and it didn't take long for us to hear footsteps on the other side.

The door opened and a large, black man in a tight, black t-shirt emblazoned with the club's logo stuck his head outside.

"Yeah?" he asked gruffly.

"We're here to see Caleb," I told the bouncer.

"Caleb's busy, and he ain't seein' anybody right now. Come back later."

He started to close the door on us, but Kane

grabbed it. The bouncer tugged on it and looked at Kane, somewhat startled when the door refused to budge in Kane's tenacious grip.

"I'm pretty sure he'll want to talk to us," said Kane evenly. "Why don't we just come inside, and you can let him know we're here."

Kane pulled the door open wider and the bouncer had to quickly let go of the handle to avoid being knocked off his feet.

"Yeah, sure, whatever," the big man said, turning his back on us. "Just wait here, I'll be right back."

We waited less than five minutes before the bouncer returned. He jerked his head in the direction of the secret hallway that led to Caleb's office.

"Come on, he doesn't like to be kept waiting," the bouncer said, obviously put out that Caleb agreed to see us after all.

Caleb's office appeared just as distractingly tacky as I remembered it, but that did nothing to diminish the air of self-satisfaction that surrounded Caleb when Kane and I walked in.

"Vanessa, so lovely to see you again, and so soon," he practically crooned, taking my hand in both of his and grasping it tightly. Bringing it to his lips, he kissed the back of it and I had to suppress another shudder of revulsion.

"Kane, so nice to see you again as well, of course," he added with a flickering glance in Kane's direction. "Now, please, what can I do for both of you?"

STEPHANIE MARKS

"We were attacked last night and separated from our people," I told him, trying not to sound accusatory. "We came here to find them."

"Oh? And how may I help with that?"

I bit down hard on my tongue and plastered a wide smile on my mouth. "Well, Caleb, and please, forgive me, I mean no offence," I forced out the words between clenched teeth, "but we followed their trail to your club. Maybe they were brought here without your knowledge?"

"I see," Caleb said, then he walked around is desk to sit down on his chair. "I'm sorry to tell you this, Vanessa, as there seems to be no point in keeping it from you, but yes, your friends are here."

"They are?" I looked at Kane and then back at Caleb. Something wasn't right, and I could practically hear the sound of the trap door closing, but I couldn't quite see it yet.

"Yes, they were brought to me for justice. They were caught breaking Coven law, you see, and are awaiting punishment." Though he tried to seem sorrowful, I detected a glint of joy in his eyes.

"What lies are those?" Kane demanded. "What laws have they broken?"

"Vampire law; and it is of no concern to you, were-wolf," Caleb told him.

"You hold my wolves as well, so I demand to know what crime they have been accused of!" He started to storm towards Caleb, but I grabbed his arm to pull him

320

back before he could do anything stupid. Like attacking a coven leader.

"What about me?" I asked quickly. "Don't I have a right to know what they are accused of?" I politely inquired.

"I'm sorry, Vanessa, but you're not a vampire either." He spread his hands, indicating there was nothing more he could do.

"But I'm here for vampire business. I belong to the Silverlake Coven Task Force. You are holding my team captive and I must know what crimes they are being accused of, or I shall be forced to take this up with Elizabeth."

"There is nothing Elizabeth can do for you. This is my area, not hers, and my word is *law*."

"So you can just hold them all here? Just like that?" I was starting to worry. I had already seen just how fast and irreversible Coven justice could be.

"Yes, I can." He paused for a moment, taking a sip of deep red liquid from a wine glass and savoring the contents. He licked his lips before setting it down and looking at us again. "Of course..." he drawled, "it's always possible that their accusers were simply trying to start trouble. Everyone was looking pretty bruised, so it's always possible that they are innocent."

"They *are* innocent," I insisted.

"Are they now?" he mused. "I suppose I could be persuaded to believe that. Of course, if I were to release these potential criminals back to you, I would need some reassurance. A sign of your good faith, you understand. And since you are serving under the orders of the Silverlake Coven, you can also negotiate on your Coven's behalf."

"And just what kind of sign of good will would you be looking for, Caleb? What do you really want?" I asked, narrowing my eyes at him.

Caleb looked from me to Kane before indicating the door. "If you would excuse us, Kane, this really is Coven business. A moment alone to negotiate, if you please."

Kane growled low and stepped closer to me. "There is no way I am leaving her alone here with you," he told Caleb.

"Kane," I jerked my head toward the door, "please, give us a minute."

"No way in hell!" Kane snapped.

"Kane! Please. Just, step outside. I'll be fine. Five minutes, that's all we need."

Kane glared at Caleb and jerked his head in a nod before leaning in closer to me. "If he tries anything, *anything*, you yell for me, do you hear me?"

"I'll be fine," I said with more confidence than I felt.

Kane's jaw clenched tightly as he struggled with what to say, but he eventually turned and stormed out the door, slamming it behind him.

"Werewolves," Caleb said, "so wild. No refinement at all."

"So what do you want from me, Caleb, really?"

"Right down to it with you, I see. I meant what I said, Vanessa. Just a sign of good will. I'm willing to release your friends back into your custody as a personal favor, and all I ask is a favor from you in return."

"And what kind of favor would that be?"

"Just a little help from time to time, you know, on some freelance projects in which your particular skill set could be of use to me. Nothing you would object to, I'm sure."

"My plate is pretty full these days with the Task Force. What if I don't have time to freelance?"

"Well, then, unfortunately, your team will have to stand trial. And due to the severity of the crimes they've been accused of, I'm afraid the penalties could very well include death. For *all* of them."

I felt the door of the trap swinging shut in my mind with a loud clank! So that was his game! Either I let him use my power whenever he needs it, or he kills them all under the guise of carrying out Coven justice.

I nodded my agreement. "Looks like you've got yourself a new freelancer then."

Caleb's mouth broke into a wide grin, and his fangs glinted in the low lamplight.

"Nice to see how agreeable you can be."

"Where are they?" I wanted to see them immediately and get out of there as soon as possible.

"They are all being held downstairs in light-free rooms. I'm sorry they could not be made more comfortable, but they had to be secured. Remember, they *were* brought in as criminals, so I'm sure you understand."

"Yes, of course," I forced out through clenched teeth. They were so close to being free, I couldn't risk insulting Caleb or swearing up my only opportunity to get them released. "So, let's go get them."

"But the sun, my dear. They couldn't possibly leave until nightfall; it wouldn't be safe." The satisfied grin on his face widened and I paused.

"They can't leave here until nightfall?"

"It really wouldn't be wise. How unfortunate if I were to release them only to have the vampires go up in flames, don't you think?" He said it as though he were explaining something very simple to a small child.

"What about the wolves? Can I take them?" I asked.

"I really think it best that they all stay until after sundown, don't you?"

The door to Caleb's office opened with a crash before bouncing off the wall behind it as Kane lurched into the room.

"You were taking too long," he said.

"Sorry. I'm fine," I reassured him.

"Really?" He examined my face, searching for signs that I could be hiding something.

"I'm all right. Caleb has agreed to let them go."

"And what did you have to give him in return?"

"That's really none of your concern, wolf. Coven business."

Kane shot him a look that said exactly where Caleb

could shove his so-called "Coven business," but he held his tongue.

"Fine, give us our people," he said.

"As I was just telling the lovely Vanessa here, they will be released to you after nightfall."

"That's not good enough," growled Kane.

"Watch yourself, wolf," said Caleb, "or you may find yourself joining them."

"Kane, don't," I pleaded. The others may have been facing trumped up charges, but if Kane threatened a coven leader, we were all truly screwed.

"I want my people back and I want them now," Kane demanded.

"I think you should listen to Vanessa, Kane, she possesses innate wisdom."

"Actually..." I looked back and forth between Kane and Caleb before pulling my gun out of its holster and pointing it at Caleb. "I think Kane may have a point. Give us our people."

"You dare to pull a gun on me?" Caleb asked, completely unfazed. "You know you cannot kill me with it."

"I know. But I'm willing to bet that no matter how old and powerful you are, a silver bullet to the head would still hurt like hell."

"You surely must realize this is a blatant act of aggression. I could kill you on the spot and still be well within my rights to do so."

"No, Caleb, no," I said sweetly. "Don't think of this

as an act of aggression. Think of it more as me renegotiating the terms of our agreement. You didn't tell me before that you wouldn't hand the others over for twelve hours. So now, I'm choosing to reject those terms. I'm sure our van is stashed here somewhere, and the windows are UV-proof. We can get the vampires out of here just fine." I knew Caleb needed me and I could only pray that I hadn't overplayed my hand.

I saw Caleb's eyes flicker towards the clock on his desk, then back to me so quickly that I almost missed it.

"You drive a hard bargain, Vanessa, but as a show of good will, I will accept your change of terms. Come; let's get your people."

Caleb rose from his desk and led us out into the main area of the club.

"Wait here, and I will go have them released."

"What if he doesn't release them?" Kane asked.

"He will," I told him, growing more anxious to leave with every passing second.

"How can you be so sure?"

"Because," I said with a smile, "he thinks he won. Quick! Go find the van and bring it around to the front."

Kane entered the club just as Caleb brought the vampires and other werewolves onto the dance floor from one of the many side doors.

"I have held up my side of our bargain, Vanessa. I

look forward to the day when I call upon you to hold up yours."

"I'll hold up my end," I told him, turning to go.

"Until we meet again then, my dear."

"I pulled the van right up to the door. Just climb in the back and you guys should be safe from the sun," Kane told the vamps.

"How did you get us out of there?" Anastasia asked.

"Vanessa made a deal," Kane told them before I could stop him.

"She did what!?" William exploded. "And you let her?"

"You think I had a choice?" Kane roared, spinning to face him. "Besides, I'm not her goddamn keeper. She can make her own decisions, no matter how stupid they are."

"Well, you should have found another way!" William continued to shout as everyone piled into the van.

"Both of you, just shut up!" I demanded. Once we were all in the vehicle, I turned to face them. "William, I promise you there was no other way, and there's nothing we can do about it now. You guys are safe and that's all that matters. I'll figure out the rest later. But that's irrelevant now because I found out something in Caleb's office. It's the only reason he was willing to let you go."

"What?" asked Michael.

"The kids are still in town. But they'll be gone any

minute; I'm sure of it. He wanted to hold you until tonight to be sure they were gone, but I saw him glancing at the time before he agreed to release you. Colleen was lying last night. And I'll bet you anything they're still in that fake office building. We have to get back inside."

"So why would Caleb risk letting us free if the kids are still here?" asked Keegan.

"Overconfidence. Now, let's go get those kids."

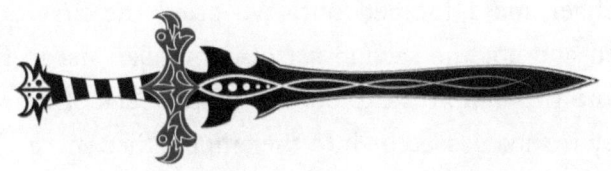

CHAPTER 30

K ane must have run through every red light we hit as we sped across town to the abandoned office building.

"There, you see!" I shouted, pointing to the semi-truck parked in front of it. "What do you want to bet they're planning on transporting the kids in that? They must be running a little behind."

"Lucky for us," said Keegan.

"I think we're overdue for a bit of luck, don't you?" I asked.

"We most certainly are," Anastasia agreed.

"Kane, back the van up to the doors. Michael and I will go in first to get the doors open and make sure the way is clear. Don't want you guys getting fried in the sun. Everyone ready?"

"Sure as shit we are, girlie," said Thatcher.

"Then let's go!"

The van flew towards the front of the building and Kane wrenched the wheel at the last moment, spinning the back end to face the doors. As the vehicle slowed, Michael and I jumped out. We pried the first doors open and got the second set of doors ajar just in time before the vampires exploded from the back of the van. They rushed passed us into the empty office space.

The empty cages were still sitting there, but now they were lined up in neat rows with the doors wide open, as if welcoming their occupants.

"They're still here somewhere," said Anastasia. "We're not too late."

"Come on then!" shouted Thatcher, rushing ahead of us to the door on the other side of the room. It was the same one that I followed Colleen through the night before.

"Stop! Who are you?" A guard stood directly on the other side of the door, a rifle in his hand pointed directly toward us.

"We don't have time for this." Thatcher was on the guard before the man could take his next breath, tearing the gun from his hands and throwing him against the wall where he landed with a sickening crunch!

Thatcher must have noticed the wide-eyed look of shock on my face as I viewed the lifeless body on the floor. He walked up to me and tugged my arm, pulling me away from the guard to follow the others.

"He's only knocked out, I didn't kill him."

"You didn't?" I asked, glancing back as we hurried down the hall.

"No, so stop looking at me like I just killed a puppy."

"I'm sorry, I guess I never thought we would have to fight humans."

"You didn't seem too worried about putting an end to that guard last night," he told me.

"I know, I was so mad that he would choose to do this. Or be a part of this. But honestly, I'm glad we weren't the ones to kill him. If we start killing humans, we're no better than the Renegades."

We passed the door that led to the side exit Colleen had escaped from after she shot me. I could instantly feel the pain of the bullet tearing through me. I squeezed my eyes shut to block out the memory and kept running.

"Up there!" shouted Michael, "That must be it." The words were barely out of his mouth before the door at the end of the hall burst open and a dozen vampires flooded the room. Behind them, I managed to see a flash of blonde and heard the crying of children.

"The kids!" Kane roared, rushing forward into the group of Renegades.

I grabbed my stake and launched myself after him into the heart of the fight. Swiftly staking the vampire that stood in my way, I was bound and determined to get into the back room. I refused to let Colleen escape this time.

Colleen was alone in the room with the children, her attention so focused on forcing them into the waiting cages that she failed to notice when I entered the room.

"Let me go! Let me go!" Christopher protested. He strained against Colleen's grasp, trying to pull his wrist free as she dragged him from the dark corner where the children were huddled together in fright.

"Colleen! Get your hands off him!"

I did the only thing I could think of to prevent the fighting in the hall from migrating to the room holding the children. I spun around and slammed the door shut.

Colleen jerked up at the sound of my voice, and the shock on her face was epic.

"Vanessa?" Her shock instantly morphed into a sneer. Colleen released Chris, shoving him backward into the frightened group of children where he landed roughly on his back. "Shouldn't you be dead by now?"

"I almost was. But then, I changed my mind. I can be fickle like that," I said lightly.

"I guess I'll just have to make sure you stay dead this time," she said, coming toward me slowly.

"I could say the same about you. I'm sorry, Colleen. I'm sorry Merrick did this to you, and turned you into a monster, but it's going to stop, and it's going to stop now. We're taking those kids back, and you're not going to stop us."

"God, Vanessa, you used to be so much fun. Now it's all blah, blah, blah, or nag, nag, nag. And you're always getting in the goddamn way!"

Colleen lunged at me and I charged forward to meet her, channeling my energy to run faster as I pushed myself harder than before. She attacked me with a fury I never before experienced. A hatred blazed in her eyes, which rocked me to my very core.

Is this what they did to her? Stripped her of everything that was beautiful and kind only to replace it with an unfeeling monster?

I knew I had to stop her. But even after everything she'd done, and all that we endured, I realized in that moment, a part of me didn't want to let her go. Or believe the only way to put a stop to all of this was for me to kill her. She was my best friend once, and I loved her. But as we crashed around the room, and I defended myself against her vicious blows, I finally had to fully accept there was no getting her back.

Killing Merrick would never be enough to release whatever grasp he held on her. He had infected her, and corrupted everything she once embodied. There was no coming back from that, and no chance at rehabilitation.

I looked at the children now cowering in the corner, observing their fear and their tears. Having been stolen from their parents in the night, and kept constantly in the dark, only to be taken away for who knows what purpose?

I thought about John and the way Colleen tore his throat out before she reveled in the joy of it.

I thought about all the countless acts of pain and horror she would inflict if I ever released her from that room. I allowed the knowledge to fill me, hardening me towards the mission I had to fulfill.

Tightening my grip on my stake, I waited for an opening, deflecting her blows until her arm went wide. Then, with a deep breath, I stepped closer to her, wrapping my arm around her back and pulling her in tightly.

Planting the stake deeply into Colleen's chest, I embraced her tightly as it pierced her heart. Her body slumped into mine and her arms came around me, clutching the back of my jacket.

"I'm so, so sorry," I whispered, burying my face in her soft, blonde hair.

"Nessa?" she whimpered.

She pulled back, and held onto my shoulders, looking directly at me with wide, frightened eyes. They accused me of betrayal. Maybe there was a piece of the old Colleen left inside her after all.

"Colleen? Oh, God! Colleen!" I pulled the stake free and let it drop to the floor. Hot tears burned my cheeks as I grabbed her face in my hands.

She clutched me so tightly, she bruised my shoulders, but I didn't try to free myself. Even as her body started to change, rapidly turning to ash, I held onto her, no longer seeing the monster she had become. I could only mourn for the beautiful person she once was.

The whimpers of the werewolf children entered my awareness as Colleen crumpled into a pile of dust on the floor. I looked up from her remains to the kids. We finally found them and now it was time to take them home.

I could hear the sounds of fighting still on the other side of the door, and the kids jumped at the loud banging when people were thrown against it. I bent down and retrieved my stake before standing guard in front of the children, ready to protect them if any of the Renegades managed to get through.

"Don't worry. I'll protect you, I promise."

A small hand slipped into my larger one and I looked down to find Chris standing next to me.

"Chris? You have to stand back," I told him softly. "It will be all right."

Instead of letting go, he held on tighter, and a look of determination appeared on his face.

"You came for us," he said, looking at the door.

"Yes, we did. And we're taking you home."

I turned around to the kids behind me. "We're taking you all home," I told them.

The kids stood together, clinging to each other for strength and courage.

"Stand back with them, Chris, and if I say, you all have to run run through that door as fast as you can and find Kane, Michael or Keegan, all right? They should be just outside the door. If I say run, you all must run, and they will protect you."

He let go of my hand and moved back to join the others. I leaned forward and crouched slightly, prepared to propel myself forward and attack the first Renegade to come through the door. No one could harm these children ever again. I would die before I let that happen.

The door to the room burst open and a vampire fell backward through the entrance with Keegan advancing on him. Running up behind the falling vampire, I wrapped my arm across his throat and shoved my stake through his back before releasing him again.

"Keegan!" I heard Christopher crying out behind me. Suddenly, his slight body was propelling past me into Keegan's open arms.

Keegan crushed the boy to him, wrapping him in a tight embrace. I looked past the pair and out into the hall, which the others had cleared. Kane and Michael entered the room next and the werewolf children rushed toward them, finally realizing they were free.

The men were surrounded by the kids who were clambering all over them. They eagerly embraced each of the children in turn, while offering them reassuring words.

"We have to get out of here now," said Anastasia, keeping her eye on the hall. "The sun is up, but there may be more human guards around."

"Let's get them out of here then," said Thatcher.

"Come on, guys," I told the kids, "we have to hurry."

The group split into two with the kids safely protected between us. Ana, Michael and William took up the rear while Thatcher, Kane, Keegan and I led the way out.

"Kane, why don't you check the semi-truck for a set of keys? If they aren't there, at least, you can still get the vehicle going," I suggested.

"Let's load the kids in the back of the truck," Kane told us. "The vampires can ride in there with them, just in case we get stopped."

"I'll ride with them in the back as well," said Keegan. "I'm not letting Chris out of my sight for a single second."

"Okay," I said, "I guess I'm driving the van then. Michael, you're with me. Let's haul our asses back to Silverlake."

We loaded everyone into the vehicles as fast as we could, the vampires diving into the back so as not to be exposed to the sun's lethal rays. I slammed the door to the trailer closed, my heart pounding rapidly in my chest.

I hopped into the driver's seat of the van and let Kane pull the large truck out in front of me before following behind. I was constantly looking over my shoulder to see if we were followed. With any luck, it would take a while before Caleb discovered his plan to transport this group of children had fallen apart. Our only hope now was that he would leave them alone after he found out, and simply consider the Silverlake Pack a lost cause.

Even if he did try again, the Silverlake Pack were now on high alert. It would be a long time before any of their children were allowed to play outside of their parents' again.

CHAPTER 31

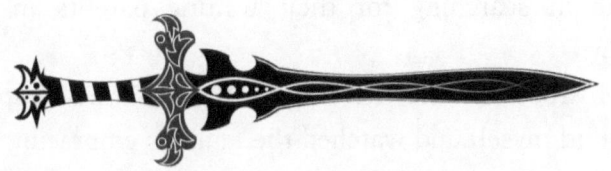

When we arrived back at the Pack lands, everyone was already outside waiting for us. Kane or Keegan must have called ahead to give them the good news.

We pulled the vehicles up in front of Kane's house. The sound of us coming up the drive must have alerted Lena and Sheena because they both came flying out of the house and up to the truck at top speed.

"Christopher!" Lena screamed as she ran around to the back of the truck "Chris!"

Michael and I jumped out of the van and ran after her, but didn't reach her in time.

"Wait!" I called, but it was too late.

She threw open the back door of the huge truck and the sunlight flooded in. I looked inside and breathed a sigh of relief when I saw the vampires huddled at the

339

other end of the truck trailer nearest the cab, safe from the direct sunlight.

The kids all shouted with joy when they saw Lena's face. We helped them jump down and they wasted no time in searching for their waiting parents in the crowd.

I stood on the driveway with my arms wrapped around myself and watched the families embracing one another. Tears ran freely, mixed with the happy sounds of laughter as the kids were led, one-by-one, back to the warmth and safety of their homes.

I turned back to look at Sheena and Lena, with Christopher safely ensconced in their arms. We came so close to losing Lena to madness and grief when her son was taken, and I could finally relax as I felt the weight and tension falling away from me at the sight of them all together again.

"Lena," Keegan said, and his voice was gruff.

Lena turned and released Chris, then stood to embrace Keegan. His arms wrapped around her back and he held her close as she cried.

"You found him," she sobbed. "You found him and brought him back to me. I can't believe you did it. Thank you, Keegan, thank you so much for bringing him home."

"Lena," he pulled away slightly so that he could look at her face, then brushed the stray hair away from her eyes. "I will always bring him back to you. I love you." His voice broke and he cleared his throat, starting again. "I love you and I should have told you sooner. I don't know why I didn't. Maybe out of respect for Ian. But I'm telling you now. I'll be a good husband to you, and a good father for Chris, if you'll both have me."

Lena stood frozen for a moment, a riot of emotions crossing over her face before throwing herself back into his arms and kissing him.

Watching them, my heart felt like a hand was around it, squeezing it tightly. It was such a beautiful scene and I felt incredibly happy for them. After everything they had endured, it was wonderful to see them all finally together. But something about watching them was painful as well. Perhaps I was watching something that would forever lie beyond my reach. Family. Children. Loyalty. *Were any of those things something a succubus could have, or even hope for? Could I ever be able to offer anyone such things, even if I wanted to?*

I looked away and caught Kane's eye. He was watching me, and a deep frown marred his face. It should have been a joyous moment for him. He protected his people, fulfilled his duty, and yet, he seemed to find no joy in it. And that was my fault.

"Let's get out of here," I told the rest of the Task Force before slamming the truck door back down to protect them from the sun.

The keys were still in the truck's ignition and I couldn't wait to pull out of there. If only to get away from the pain I saw in Kane's eyes. The sooner we were gone, the sooner I could put it all behind me. I was more than thankful that I wouldn't have to speak to him any time soon.

"Do you even know how to drive this thing?"

I jumped at the sound of Kane's voice floating in from the window. Sticking my head out, I looked down at him, and saw the blank expression on his face.

"Move over then, I'll drive it back, and you drive the van."

There was no point in arguing, since I couldn't drive the big truck myself. The only thing I could do was let him follow me out to Elizabeth's manor. That was about the best place I could think of to keep the truck without it being seen. All the vampires could remain safely inside until the sun went down. While the van had UV-proof windows, the truck allowed them much more room in which to pass the time.

I could feel him in the truck behind me the entire way back to the city and out to Elizabeth's property. What would I say to him once we got there? What could I possibly say?

Once we finally arrived, I sat in Elizabeth's circular driveway, staring at the dashboard. It was done; it was finally over. Now that I was sitting back home with the vampires, I actually believed the mission was at an end. We got the kids back, and we all made it out alive.

Taking a deep breath, I jumped down from the van and walked over to the back of the truck while Kane stayed sitting behind the wheel.

I knocked loudly three times on the door and waited for a reply.

"We there yet or what?" barked Thatcher.

"Yeah, we're here. Umm, what did you guys want me to do?"

"Just leave us here, love, we'll be just fine in here for the day. We'll head out once the sun goes down," came William's voice.

"Are you sure? I feel kind of weird leaving you all in the back of a truck."

"We'll be fine, Vanessa," said Anastasia with a laugh. "Trust us, we have all been trapped in places much less comfortable. If there is any problem, we will call you."

"Okay, well, stay safe," I said, still hesitant to leave them behind, but backing away from the truck anyway.

"So they're staying in there then?" asked Kane when I came around the other side.

"I guess so. They said they're fine."

"Are you staying too?"

"No, I need... ummm a lift back to my place, if you don't mind."

He grunted, but didn't say anything, and nodded his head as he walked toward the van.

I took that as a reluctant yes and followed after him.

"Thank you," I said as I climbed in behind him.

"You're welcome," he replied without looking at me.

"Kane, please--"

"Stop, Vanessa. Will you please just stop? I can't do

this with you right now." He bowed his head and closed his eyes, letting out a weary sigh.

"But--" I tried again.

"Why now?" he shouted. "Why do we have to do this now? I wanted to talk before, Vanessa. You knew how I felt. I wanted you to be honest with me, and you kept blowing me off. I saved your life and we had... we had sex, and then you treated me like crap. And *now* you want to talk?"

"Yes," I said quietly, a tear slipping down my cheek.

He stared at me for a moment and then looked away before switching on the ignition with a rough twist of the key.

"Well, I don't."

Unlocking the door, I entered my cold, dark apartment. Having forgotten to turn the heat on before I left, my place felt like an icebox. Now that Karen was sleeping in her own home again, I would have to remember things like that. It was easy for me to forget such little things when I was so caught up in Coven business.

I removed all my weapons and dropped them on the counter. Stretching, I enjoyed the newfound feeling of freedom. It felt like I had been wearing my weapons non-stop for weeks. All I wanted now was a nice, long bath and then to sleep for a week.

I stripped down, leaving a long line of discarded

clothing from the kitchen to the bedroom, and changed into my pajamas, suddenly too tired to drag my weary body into the bathroom for a bath. I was crawling under the covers when my cell phone buzzed on the bedside table. I closed my eyes and waited for it to stop. It was too soon for another disaster, and we had only just finished dealing with the last one.

My phone stopped and then immediately starting buzzing again. I pinched the bridge of my nose and counted to ten under my breath, forcing myself to stay put. I refused to answer it. The phone stopped and I rolled over onto my other side with my back to it, snuggling deeper down into the blankets. I was finally starting to feel the tension ease from my shoulders when my phone went off again.

"Oh, goddammit!" I shouted, rolling over and snatching the phone off the table.

Iris's name flashed up at me from the screen and I answered it immediately.

"What's wrong?" I asked her.

"Just checking in. Wanted to make sure you didn't forget about me."

"I didn't forget. We got ambushed. Whoever was working with that guard probably sold you out. They were waiting for us when we got there."

"Are you all right?" I heard what sounded like genuine worry in her voice.

"Yeah, we're fine. We got the kids out of there before they were transported. I suggest you stay out of

Caleb's way tonight. I'm sure he's going to be on the warpath when he wakes up and finds out about it."

"Well, at least, you won't have to worry about him for a while, and he didn't get his hands on you," she said.

I didn't say anything, unsure of whether or not to tell her about the deal I had to make with Caleb before he let the others go. The silence lasted way too long while I tried to think of something to say.

"Vanessa... are you still there?" she asked hesitantly.

"Yeah, I'm here. So about Caleb..."

"What the hell happened?" she snapped at me.

"I had to make a deal with him."

A loud thud came from the other end of the line and I wondered if she just punched a wall.

"You *promised* me you wouldn't get tangled up with him. You promised me you would keep yourself safe."

"I didn't have any choice."

"Of course, you had a choice! You just made the wrong one!"

"He would have killed them, Iris. My team, the wolves who came with us, he would have killed them all, and then we would have lost the kids. I had to do something. And how about you? What dumbass choice did you make to land yourself where you are, huh?"

She didn't respond and I continued. "See? Exactly. I got myself into this mess with Caleb and I'll get myself out of it."

"And us? How are you going to help us if you're so busy trying to save yourself? He will ruin you, Vanessa; make no mistake about that. Whatever deal you made, whatever you think you'll have to do, I promise you right now it will be so much worse."

"I'll get you all out of there. I made you a promise and I plan on keeping it. We'll bring Caleb down. I'll find a way. There's no doubt that he's entangled with the Renegades, we just have to find a way to prove it. If we can just tie him to the kidnapped werewolf kids, maybe it will be enough for Elizabeth to step in and do something. But there's no way we can go after a coven leader without proof. Real solid proof. Otherwise, it's more likely that we'll be the ones to lose our heads instead of him.

"Well, since it sounds like you're going to be around here pretty often, maybe you can help us figure something out before too long."

"We can only hope."

There was a knock on my door and I left my bedroom to go answer it.

"Iris, someone is here, I've got to go."

"Take care of yourself, Vanessa. Don't let your guard down around him. Not even for a second, do you hear me?"

"I hear you."

I grabbed one of my guns off the counter as I walked past and flipped off the safety lock while checking the peephole on my front door. To my surprise, Kane was standing on the other side.

"I'll talk to you soon. Call me if you hear anything interesting, okay?" I told Iris as I unlocked the deadbolt.

"I will. Bye."

The line went dead and I stuffed my phone into the pocket of my pajama pants before opening the front door. I was holding my gun behind my back, out of view.

"Kane? What are you doing here?" I opened the door wider, but not wide enough for him to enter.

"I was on the highway, on my way home and planning to forget about you," he said. The hair on his head was sticking up in messy spikes as if he'd been running his fingers through it. "I was going to forget about you because of this," he said, gesturing with his hand back and forth between us. "I don't need this."

"Then why are you here?"

"Because I'm an idiot."

My hand dropped to my side, exposing my gun and he looked down at it in mild surprise.

"Oh," I glanced down at the gun, then back up at him, "sorry."

I turned and walked away from the door, leaving it open so he could follow me inside while I placed the gun back on the counter.

"Can I get you anything?" I asked. I had no idea what to say to him. Having him in my apartment reminded me of the first time he was there. Even with all the clumsiness and tension, there was an innocence about it then that simply vanished. Now, I was just itching for him to go. We could never go back to what we were, or what we could have been. I ruined that.

"No, I don't need anything."

"So is there any other reason for your being here other than the questionable state of your mental health?" I asked with a small smile, trying my best to ease the thickening tension.

"I didn't really think it through. I just..." he broke off, clenching his fists and looking around the room. "You wanted to talk, so talk."

I opened my mouth and shut it again. I didn't know how to reply to that. Letting out a defeated sigh, I stared down at the grain in the hardwood floor.

"This was a bad idea," he said. "I shouldn't have come."

"No, I'm sorry. I don't... I don't know how to handle this. I've never had to... I've never been... Dammit, Kane, I'm a succubus!" I threw my hands up in frustration.

"I know you are."

"No, you don't. I mean, you know what I am, but you don't know what *that means*." I paced back and forth, searching for the words, trying to get it straight in my head. "I'm a succubus. I feed off people. I need to survive by taking from people in the most intimate way possible. *Lots of people.* I'm always hungry, Kane. I always need to feed. I've only just discovered what I am and what that means, and I'm still learning things. Not only that, but for the first time in my life, other people know what I am too."

"You're not alone anymore, Vanessa, you don't have to hide that side of yourself." He took a step toward me, but stopped, seemingly unsure of how to comfort me.

"But that's just it, Kane. I don't know how not to be alone. Other than William, I've never been with a man before that knows what I am. I kept putting you off because whatever you're looking for isn't casual, and I don't know if I can give you that. Everything is still so new. I just, I don't want to make you a promise that I don't know if I can keep. I'm not sure if I even want."

"Vanessa—"

"No." I held up my hand to cut him off. "Please, just let me finish. "I like you, Kane, I do. But I've only known you for what, a few weeks? You're a good man, and I could easily see my feelings for you growing. But I have feelings for William too. And even though he and I haven't spoken about our relationship, we do mean something to one another, and I don't want to hurt anyone. I'm not saying that I'm choosing him over you, I just don't want to cause you any pain."

"Vanessa?" he growled in annoyance.

"What?" I asked, praying that he understood.

"Just shut up."

He grabbed me and pulled me closer, crushing his

mouth down on mine. I moaned in frustration before giving in and kissing him back. One of his arms wrapped tightly around my waist while his other hand tangled in my hair, forcing my head back.

"Kane," I said, panting, and pulling my mouth free. "This is a really bad idea."

Kane pressed his forehead against mine and released a deep sigh.

"Yes, it is. But I'm not ready to let you go. I'm not giving up on this, not just yet."

"I can't be with you, not the way you want," I told him sadly.

"I know. But this will just have to be enough for now. I can't promise I won't get jealous, but I'll try to understand. And I'll keep proving to you that I'm the right choice for you in the end."

"Kane," I said, a hint of warning in my voice. "You don't know that."

"I wouldn't be me if I didn't try, Vanessa. I want to see where this goes, and I'm willing to be patient, for now. I know we haven't known each other long; and yes, you're right, what I'm feeling is crazy. But I do feel something between us, and I like it."

"This might end really, really badly," I said as he pulled me close again and wrapped me in his arms.

"It might, but I guess we'll just have to wait and see."

COMING SOON

BOOK 3 OF
THE VANESSA KENSLEY SERIES